Readers love

'If you like getting your history from fictional stories rather than dry tomes then this is the book for you. I'd highly recommend it!'

'I was transported back to the age of the giant steamships crisscrossing the Atlantic, and to the ill-fated voyage of the Titanic. The author has done an immense amount of research and really brings this event and era to life – I truly felt as though I was there in that moment with the heroine . . . An emotional roller-coaster that will keep readers turning the pages – highly recommended!'

'Heartwarming and loved the twist in the tale. Couldn't stop reading, so some late nights for me!'

'The mark of an excellent book – when you don't want it to be finished and when you want to find out more about the subject . . . This book was an education as well as entertaining – as always well written and one not to put down until it was finished'

'It was highly captivating, dramatic and an emotional read in places. I literally could not turn the pages fast enough, with wanting to find out what happens next and as to how it would all end'

KATHLEEN McGURL lives in Christchurch with her husband. She has two sons who have both now left home. She always wanted to write, and for many years was waiting until she had the time. Eventually, she came to the bitter realisation that no one would pay her for a year off work to write a book, so she sat down and started to write one anyway. Since then, she has published several novels with HQ and self-published another. She has also sold dozens of short stories to women's magazines, and written three How To books for writers. After a long career in the IT industry, she became a full-time writer in 2019. When she's not writing, she's often out running, slowly.

Also by Kathleen McGurl

The Emerald Comb
The Pearl Locket
The Daughters of Red Hill Hall
The Girl from Ballymor
The Drowned Village
The Forgotten Secret
The Stationmaster's Daughter
The Secret of the Château
The Forgotten Gift
The Lost Sister
The Girl from Bletchley Park
The Storm Girl
The Girl with the Emerald Flag
The Lost Child

The Lost Diamond

KATHLEEN McGURL

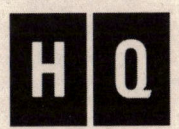

ONE PLACE. MANY STORIES

This novel is entirely a work of fiction. The names, characters and incidents portrayed in it are the work of the author's imagination. Any resemblance to actual persons, living or dead, events or localities is entirely coincidental.

HQ
An imprint of HarperCollins*Publishers* Ltd
1 London Bridge Street
London SE1 9GF

www.harpercollins.co.uk

HarperCollins*Publishers*
Macken House, 39/40 Mayor Street Upper,
Dublin 1 D01 C9W8
This edition 2025

1

First published in Great Britain by
HQ, an imprint of HarperCollins*Publishers* Ltd 2025

Copyright © Kathleen McGurl 2025

Kathleen McGurl asserts the moral right to be identified as the author of this work.
A catalogue record for this book is available from the British Library.

ISBN: 9780008591700

This book contains FSC™ certified paper and other controlled sources to ensure responsible forest management.

For more information visit: www.harpercollins.co.uk/green

Printed and bound in the UK using 100% renewable electricity at CPI Group (UK) Ltd

All rights reserved. No part of this publication may be reproduced, stored in a retrieval system, or transmitted, in any form or by any means, electronic, mechanical, photocopying, recording or otherwise, without the prior permission of the publishers.

This book is sold subject to the condition that it shall not, by way of trade or otherwise, be lent, re-sold, hired out or otherwise circulated without the publisher's prior consent in any form of binding or cover other than that in which it is published and without a similar condition including this condition being imposed on the subsequent purchaser.

*For everyone I worked with during
my 31 years at John Lewis*

Prologue

1947

A storm rages over the Alps; a fierce storm, one that no one in their right mind would want to be out in. Least of all, in an aeroplane, flying high above the mountains in the midst of the storm clouds, buffeted by winds and beset by turbulence.

Yet this is where Wilfred Fforbes-Whyte is, flying a route he has taken several times before, between London and Delhi, between the place he always insists on calling 'home' and the place where he has lived almost all his life.

The plane is a Lockheed Constellation, a workhorse of its time, with about fifty people on board. Some are businessmen, some are like Wilfred – a member of the British Raj, employed in the Indian Civil Service (though not for very much longer, for India is about to gain independence from Great Britain). Wilfred and others like him will then decamp to England to begin a new life in a country they barely know.

As the plane lurches sickeningly yet again, Wilfred leans forward to clutch at the metal briefcase by his feet and holds on to it tightly. It wouldn't do to lose the case, or more precisely, its contents. All that Wilfred considers most precious in his life is bound up with that case, and its safety is of paramount importance. The case and its contents *must* reach their destination, otherwise everything he holds dear will be lost.

All this is the diamond's doing. The diamond that nestles in its velvet box inside his briefcase. The legend says that it is cursed, and Wilfred has been warned that bringing it out of its native India will lead to no good. Maybe it has caused this terrible storm. Or perhaps he is being fanciful and this brush with danger is robbing him of reason. He can no longer think straight. He is sweating profusely; he is scared, no, terrified, that this might be the end. It's not himself he worries about. It's the diamond. It's his daughter, Celia.

The plane tips sideways, sending loose items flying around the cabin, then rights itself once more. Some passengers scream, some are crying, some are praying. Across the aisle a young girl stares at him. She has long black hair. She is young and beautiful. For a moment Wilfred thinks it's his wife, dear Alice, but then he blinks and remembers it cannot be her. It must be Celia, then, and he reaches out to her to touch her hand, to reassure her that all will be well. It has to be.

But then the plane plummets once more in an air pocket, and this time it is directly over western Europe's highest mountain – Mont Blanc. Wilfred's grip on the briefcase loosens and it slides away from him, down the aisle, past the dark-haired girl who watches it go past her towards the cockpit of the plane where the pilots are wrestling with the controls. Wilfred screams out in horror, and through the window beside him he sees the mountain, its jagged rock and icy glaciers coming up far too fast towards him. *This is it*, he thinks. *This is the end.* And his final thoughts are of his darling Celia, though there is nothing he can do now to save her.

Chapter 1

Lisa, 2023

'This,' Lisa said, as she gazed around at the magnificent Alpine scenery, the snow-capped peaks under an azure sky, green valleys below and a glacier tumbling down the mountain to her right, 'is exactly what I needed.'

Gaby grinned at her. 'Told you. Mountain medicine. It always hits the spot.'

'Thanks for insisting I came on this holiday with you.' Lisa stepped off the path and found a flattish rock, then took off her rucksack and sat down. It had been a last-minute decision to come with Gaby. 'I needed a short break, though I'm not as fit as I'd like to be.' She pulled her water bottle out and took a long swig. The water was warm but she knew she needed to take on more liquid. It was a hot day and they'd been climbing steadily for four hours.

'That,' Gaby said, pointing at a rounded summit ahead, 'is Mont Blanc.'

Lisa looked up at the mountain. From where they sat, it appeared not to be too far off. She had the impression that if they kept walking steadily, they'd be on its summit by mid-afternoon and down again in time for tea. But she knew that was an illusion – the mountain was several miles away and it was certainly not one that two women in summer hiking boots could manage. Gaby, though, was an experienced mountaineer and someone who was always up for a challenge. 'Would you ever want to climb it, Gaby?'

Gaby smiled. 'God, yes. I'd love to. But you need a guide, and you'd need to spend a week or so climbing at altitude to acclimatise, and I can't afford the cost or the time. One day, maybe. Before I'm too old for that kind of thing.'

'You've got years yet. We're only twenty-eight.'

'Mmm.' Gaby looked thoughtful. 'Maybe I'll do it in two years' time. When I turn thirty. Yes – that's a plan. If Josh doesn't decide to whisk me away to some exotic and romantic resort, I'm going to book a guide and climb Mont Blanc. Fancy coming with me?'

'It'd take me two years to get fit enough to even consider it!' Lisa laughed. 'And don't you need to be roped up and use crampons and ice axes and all that sort of thing?'

'Yes, but we could get some training from the guide. It'd be a challenge, but we could do it!'

Lisa thought for a moment then made a snap decision. 'Well, all right then! Here's the deal. If I'm still single at thirty I'll climb Mont Blanc with you. It'll be my way of sticking two fingers up at life, eh?'

'You're on.' Gaby high-fived her. 'Right then, shall we continue?'

Lisa pushed her water bottle back into the pocket on the side of her rucksack and stood up, swinging the pack round onto her shoulders. 'Sure. This mountain's not going to climb itself, is it?'

They walked on, the path rising steadily as it zigzagged its way up a ridge of land between two glaciers. The views were stunning. Every so often there'd be a view of the Bossons glacier on one side, or the Taconnaz glacier on the other. Both originated on Mont Blanc itself. Behind and below them, the Chamonix valley opened up with the town itself a little way further along. It was a hot June day but as they'd climbed out of the valley, higher and higher, the temperatures had dropped to a reasonable level. With a hat to keep the sun off and plenty of sunscreen and water, Lisa felt well equipped for the day. She'd always loved walking but was more used to the lower peaks of the Lake District or the rolling hills of the South Downs. This was her first walking trip in the Alps. Gaby had persuaded her it was the best way to put her recent break-up behind her.

And Gaby had been right. Every step Lisa took was a step up, a step away from Rupert and towards a better future. She'd been with him for the best part of two years. Why had it taken her so long to recognise what everyone else – certainly Gaby and some of her other friends – had seen from the start? Rupert had seemed charming and was definitely handsome, and for a while she'd thought she loved him. 'He's not good for you,' Gaby had told her more than once. But it had taken her a long while to see that for herself, to see the real Rupert behind the charming facade. It had knocked her self-confidence badly, and she knew it would take time to heal. This trip away was just the start of a long process to find herself a new path in life.

A little further on, Gaby stopped beside a huge boulder that must have fallen down the mountain hundreds of thousands of years ago. A little wooden sign was attached to it, that read: *Gite a Balmat*.

'Balmat, with another fellow – Paccard – was the first to climb Mont Blanc,' Gaby explained. 'Balmat would shelter overnight under this rock on his reconnaissance trips to work out the best route up the mountain.'

Lisa peered beneath the overhanging rock. It didn't look too comfortable. 'Is this the way most people climb to the summit?'

Gaby shook her head. 'Not these days. I think the usual route is over there somewhere.' She waved a hand vaguely. 'You go up to a mountain hut, spend the night there, then get up at stupid o'clock to climb to the summit. I'll have to look into it if we're going to do it.'

'Steady on!' Lisa laughed. 'I'm not fully committed to the idea.'

'There's no Rupert Wossname-Thing to stop you now. What was his surname again?'

'Wyndham-Royce. No. Thank God.'

'You are *so* much better off without him, mate,' Gaby said. 'You seem happier, too.'

'I am. At least I think I will be, eventually.' Lisa took a last look at the spot where the mountaineering pioneer had spent his nights over two hundred years ago and carried on, following Gaby. She was beginning to feel happier, it was true. Life with Rupert had been one long round of parties, clubs and expensive meals, plus city breaks during which they went to more parties, clubs and restaurants, and never managed to see any sights. He was a city boy through and through: working for an investment bank, driving a red Ferrari and wearing sharp Italian suits. He couldn't have been more of a caricature of his 'type' if he'd tried; Lisa realised that now. And while that lifestyle had been enormous fun for a while – those extravagant gestures he'd make sending her huge bouquets of exotic flowers, booking entire restaurants to take her out for her birthday – she now knew it wasn't who she really was.

She fully intended to move out of London, find a cottage on the edge of a village in some pretty county, and take up baking and cross-country running before she was very much older. But for now, her job as a data analyst with the Civil Service meant she was tied to her London flat and the daily commute to work by tube.

This holiday, in the magnificent setting of the Alps, with distant horizons that soothed her soul, was a welcome change. She was able to de-stress, to consider her future now that Rupert was at last out of the picture. Doing it while hiking up mountains with her best friend in spectacular scenery was an added bonus. They had rented a small apartment in Chamonix down in the valley and were spending every day walking. The exercise was paying off too – both mentally and physically Lisa felt better than she had for years. She was sleeping better, and the anxiety attacks that had plagued her immediately after the break-up were becoming less frequent.

'Look at that.' Gaby had stopped at a turn in the path, at a spot that overlooked one of the glaciers. 'See how the edges of the glacier have receded? And down there you can see that the nose of it has receded too.'

Lisa looked where her friend was pointing. The glacier was indeed shrinking noticeably, with bare shattered rock exposed at its edges. 'Global warming?'

'Yes. Really brings it home to you when you see incontrovertible evidence like that right in front of you, doesn't it?'

'Yes.' The two women regarded the diminishing glacier sadly for a moment, then turned to continue walking up the trail. They were heading for the spot, known as La Jonction, at which the two glaciers diverged, one going down the left-hand valley and one down the right. That would be as far as they could safely walk, as it was all ice beyond there and they weren't equipped for it. Still, with a total height gain of 1,600 metres above the valley floor it was a tough enough walk.

And the views, oh the views! Lisa lifted her head to regard the towering Aiguille du Midi to her left, its sharp spires of rock piercing the skyline, starkly beautiful against the stunningly blue sky. There was a cable car that ran to the summit of that peak that they'd earmarked for a possible rest-day activity, but so far they'd preferred to walk every day. Now it was the last day of their trip, so taking that cable car would have to wait for a future holiday.

There *would* be more holidays like this one, Lisa promised herself. Rupert hadn't allowed her to go away without him. 'Why would you want to, babe,' he'd said when she'd once broached the subject of a Lake District walking trip with Gaby. 'You know I'll take you somewhere far more exotic and much more fun.' And then he'd booked a week partying in Palma that clashed with Gaby's trip, so that she'd had to choose between them. She'd told herself at the time she was lucky to have him but looking back she realised she'd been far too much under his control. She shuddered at the memory, then forced herself to concentrate on the action of walking, one foot in front of the other, ever onward, ever upward, to stave off the anxiety attack that would no doubt arise if she kept mentally going over her time with Rupert.

A little further up, Lisa and Gaby had to scramble up a rock face. A rope handrail in places hinted at the popularity of this walk, but they'd been lucky – it was midweek and not yet the main holiday period, so there weren't too many other hikers. Also, they'd left early and made good time. Lisa expected that later on in the day there'd be many others on their way up – it was too good a day to waste.

And then they reached La Jonction itself – a vast expanse of ice crevasses ahead of them, stretching away left and right to form the two glaciers.

'This is it for us,' Gaby said. 'We'll have our picnic here. But don't go on the ice – it's not safe.'

'Don't worry.' Lisa was standing gazing at it, and saw that in places a thin layer of snow covered the cracks and crevasses. She could see how you might step onto it thinking it was firm and fall down, breaking a leg, or, further out on the ice, even get stuck at the bottom of a deep crevasse.

She approached the edge of the glacier and poked at it with her walking pole. On the very edge it was loose, slightly melting in the heat of the day. It was dirty; not the brilliant white it looked from further away. Embedded in the ice were gravel, chunks of rock and soil. Even so, in places it sparkled and glistened in the sunlight. She walked along beside the edge of the glacier, picking her way over the loose rock and stones. Lateral moraine, it was called – the term coming back to her from school geography lessons with Mrs Leeming so long ago.

A little further along, something caught her eye. A metallic glint from the side of the glacier. At first, she assumed it was ice catching the sunshine, but as she came closer, she realised it was something else. A corner, a box or case made of some sort of metal, poked out of the edge of the glacier. It was not deeply buried and around it the ice seemed to be melting away. 'Gaby! Look at this!' she called, and Gaby came hurrying over.

'Wow. How did that get there?' Gaby took a step closer and touched the exposed metal.

'Reckon we could pull it out and see what it is?' Lisa said.

'I should think so. Whatever it is has been carried down the mountain by the glacier. Perhaps it's some sort of mountaineering equipment, abandoned up near the summit years ago.' Gaby was already stabbing at the ice around it with her walking pole, loosening it so that chunks fell away.

Lisa moved beside her and joined in, and before long they could see it was a metal case, the size of a briefcase, fastened by two catches either side of the handle. The surface was pitted and dented, presumably the work of ice over the many years the case had been trapped in the glacier. Lisa reached out and ran a hand over it, wondering who last touched it, and when and how it had been lost.

'What do you think it is?' she asked. 'Some sort of camera case, perhaps?'

'It's kind of a heavy thing for any mountaineering expedition to carry up. Could be scientific equipment, perhaps? We need to get it out and open it up.'

'Looks like it's locked.' Lisa pointed at a keyhole they'd just uncovered beside the handle.

'Might not be. We'll just have to get it out and see.'

Lisa could now get her hands around it, jiggling the case within its icy tomb. It would be so much easier to crawl onto the glacier so they could dig the case out from the other side but she didn't dare. Gaby kept digging with her pole until she found it was gradually coming free, and then with one last concerted effort from both of them pulling at it, the case popped out of the ice, sending them both sprawling backwards onto the ground.

'Ouch! You OK?' Lisa asked, as she rubbed her leg where she'd landed on a protruding stone. That would leave her with a nice bruise in a day or two.

'Yes, fine. Only my dignity dented,' Gaby replied.

They scrambled to their feet and Lisa carried the case away from the ice, to a flattish piece of rock beside their rucksacks. 'Let's see what's inside, then.'

The catches were stiff and wouldn't release until Lisa pulled out her Swiss army knife and prised them free. But the case wouldn't open.

'It's locked, isn't it?' Gaby said, sounding disappointed.

'Not sure.' Lisa was still poking at the seal with her penknife. 'If it's been there years as you suggested, it might just be stuck . . .'

'Hit it with a stone to break the lock?' Gaby helpfully held out a stone, but at that moment the lid of the case released a little.

'Here, get the blade of your penknife in that side, and I'll do this,' Lisa said. Gaby knelt down to help and shortly after they had the lid freed all around. 'Now then, let's see,' Lisa said as she eased it open.

Inside were notebooks, envelopes, and bundles of papers held together by paper clips. The kind of contents you'd expect in any businessman's briefcase. But how had it come to be half-way up Mont Blanc?

'There's a newspaper here . . .' Lisa tugged it out from beneath other papers. Everything was in good condition – the case had kept all moisture from the glacier out. She opened the newspaper, which was an edition of the *Times of India*, to check the date. 'Wow! It's from July 1947!'

'That's older than I was anticipating!' Gaby reached into the case and pulled out a handful of documents which she rifled through. 'We could probably work out who this belonged to from these papers. Though God knows how it got here. It definitely doesn't look like something left over from a mountaineering expedition.'

Lisa noticed a small pocket stitched to the lining of the case. She pushed her fingers in and rummaged around. 'There's something else in here.' It was a small black velvet box, a little larger than a ring box.

'Well, you have to open that!' Gaby said, putting the papers back into the case.

The box had a tiny hook to fasten it, and carefully Lisa eased it back and opened the box, mindful of the fact that if whatever was in it fell out it could be hard to retrieve from among the gravel and stones at their feet. She kept the box level as she opened it.

And then both women gasped when they saw what the box held.

A brooch – a ring of green stones that Lisa assumed were emeralds, set in gold, surrounding the largest diamond she had ever seen.

'If that is real and not paste—' Gaby began.

'—then it must be absolutely priceless,' Lisa finished, breathlessly, staring at it in awe.

A shiver ran through her as she gazed at the diamond, watching how the sunlight made sparkling colours appear deep inside the gem, as though it had a hidden life or even a mind of its own.

Chapter 2

Wilfred, March 1947

The diamond sparkled in the light of the setting sun, as Wilfred Fforbes-Whyte held the brooch up to the window. He turned it one way and then the other, admiring the rainbow it cast onto papers on his desk. It was beautiful. His grandfather had had it set into a brooch surrounded by bright emeralds, and had given it to his grandmother as a token of their love. As a child, Wilfred had loved it when his mother wore it, and then his beloved Alice, God rest her soul, had pinned it to her gown for every grand, official occasion they'd been invited to. The diamond was truly magnificent, and lived up to its name – Shining Star, or *Chamakta Sitara* in Hindi. Wilfred worshipped it. In a few years, his daughter Celia would be old enough to wear the brooch and until then, it was his job to keep it safe at any cost. That meant, he realised with a sigh, that he should take it somewhere else, away from his home here in Agra, and sooner rather than later. He would hate being parted from it. Eventually he'd take it home to England.

It was funny, he mused, how he always referred to England as 'home'. He'd been born in India and had lived there all his life apart from a few years at an English boarding school and then three years up at Oxford University. His entire career had been spent in the Indian Civil Service, like his father and grandfather before him, and other than annual visits home he'd thought he would never leave India. But now, the political situation meant his job would presumably come to an end once India achieved independence. And then, what else was there for him to do, but to pack up and take Celia back to England?

She'd hate it – he knew that. She'd really only ever known India. When Alice had been alive, they'd taken annual trips back home. But those had stopped after her death, and of course the war had made everything more difficult. They'd had one brief visit last year, during which Celia had appeared to hate every minute of it. She would, he knew, put up quite a fight when the time came to move back for good.

He sighed. He'd cross that bridge when he came to it. For now, his priority was to pack what he needed for this short trip home. He was only planning to stay in London for a few days. Just enough time to take care of a little business at his bank and to attend a few meetings. He'd also have to see his brother Cyril and try to start the process of mending their long-broken relationship. For so many years they had been in contact by letter only. Last year's visit hadn't helped – they'd met up but barely spoken.

And it wouldn't hurt to spend a bit of time working out where he and Celia would live when they were finally forced to return to England forever. Wilfred owned no property there. Cyril had inherited the family home in Hampshire. His brother had never much liked India and indeed, despite being born there like Wilfred, had never gone back after boarding school days. In that, as in so many other aspects, they were completely unalike. Wilfred had already decided to spend the minimum time possible with Cyril. Just long enough to remind him that he had a brother, and to sound him out for advice on buying a decent house in England, somewhere within easy reach of the capital.

He took a last look at the brooch then returned it to its little velvet case. He bundled up some documents he needed to take with him, together with the latest edition of the *Times of India* that he hadn't finished reading, and put those in his metal briefcase that he kept with him at all times on these trips. He had a long journey ahead, with two stops for refuelling. Still, it was better than the old days when you had no choice but to go by sea – a journey that took weeks.

His suitcase was packed; more or less. Sanjit had seen to that, earlier in the day. Wilfred would be leaving early in the morning to catch the train to Delhi, a taxi to the airport and then the flight to London.

A distant gong sounded, alerting him to the fact it was dinnertime. It would only be himself and Celia eating. The servants ate separately. Until recently, Celia had eaten her meals with her *ayah*, Sita, but now that she was fifteen, Wilfred had thought she was grown-up enough to eat in the formal dining room with him. Meals since Alice's death had been lonely affairs, so he was glad of Celia's company, even if she was still a child, and could sometimes be argumentative or sulky over dinner. She needed to learn how to behave in formal and social situations, and without a mother to teach her, it was up to him.

He checked his appearance in a mirror, straightened his tie and left his office, heading out through the door that led to the veranda. He followed that around the bungalow and into the dining room, where the table was neatly set for two and Sanjit was already standing, waiting to serve him, wearing a fresh white *lungi* and *kurta*. He bowed as Wilfred entered.

'Evening, Sanjit. Where's Celia?'

'She is coming, *sahib*. She is in the house.'

'She's always late. I must have a word with her.' Wilfred sat in the chair Sanjit pulled out for him, and as he'd done so frequently in recent months, wondered whether he'd be able to afford servants when he moved home to England. From what Cyril had told him last year, these days very few people had live-in servants. Typically, the middle classes might employ a cleaner and a gardener who'd come once or twice a week, but that was all. After the war, there was a shortage of people for domestic work in any case. Here in India, he employed a cook plus two kitchen boys; a *dhobi wallah* who took care of their laundry; a woman who cleaned the house; Sanjit who functioned as his driver and butler; and of course Sita, to take care of Celia. Wilfred would miss being waited on.

But with no wife, once they were back in England he'd have no choice but to employ a cook-cum-housekeeper at the very least. He was pretty certain Celia wouldn't want to cook every day for him. Many widowers in his situation would remarry, but he knew Celia wouldn't like the idea of a stepmother. Besides, how he could ever find anyone to step into Alice's shoes he had no idea.

The door to the hallway burst open at that moment, and Celia charged through it, panting. She threw a look at Sanjit who gave a tiny nod, which Wilfred guessed he was not supposed to see. Celia's hair was awry; she was wearing a *salwar kameez* and there were dirt marks on her knees and hips. She had most definitely not been in the house as Sanjit had said.

'Evening, Celia. Nice of you to join me.'

'Sorry, Papa. I am only two minutes late.' Celia plumped herself down into the chair opposite him, picked up the bread roll from her side plate and tore into it, as though she hadn't eaten for days.

'You are six minutes late,' Wilfred replied, consulting his watch. 'And you are in dirty clothes, which tells me you did not return to the house in time to change into proper English clothes, prior to the dinner gong. It's disrespectful to me, Celia, and unbecoming. You are a young lady now and should behave like one.'

Celia tilted her head on one side. 'I can behave like one when I want to, Papa. I know how to. But today I was out with Vijay and we were down by the river bank and I did not have a watch on and—'

Wilfred held up a hand to stop her. 'I gave you a watch. Wear it, please. I allow you to run wild in the afternoons still, but if you fail to be back in time for dinner I shall put a stop to that. And it is time you stopped wearing these Indian clothes.'

Celia pouted. 'I hate wearing dresses.'

'You will have to wear them in England. All the young ladies wear dresses or skirts, all the time.'

'I know, I remember from last year. I hate them. I never want to go to England again.'

'Sooner or later, Celia, we will have to. For good. We've talked about this.'

At that moment the kitchen *wallahs* entered bearing dishes of food, which they placed on the sideboard for Sanjit to serve from. 'Ah, splendid. Here we are at last. What is it tonight, Sanjit?'

'Lamb chops and potatoes, *sahib*,' came the answer.

'Ugh.' Celia pulled a face. 'I would much prefer the *dal bhat* I bet Sanjit and Sita and the others will be eating later.'

'Well, I wouldn't. And this is my house, my table, my food. So eat it like a lady, my girl, and be thankful for it.'

Celia picked up her cutlery and began to eat, making a big show of how much she disliked the food. Wilfred ignored her. She was too 'native' for her own good. He should have sent her to school in England, he thought for the umpteenth time. There, she'd have been taught what to wear, how to behave and what she should enjoy eating. But he'd kept her in India for his own selfish reasons. His beloved Alice had been dead eight years now, and Celia was all he had left of her. And so he'd kept her with him, at the expense of her having a decent English education.

He just hoped that a couple of years at school in England, then maybe a spell at a finishing school somewhere else in Europe, would be enough to knock the rough edges off her and turn her into someone who might manage to make a good marriage. She was pretty enough and had a caring nature. She'd make a decent wife and mother if only she could be tamed a little.

Dessert was brought in – a banana *lassi* spiced with cardamom. When the kitchen *wallahs* and Sanjit had left the room, Wilfred cleared his throat. 'Celia, there is something I must speak with you about. I have to go to London tomorrow. Just for a brief trip. I expect to be back within a week. Ten days, perhaps, at the most.'

'You're going to England?' The girl looked up in surprise. 'Why did you not tell me before?'

'It was a last-minute decision.'

'Why are you going, Papa?'

'To make a start on putting arrangements in place for when we move back. Looking at suitable houses, and a school for you. Sounding out acquaintances regarding business opportunities. Meeting your uncle Cyril. And I will use the opportunity to take some items to my bank there for safekeeping. What with the problems in India, the independence movement and so forth . . . there are items that are better off in English banks.'

'Such as?'

'Just some important papers.'

'Can't you send someone else?'

'No, I cannot trust anyone else. You have heard of the riots and violence that is all too prevalent across the country? Mr Gandhi's followers are becoming more and more dangerous. I fear that should anything happen here, this house might be a target and valuable items stolen.'

'Papa, if this house could be a target, doesn't that mean that we are all in danger here? You, me, Sita, Sanjit and all the others? Do you care more about important papers than you do about us?' Celia clattered her spoon down onto her plate as she spoke, glaring at Wilfred.

It was typical of the girl to misunderstand, he thought. She'd always been a lively child, but these days she seemed to take every opportunity to be confrontational towards him. 'Of course I don't. But I will let it be known that all valuables have been removed from the house and lodged elsewhere. And that will reduce the chances of any mob attacking us.'

She stared at him, and a worried expression crept into her eyes. 'Papa, might they attack you on the way to the airport tomorrow?'

'No, I don't think that is at all likely.' He smiled at her, feeling oddly pleased that she'd shown concern for him. Perhaps it was just her age, being at that awkward stage between childhood and adulthood. He'd heard from friends that children often became rebellious or difficult at this age, but that they pulled through all right and became decent adults in the long run.

It was just tough having to deal with it all alone. Alice, he was sure, would have done a much better job. She would have known how to handle Celia.

'Anyway, as I say, Celia, I shall be gone tomorrow morning by the time you get up. Sita and Sanjit will look after you, and I shall be back in no time once my business is concluded. Is there anything you'd like me to bring back for you from London?' He had in mind some sort of gift, something with 'London' written on it, something quintessentially English that you couldn't find in India.

She shrugged. 'What on earth do they have there that we don't have here?'

'Well, um, I don't know what girls your age like . . . a dress, maybe? Or . . .' He'd been about to say stockings, or lipstick, remembering the sorts of things Alice would shop for on visits home. Actually, he had no idea what could be obtained in England these days. There was still strict rationing in place, a leftover from the war.

Celia smiled at him, a hint of triumph in her eyes. 'Anything I want, Papa, I can buy from the bazaar here. I don't like English things anyway.'

'Darling, you are English. Never forget that.'

'I feel more Indian.' She raised her chin as she spoke, defying him. It wasn't the first time she'd said this, and it wasn't the first time he'd admonished her for it.

He pushed back his chair and stood up. 'Don't ever say that. Don't think it. You are *not* Indian, despite where you were born and where you live. You are English. And before very long, you will be living in England, so you had better get used to the idea. For a start, stop wearing those *salwar kameez* and put on a dress, for goodness' sake! Stop running around wild with Vijay. Act like an English lady.'

'You mean I should spend my days playing the piano and reading romantic novels? Is that what you want? So I can ensnare a good husband?'

Precisely so, Wilfred was on the point of replying, but that would only inflame the situation further. And he was leaving tomorrow. He wouldn't see her again for a week or more, and he didn't want them to part on an argument. He sat down again, sighing heavily. 'Celia, you know I only want the best for you. I am sorry if I was a little harsh just now. Let's leave the subject for now, as I am going away. But we will talk more on it when I am back. You are growing up so fast, my dear, and people have expectations of you and . . .' He broke off. She was rolling her eyes, again, and through the glass-panelled door he could see Sanjit waiting to come in to serve his coffee and brandy. Sanjit may have worked for him for twenty years but there were some discussions one simply didn't have in front of the staff, and this was one of them.

Celia turned round as though checking what he was looking at, then she pushed back her chair. 'Well, it looks as though it's time for your brandy. Which means it's time for me to leave the table. I wish you weren't going away, Papa. I always worry that perhaps you might not come back, and what would become of me then? I'd have to go to the residence and throw myself on the mercy of the governor, I suppose. Or else go to the maharajah and see if he'll adopt me as a kind of sister to Vijay. Hmm. English, or Indian. It'd be a tough decision for me, don't you think?'

Without waiting for an answer, she walked out of the room.

Wilfred was left sitting at the table, shaking his head. But he was smiling – her tone had been teasing in those last remarks. Beneath it all, they had a good relationship and only wanted the best for each other. He'd see her before he retired to bed that evening, to say goodnight and goodbye, and they'd put the little spat behind them.

He beckoned to Sanjit to come in to serve the brandy. As he drank it, he switched his thoughts away from Celia and on to what he needed to achieve on this trip home. As well as his business interests, he needed to make a start on planning for his and Celia's futures, in a country he might call home but which, if he was honest, he barely knew.

Chapter 3

Lisa, 2023

'What are we going to do with it?' Lisa asked, staring down at the metal briefcase and its precious contents. She'd tucked the diamond brooch back into its box and into the pocket inside the briefcase, refastening the catches.

'What are *you* going to do with it, you mean. You found it. I reckon it's a case of finders keepers.' Gaby raised her eyebrows at Lisa.

'No, surely not! I must have to hand it in, somewhere. A police station or something. And then using my appalling French, explain where we found it.' Lisa grimaced at the thought. It was not an enticing prospect.

'It'll be late in the day by the time we get down the mountain, and we fly home tomorrow. Honestly, Lisa, I don't think we've time for all that. Besides, that newspaper is from India and the documents in the case are all in English, so it almost certainly doesn't belong to anyone French.'

'I suppose,' Lisa said, the idea forming in her mind as she spoke, 'I could take it home, go through the papers and see if I can find out who it belonged to. And then, you know, repatriate it all.'

'Or sell that brooch, which must be worth a fortune, if it's the real thing.'

'I couldn't. Something like that – it'd need provenance. Maybe it was stolen, and trying to sell it would alert the authorities and I'd be arrested for handling stolen goods . . .'

Gaby laughed. 'You've watched far too many crime dramas. If it was stolen, that would have happened back in the 1940s judging by the date on that newspaper. So I doubt anyone would care anyway.'

'Well, first things first,' Lisa said. 'We are several hours' walk up a mountain. How are we even going to get the case down?' She was thinking of the section where they'd had to scramble up a rock face. They'd need their hands free to get down that part.

'Let's consolidate our stuff into one rucksack, and then I think we can get the case into the other. Yours is larger – it'll fit in there I think. But let's eat our picnic first, eh?'

Lisa grinned and nodded. In all the excitement of finding the case she'd forgotten about eating. They'd made sandwiches in their apartment that morning – a fresh French baguette filled with ripe brie and tomatoes – and she was starving. They also had a flask of coffee, an apple each and some energy bars.

Twenty minutes later, with the food eaten and rucksacks repacked, Lisa hoisted her pack onto her shoulders. It was heavier than before and uncomfortable now that it contained the briefcase, but at least they were going downhill. She shifted it around on her back until it was as comfortable as it was going to get, and after taking a few more photos of each other grinning beside the glacier, they set off back down the mountain.

Back down in the valley, they caught a bus into the centre of Chamonix and walked through the town to their apartment. Lisa kept half expecting someone to stop her, put a hand on her shoulder and accuse her of stealing the jewel. It was hard to believe she possibly had a priceless diamond brooch in her rucksack. But, she kept reminding herself, it may very well be imitation and besides, it had almost certainly belonged to someone British. Surely in among all the papers she'd find a clue as to whose it was. She had no intention of keeping it or selling it. She would do all she could to find the owner, and if she had no luck, she'd give it to a museum or something like that.

She realised with a jolt that for the entire descent she'd only thought about the brooch, and it had chased all thoughts of Rupert out of her head for the first time since the break-up. She smiled. It was a good sign. It was almost as though the brooch had been sent to help her find her way forward in life. A fanciful idea, but one that she found oddly exciting.

As they passed through a central square in the town, Gaby stopped by a statue of two mountaineers, who were pointing up at the skyline. 'Look, its Balmat and Paccard. They're pointing at Mont Blanc.'

'I wondered who they were when we saw them the other day.' Lisa stopped to read the plaque, which was of course in French but she could make enough sense of it. 'Early adventurers. And now we've been part the way up, too.'

'Ha. The easy part.'

'It was hard enough! Come on. I need a shower, a cold beer and a large meal. Not necessarily in that order.' Lisa felt exhausted after the day's hike. She was more than ready to get the uncomfortable pack off her back and collapse onto the sofa in their apartment. It was the last night of the holiday; she'd be back at work in two days and she wanted to relax and enjoy the end of their trip.

'Shall we start looking through the papers in the case tonight?' Gaby asked as they let themselves into the apartment building and climbed the stairs.

Lisa shook her head. 'I'd rather leave it until I'm home, unless you particularly want to do it today. I'm too tired now. I'll have all day Sunday to go through it, in between putting machine-loads of washing on.'

'I'm glad you said that. I'm pretty exhausted too. You'll keep me up to date on any discoveries, though?'

'Will do.' Going through the contents of the briefcase would be a good way to keep her mind occupied and stop her brooding about Rupert.

'Bagsy first in the shower!' As they went into the apartment Gaby barged ahead of Lisa, straight into the bathroom.

'Be my guest,' Lisa called to her, laughing. 'I'll be first in the kitchen then, where I believe there's only one cold beer left in the fridge.'

Gaby poked her head around the bathroom door as Lisa opened the bottle of beer and took a long, refreshing swig of it. 'Aw! Oh, well. I guess I'll have to wait until we go out. Enjoy your beer.'

'Enjoy your shower!' Lisa laughed again.

They had a fabulous last night in Chamonix – finding a restaurant that served them a meal of *Tartiflette* and salad followed by profiteroles smothered in chocolate sauce, then going on to a bar for a few drinks where they were chatted up by a group of Australian climbers.

'If only we weren't going home tomorrow,' Gaby said, with a wink at Lisa, as they left the bar. 'You could have taken your pick of that crowd.'

'Hmm. They're all a bit loud for me,' Lisa replied. 'Besides, I'm not ready for a new man! I can cope on my own, you know. And actually, now that I'm all re-energised after this holiday I'm looking forward to being on my own, doing my own thing.'

'I know. Didn't mean to imply you're desperate. After Rupert, God knows you need a break from men. And of course, any time you want a girls' night out, I'm your woman.'

'Thanks, mate.' Lisa smiled at her friend. It had been a

wonderful week and she felt lucky to have a friend like Gaby who liked the same things she did, and was always prepared to spend a bit of time away from her long-term partner Josh.

The following morning, they got up early, ate a rushed breakfast, then took a bus to Geneva to catch their flight back to London. Lisa barely had time to think about the briefcase and its contents, which were inside her suitcase, checked in as hold baggage. She'd had to cram her clothes in around it. She and Gaby were far too busy chatting about the climbs they'd done, the views from the tops, and where they'd go for the next walking trip. 'Dolomites, I think. Or Pyrenees. Or some other part of the Alps. Honestly, as long as there are mountains I don't really care!' Gaby said, with a chuckle, as they flew over France.

'Wherever we go, I'm going to be sure to be fitter before the start. I am so stiff this morning.'

'It was a big walk yesterday. I'll let you into a secret. I'm stiff as a board too.'

Lisa smiled. 'That makes me feel better.'

They parted at Heathrow with plans to get together soon to reminisce and look at each other's photos again. 'But keep me updated on what you find in the briefcase, and what you decide to do with that brooch,' Gaby made Lisa promise.

Lisa returned to her flat in Battersea and spent the evening unpacking and making a start on the washing. The briefcase she put on her coffee table where it caught her eye every time she walked through the sitting room. 'That's a job for tomorrow,' she promised herself. She'd have time then to dedicate to going through all the papers and having a good look at that diamond brooch. She still had no idea what she'd do with it.

On Sunday morning her first job, after making herself a coffee, was to try to find out how the briefcase could have found its way onto a glacier high in the Alps. It just wasn't the sort of thing a mountaineer would take up there. The date on the newspaper she'd found inside was July 1947, so that was a huge clue she could follow up. She fired up her laptop and spent some time on Google, searching groups of terms including 'Mont Blanc', the names of the two glaciers, '1947'. She found several interesting websites that described walks up Mont Blanc including the exact walk she and Gaby had done to La Jonction. And she found other websites that told the story of Mont Blanc's first ascent. All very interesting but not what she was looking for.

At last, after a third cup of coffee she spotted a link to a Wikipedia page about an aircraft that had crashed on Mont Blanc in 1947. 'That must be it!' she said aloud, as she opened the link and skimmed through the article. The plane was a Lockheed Constellation with about fifty passengers on board. It was a BOAC plane that regularly flew a route between London and Delhi, with stops for refuelling in Milan and Beirut. It had crashed during a storm – investigators had postulated that it must have been flying too low and with poor visibility. Lisa supposed that in those days aircraft instrumentation wasn't as good as now. The plane had crashed near the summit of the mountain, and because of the storm no one had been able to reach the wreckage site for days. There were no survivors and no chance of recovering bodies from that altitude as everything had already been covered by several feet of new snow. Over time, everything – wreckage, bodies, luggage – was claimed by the glacier and entombed in ice.

It seemed that her briefcase wasn't the first item from the crash to have been recovered decades later. A plane seat, a few pieces of metalwork from the plane's fuselage and a wristwatch had all been found, just as the briefcase was, brought down by the glacier and recovered from its edge. It was expected that more would surface in time, especially with the effects of global warming meaning the glacier's leading edge was retreating.

As she read about the discoveries, Lisa gasped. The watch had been engraved on the back, and the finder had managed to use that engraving to track down descendants of its owner, to whom the watch was returned.

'So it is possible! And I have a case full of papers to help me, not just a brief inscription on a watch.' She sent a WhatsApp message to Gaby to tell her what she'd found out so far.

Gaby was on the phone to her in minutes. 'That's an awesome discovery, mate! Makes perfect sense as well, given where we found it. So the owner of the briefcase was probably some businessman. Wonder why he was bringing such a valuable jewel with him?'

'Perhaps he'd bought it to give to a woman?'

'Lucky woman! Wonder who she could have been to warrant a gift like that? Have you read through any of the papers yet?'

'Give me a chance! First of all I wanted to work out how the briefcase came to be half-way up Mont Blanc. With that mystery solved I can then work on the documents. Hey – the newspaper is the *Times of India* and dated 1947. And the flight was between Delhi and London. Which means . . .'

'Yeah?' Gaby sounded confused.

'Indian independence was in 1947, right?' As she spoke, Lisa opened a new browser tab on her laptop and quickly ran a search. 'Yes. August 1947.'

'So . . . what does that mean for us?'

'Nothing really. Just interesting that it's from that time, is all.' Lisa smiled. Gaby never had much interest in history, unless it was related to mountain climbing. That was her specialist subject.

'Right. Listen, mate, I've got to go. Josh and I are having a date night tonight, to make up for me abandoning him for a week. And after a week in the mountains, I need a lot of pampering time to make myself look presentable.'

'Ooh, nice. Have fun! Bye.'

As she ended the call, Lisa felt a pang of regret that she no longer had anyone to go out on a date night with. But then she remembered Rupert and shuddered. Better that she was alone than still with him.

And, actually, the idea of going out tonight didn't appeal. She'd be much happier staying in, perhaps pouring herself a glass of wine, and rummaging through the papers in that briefcase. It was certainly doing a good job of keeping her mind off Rupert.

Chapter 4

Celia, March 1947

Celia woke late the next morning and it took her a moment to remember that Papa was leaving for England. He might well have left the house already. Usually he woke her, clattering around outside her room. He probably did it on purpose, she'd always thought. She knew he was setting off early so presumably today he'd tiptoed about, not wanting to wake her, for once. He'd said goodbye the night before, and she'd hugged him and told him to come back soon, and to be careful. He'd kissed the top of her head in response. He might worry about the riots in India, but she worried about what might happen to him in faraway, grey London where pickpockets were everywhere, where trains ran underground, where unexploded bombs from the war were constantly turning up. Not to mention the dangers involved in getting there and back again by aeroplane.

She swung her legs out of bed, stretched, and pushed open the blinds at the window. It was March, and the year was already beginning to get hot. The atmosphere felt thick with dust, and that would only become worse until the monsoon rains arrived in June. They'd go to the hills before then, to escape the heat and then the deluge, as so many family members of the British civil servants did. Celia liked the monsoon. She loved the way it washed the air, leaving everything feeling fresh and clean. And the weather post-monsoon was perfect. The sky would be a sparkling blue, the temperatures just right, the days full of promise. The worst time of the year, in Celia's opinion, was the two or three months immediately before the monsoon, when the heat of the year had set in and every day was hot and sticky, the sky was a dull orangey-pink full of dust and everyone was short-tempered.

In other words, now.

She shrugged on a light cotton dressing gown and left her room, walking barefooted along the veranda and across the central courtyard. With Papa not around there was no one to tell her off for not putting shoes on. Sita was sitting on a chair outside her own room in the servants' wing, dressed in a pink and brown sari. She was sewing something with small neat stitches, the way she'd tried but failed to teach Celia. She smiled as Celia approached.

'Good morning. I didn't wake you today. I thought you would want to sleep longer as the *sahib* is away.'

'Thanks, yes, the lie-in was lovely. Are you going to the bazaar this morning? Can I come?' Celia had free time until two o'clock, when a tutor was due to come to the house to spend a couple of hours teaching her history and mathematics.

'Of course. We will buy some mangoes, yes?'

Celia grinned. Mangoes were her favourite thing to eat and Sita knew it well. But her main reason for wanting to go to the bazaar that day was simply to get out of the house, to take the opportunity to go to the bustling, busy market while Papa was not around to tell her not to. He'd been uncomfortable about her going to busy places lately, since the rioting had intensified. It wasn't safe, he'd told her. But she couldn't stay home every day, protected by the high white-washed walls that ran around the perimeter of their grounds. Life was out there, in the bustling streets of Agra, in the villages surrounding it, in the lazy Yamuna River running through the city past its most famous monument, the Taj Mahal. A building Celia loved, and visited as often as she could. Something about its perfect symmetry and glowing dome made her feel at ease with herself and her life. It was a place of healing, she'd always felt.

'I'll get some breakfast; then can we go?'

Sita looked her up and down, raising an eyebrow, and Celia laughed. 'Oh, yes. I suppose I should get dressed first. What would I do without you?' She kissed the top of Sita's head and ran back across the courtyard to her room to dress.

Sita had been part of the family since Celia was born – employed first as a nursemaid, or *ayah*, but these days her role was simply to be a companion for Celia. When Celia's mother had died it had been Sita who came to tell her, Sita who'd held her tight while she wept, Sita who'd slept in her bed comforting her night after night until the tears finally ceased. Papa had barely wanted to see her during those first few weeks. He'd been thin-lipped and silent, waving her away whenever she tried to approach. She'd wanted – *needed* – a hug from her remaining parent, reassurance that he wasn't going to leave her like Mama had, but he'd seemed unable to offer it. It was Sita who'd stepped up to the role of comforter, caregiver and, as Celia grew, confidant.

Celia tore off her pyjamas and stuffed them under her pillow, then opened her wardrobe to decide what to wear. With Papa away there was no one to disapprove if she wore Indian clothes, so she pulled out a turquoise *salwar kameez* set and a pair of flat leather sandals that had a matching strand of turquoise silk threaded through. She tugged a brush through her long dark hair and draped it over her shoulder, plaiting it. She checked her appearance in the mirror and smiled. A little more tan, a *bindi* on her forehead, and she could pass for a north Indian girl, she thought. The idea pleased her. Who cared about faraway, cold, grey England? This was her home. Colourful, chaotic, warm and wonderful India.

Soon after, she left the compound with Sita, who was carrying a wicker basket. They walked along the wide tree-lined avenues of the prosperous British area of the city towards the part Celia loved the best – the narrow alleys of the bazaar where you could wander for hours and find something new around every corner. She loved the hustle and bustle; the bullock carts and rickshaws; the ramshackle houses; the canvas-covered stalls selling roasted nuts, paper bags of spices, exotic fruits, lengths of cotton, copper pans and so much more; the women in their colourful saris and men in white *kurtis*; the beggars with their endless calls for *baksheesh*; the scruffy children chasing each other in and out of buildings; the dogs, cats, chickens, goats and cattle wandering freely; the smells, the noise, the life that was everywhere – Celia loved it all.

'Oof, it is becoming hot!' Sita said, fanning her face with her hand. 'Two or three more months and we will be going to the hills. I will be glad when that time comes at last.'

'I won't be,' Celia said, pouting. 'I wish we could just stay here.'

'It is too hot, *meri jaan*. No English ladies stay down on the plains in the monsoon, and you are an English lady. Besides, I go where you go, and I prefer the hills.' Sita flashed a smile at Celia.

'All right. For you, I will go to the hills. Just for you.' Celia linked arms with Sita and pulled her close. It was true, she would do anything for Sita, and she knew Sita would do anything for her. Sita had family in the city – a brother, his wife and their several children, and elderly parents. But she'd said many times that Celia was also her family, the baby she'd more or less brought up, the child she'd cared for and loved with all her heart.

They rounded a corner and reached the beginnings of the bazaar – streets and alleys lined with stalls packed tightly together, the shops behind them also open with goods displayed on tables spilling out onto the road. Sita crossed to a stall selling silk saris and fingered a few. 'Beautiful, yes?'

'Simply gorgeous,' Celia said, picking up a bright green one threaded with gold. 'I would love this but Papa would definitely never let me wear it. He doesn't even like it when I wear this.' She indicated the baggy trousers of her *salwar kameez*. 'Maybe I should buy it anyway and wear it when he is away.'

'It is too expensive, *meri jaan*. I was looking at it only because I will perhaps buy a new sari for my nephew's wedding.'

'Nephew's wedding? You never told me! When is that?'

'I do not know, but Bhavik is searching for a wife for him, so it might be soon.'

'Your nephew is not even betrothed?' She should be used to it, but it never ceased to amaze Celia how marriages were arranged, sometimes at short notice, within Indian families.

'Not yet.' Sita smiled. 'But he is a good boy and it will not be long before Bhavik finds him a suitable bride. And I wish to be ready with a suitable outfit as auntie of the groom.'

'That green one would suit you.'

Sita began to move away, to browse the next stall where spices of all sorts were being sold. But Celia stayed where she was, handling the green sari, admiring the way its fine silk slipped through her fingers. It would suit Sita, and would be lovely for her to wear at her nephew's wedding. On a whim, Celia pulled out her purse, haggled a little with the stallholder and agreed a price for the sari and a matching blouse.

'*Meri jaan*, what are you doing?' Sita was back at her side.

'Buying this.'

'But . . . please, no, not for me . . . I couldn't accept it . . .' Sita shook her head and held her hands together in a gesture of pleading.

Celia cocked her head on one side and regarded her *ayah*. 'Not for you, then. For me. I have always wanted to own a sari, and this one is simply beautiful.' She gave the stallholder the money and tucked the sari into Sita's basket, taking the basket from her. 'I'll carry this, now.'

Sita looked as if she was about to reply when a crowd of people came running around the corner, careering into stalls and knocking them over, shouting. A basket of oranges fell, scattering across the street. One man was brandishing a stick, shouting in Hindi.

Celia stood and stared, trying to make sense of what the men were shouting. Sita had taught her Hindi but she couldn't always make out the local accent.

'Celia, come! We must run!' Sita grabbed her by the arm and pulled her away, out of the path of the oncoming mob.

'Who are they? What are they doing?'

'They are protesting . . . they are starting a riot . . .' Sita was panting, still clutching Celia's hand. The poor woman was not made for running, Celia thought, as they dodged between stalls to get out of the way. She'd been taller than her *ayah* since she was ten years old. The basket over her arm was being knocked about and Celia was worried her new sari would fall out. The mob was very close, knocking over everything in their way and she could smell that something was on fire, a stall, perhaps. At that moment she spotted an escape route and pulling on Sita's arm said, 'In here.' She darted through an open archway that led along a passage and into a quiet courtyard of an abandoned house. It was somewhere she'd sometimes been with Vijay, before these days of riots and protests had begun, playing make-believe games where the house would be their fortress, to be defended against tigers, pirates or evil magicians.

'What if the rioters come this way?' Sita panted, looking around at the enclosed courtyard.

'Upstairs.' Celia tugged again on Sita's hand, pulling her towards an external staircase that was tucked away in a hidden corner of the courtyard. It led to a roof terrace, that in the old games had been their last stronghold, the place where she and Vijay finally defeated whoever the baddies were that day. 'We'll be safe up here. And we can see what's going on.'

They hurried up the steps, Sita clutching at the hem of her sari. Once on the terrace the Indian woman sat down heavily on an old wooden chair. 'Oof. I cannot run like you, young thing.'

Celia put the basket down beside Sita then approached the edge of the terrace to peer over the low wall, down into the streets below. She could just about see into the street where they'd been shopping, where rioters were passing through, seemingly intent on destroying everything in their path. There were dozens of them, and fights had broken out up and down the street with stallholders trying to protect their wares. She shuddered. It was certainly getting ugly.

Sita called to her. 'Come away from the edge, *meri jaan*. You might fall. Or they might see you and come up here to find you.'

Celia took a step back and then sat down cross-legged on the floor in front of Sita. 'I suppose we just have to wait until it all calms down. What are they rioting about this time?'

'I heard – they are shouting – there are the Muslims and the Hindus and they are fighting each other. They do not want the country to be divided in the Punjab.'

'Why not?'

'They do not want to have separate countries.'

'So they fight each other to prove they can live together?' Celia pulled a face. It made no sense. She was only vaguely aware of what was going on in Indian politics. Papa kept talking about *when* India achieved independence but she tended to switch off and not listen to him. She just wanted things to continue as they had been all her life – with Papa working for the Civil Service and attending formal dinners at the governor's residence, her spending time with Vijay and going to the bazaar with Sita, and most of all, she and Papa remaining in India.

'I do not know why they fight each other,' Sita said, sadly.

Celia shifted so she was kneeling in front of Sita and pulled her in for a hug, resting her face on Sita's shoulder. She could smell the scented hair oil her *ayah* used. 'Will it end, do you think, when India gets independence?'

Sita shrugged. 'I do not know. You could ask the *sahib* what he thinks. I hope it will end.'

'And do you hope that independence will be soon? They've been talking of it for years.' All her life there had been mutterings. Ever since Mr Gandhi started stirring things up with his salt marches. What had started out as a peaceful movement was certainly not entirely peaceful now.

'I think it may be soon. Next year, perhaps.'

'Next year.' Celia stared across the rooftops of Agra. In the distance she could see the dome and minarets of the Taj Mahal and beyond it, the brown waters of the Yamuna River winding its way through the town. Next year was so soon. Whenever Papa spoke of Indian independence, he went on to say that when it happened there would be no job for him in India and that they would return 'home'. To England, he meant. Celia had tried not to think of it. It was not what she wanted, ever. 'Sita, if it happens, and Papa takes me to England, will you come with me?'

Sita gave a little chuckle and shook her head. 'Ah, *meri jaan*. I cannot come to England. My parents are here, my brother is here, and my nieces and nephews are here. I am Indian. I must stay here, in India. It is where I belong.'

Celia gasped. 'But I can't go without you! You have always been with me.'

Sita picked up her hand and kissed it. 'I know. But I am not English like you and I would be unhappy in England. Besides, you are almost a woman. You will not need your old *ayah* soon.'

'If you're not going to England then I don't want to go either.' Last year she and Papa had made a short trip to England, the first since Mama died. He'd been testing her, she thought, trying to discover how she'd like England when the time came to move for good. He'd introduced her to girls her own age, daughters of old friends who'd already moved back to England, but she'd found she had nothing in common with them. It had rained every day of their stay — not furious downpours like the Indian monsoon but damp, penetrating, depressing drizzle. Life was lived indoors, with curtains drawn and fires lit, and she'd hated every minute of it. Worst of all, she'd missed Sita and Vijay. It had hurt so much, the intensity of her longing for their company. If England meant no Sita and no Vijay, then Celia wanted none of it.

'But you must do what the *sahib* says.' Sita turned away, staring at the distant horizon, then looked back at Celia. 'It might be a long time yet. Let's not worry, eh, *meri jaan*. Listen, I think the street is quiet. We can leave and go home now.'

'What about the shopping?'

'I fear the stalls are all broken. We must go straight home where it is safe. We will shop another time.'

Celia got to her feet and helped Sita up. She looked over the parapet once more and could see Sita was right, the rioters had dispersed or moved on. Market stallholders were retrieving what was left of their goods, packing things away. Further across the city there were shouts and then the sound of gunfire. It wouldn't be the first time police had opened fire on rioters. Sita was right: they had better just get themselves safely home as soon as they could.

Everything was changing. Celia felt alone and frightened without Papa there to look after her. And yet she knew that she'd feel even worse if she was taken back to England without Sita. Life in a strange and distant country, even if it was the mother country, without her *ayah* was a terrifying prospect.

Chapter 5

Lisa, 2023

Lisa spent most of the rest of Sunday unpacking, dealing with the washing and putting her flat in order. There was nothing worse than spending a long hard day at work and coming home to mess and clutter, she always thought. She liked to come home to a tidy, clean sanctuary. It was one of the things she'd hated about Rupert. He lived in an apartment where a cleaner came in daily to tidy up after him, wash the dishes, deal with his washing. Whenever he'd stayed with Lisa, he seemed to assume she had the same set-up. Despite her telling him many times that in her flat there was only herself to pick dirty clothes off the floor, load the dishwasher and wipe the kitchen surfaces, he still left mess everywhere. And he never once helped her to tidy it up.

Yet somehow, she'd allowed him to act like this. She'd told herself that clearing up after him was a way of paying him back for all the lavish gifts and expensive nights out that he insisted on paying for. She'd let herself slip into the role of trophy girlfriend crossed with 1950s housewife. And it wasn't who she really was.

As she stowed her rucksack at the back of her wardrobe and

put the last load of washing into the drier, she gazed around the flat. One thing was certain, without Rupert in her life it was much easier to keep the place clean and tidy.

There was no more housework to do now. She glanced at the metal briefcase that was lying on one end of her sofa, teasing her with its contents.

'Time to go through your paperwork,' she told it, and made herself a cup of tea to drink while she looked through it. Returning to the sofa, she unclipped the briefcase's catches and flipped open the lid, which opened easily this time. It was far from full, which was odd. For a man on a business trip that would take him halfway around the world, you'd expect him to fill his briefcase with papers, especially in the days before computers. On the top was the *Times of India* newspaper that she and Gaby had already seen while on the mountain. She scanned the headlines, which were all about the progress of Indian independence and the engagement of Princess Elizabeth to Philip Mountbatten, then put it to one side to look through more thoroughly later.

Under the paper was a sealed envelope of thick, cream-coloured paper. In fountain pen, someone had written *Celia* on the front. 'Bet that's a love letter,' she muttered. What a shame the addressee, this Celia whoever she was, had never received it. Perhaps the brooch was a gift for her. Beneath the letter was a pad of the same paper and a few matching envelopes.

Then there were a couple of sheets of paper, stapled together. The sheets were headed with a crest and the words *Grosvenor Hotel, Buckingham Palace Road*. Lisa studied the typewritten details. It was an invoice, for a three-night stay in the hotel and dated March 1947. The guest had eaten breakfasts and a dinner there too, and had drunk several whiskies in the bar.

On the second page was what Lisa was hoping for – confirmation of the guest's name. Mr W Fforbes-Whyte. No Mrs, only a Mr. That lent weight to the idea he was travelling for business purposes.

'So I have your name, Mr Fforbes-Whyte.' Lisa grinned and jotted the name into a notebook. 'But where did you live in England? Obviously not in London as you needed to use a hotel there. Who were your family members? Why did you have a valuable jewel in your briefcase?'

There was also a business card from a hotel in Delhi in among the London hotel paperwork.

She picked up the next document and studied it. 'Ah-ha. Another clue.' It was a letter from a bank confirming the reservation of a safe deposit box and detailing instructions of how to access it.

Lisa tapped a fingertip against the letter. Had he been planning to deposit the diamond brooch at his bank? If the jewel was genuine, it was certainly the sort of thing one might keep in a safe deposit box. Or had he perhaps collected it from there?

Beneath the letter was a sheaf of papers in a folder. They were all house details. None had photographs of the property, they comprised only a typewritten description of the house and the dimensions of each room. She supposed that in the 1940s there were no photocopiers, therefore, no chance of illustrating house details with pictures.

The properties all looked to be in Chelsea and Pimlico. 'Expensive part of town,' she mused. At least it was an expensive part of London these days. Among them was a brochure for a girls' school – the Lady Margaret – in the same area.

At the very bottom of the briefcase was a paperback book – a Penguin edition of *Brideshead Revisited* with a bookmark tucked inside at page forty-two. 'You didn't get too far with this,' Lisa told the unknown man.

That was everything that was in the case. She'd hoped, she supposed, for some sort of family photograph, or something with his home address on. But she had his name and she'd come up with a theory as to why he was flying between London and Delhi. Even though she had no idea why he was taking such a valuable jewel with him.

She felt around the sides of the case, feeling unsure why she was doing so but with the vague idea there might be some secret compartment that would spring open if she pressed at the right place . . . but nothing happened. There was only the internal pocket in which the brooch's box had been tucked. Besides, she told herself, there was no space for any more compartments. The case was lined with a black fabric but she could feel the metal through it all the way around.

She picked up her notebook in which she'd jotted down the few definite things she knew about the owner of the case. The hotels he'd stayed at, the branch of the Midland bank he used. Would there be any way to find out more via the London hotel or the bank? She knew that the Midland had become HSBC years ago. She checked the address of the branch that had written to Mr Fforbes-Whyte on Google Maps and discovered it was no longer a bank. Now it was a pub – one of a cheap chain.

But the man's name. It was an unusual one. She felt a shiver of distaste at the double-barrelled name – Rupert Wyndham-Royce had put her off those for life. Something about the name Fforbes-Whyte rang a distant bell, but she couldn't put her finger on why that was.

'Where have I heard that name before?' she wondered. The answer would no doubt come to her at about three o'clock in the morning. Or not at all.

The name didn't come to Lisa at three o'clock in the morning, though. She slept straight through. *Must have been more tired than I realised*, she thought, as she dragged herself out of bed on Monday morning. Back to the grind, after such a restorative holiday. As she left her apartment block and walked the short distance to Battersea tube station, she already felt she was missing the mountains. London was all very well but there were too many people, too many buildings and not enough air. And too much of city life reminded her of her time with Rupert. This was his domain.

Work was . . . well, work. Spreadsheets, numbers, meetings, discussions about future strategy, reports. And catching up on what she'd missed while on holiday. Lisa found herself gazing out of the window far too much. But the view was only of the building across the street and the traffic below.

She sent Gaby a WhatsApp message. *Missing the mountains. You?*

The reply was almost instantaneous. *God yes. Let's plan another trip ASAP. Any more news on the mysterious briefcase?*

I have a name for the owner, Lisa replied. *Mr W Fforbes-Whyte.* It was too complex to type all that she'd discovered or guessed at into her phone. Gaby would have to wait until they could call each other or meet up, before she passed on the rest of what she'd found out.

There was no immediate response. Presumably Gaby was now in a meeting. She'd reply later.

Lisa sighed and returned to her work. Beside her, Justin Beale, who'd worked for the department as long as she had, turned and gave her a wry smile. 'Post-holiday blues, eh, Lisa?'

'Yep. London's so . . . built-up. I can't get used to it again.'

'Where were you?'

'French Alps.'

'Ah, yes. Not so built-up. Well, I have a suggestion for you that'll help ease you back into London life. If you're not doing anything tonight it's Amanda's birthday, and we're going for drinks after work in the King's Arms. There's a bit of a crowd coming, and you'd be very welcome to join us.'

'Oh! Thank you. Yes, I might just do that.' Something to look forward to that evening. She liked Justin and his girlfriend Amanda. She decided to pop out in her lunch break and buy a card and some small gift for Amanda.

'Great! See you there from about six-thirty then.' Justin grinned and turned back to his computer to peer at a complex-looking spreadsheet. Much the same as the one Lisa herself was poring over. The numbers were all blurring into an amorphous mass, as all she could see in her mind's eye were the glaciers at La Jonction and the beautiful diamond brooch they'd yielded up to her. At least thinking about the mountains meant she wasn't dwelling on Rupert and how many years of her life she'd wasted on him.

The day passed more quickly now that she had something to look forward to in the evening. At lunchtime she managed to buy a card and a gift box of Molton Brown toiletries – unoriginal but everyone liked nice shower gels in pretty packaging, didn't they? She touched up her make-up in the office loos and arrived at the pub at quarter to seven. Justin and Amanda had requisitioned a couple of tables near the back, and there was a good crowd already there. A few were from her office and the rest were Amanda's friends. Lisa said hello to everyone she knew and passed Amanda the little bag containing her gift and card.

'Hi, Lisa, oh, you didn't have to get me anything!' Amanda peeked inside and squealed in delight. 'Molton Brown – oh I adore their stuff. Perfect, thank you!'

'You're very welcome. Happy birthday!' Lisa kissed her on both cheeks and found a seat at the table.

'Is Rupert coming tonight too?' Amanda asked.

'Ah, no. We've split up,' Lisa replied with a smile that she hoped indicated she didn't need sympathy.

'Oh! So sorry to hear that.'

'Don't be. Honestly he was—' Lisa stopped just in time. She'd been about to say, 'he was a wanker,' when she remembered that she'd originally met Rupert at another occasion with Justin and Amanda. She couldn't remember exactly, but possibly it had been Amanda who'd introduced them. If he'd been a friend of Amanda's then it was probably best not to say anything bad about him. In any case, she didn't want to talk, or even think, about him.

But Amanda was nodding sagely. 'He was indeed.' And then she spotted someone else coming into the pub and turned away to greet them.

Justin was by her side. 'You've no drink! What would you like?'

'Oh, I'll pay . . .'

'No, you won't, we've got a tab running behind the bar. Gin and tonic, am I right?'

'Sure, thanks.' Lisa smiled at him as he went to fetch her drink. Justin was one of the good guys. It was nice to know they still existed after her experience with Rupert. Her smile faltered as she pondered why she'd taken so long to ditch Rupert.

'What are you looking so serious about?' Justin said, returning with her drink.

'Oh, nothing. Nice to be out.'

'You broke up with Rupert, Amanda says?'

'Yes. Not long before my holiday.'

'So you're back on the market. I'll let my single mates know,' Justin said, with a wink.

'Only if they're really nice, decent blokes, good-looking with a fit body. Oh, and they need to be into mountain walking.'

'Hmm. I'll see what I can do, madame.' He gave her a mock bow.

Lisa laughed and sipped her drink. Around her the buzz of post-work, early evening socialising was well under way. This was the part of London living she enjoyed. The part she'd miss if she moved to a quiet little village in the country.

And then she heard a voice at the other side of the pub, a voice she recognised ordering drinks loudly. She glanced across. Rupert. In a shiny suit over a bright pink shirt, and flourishing a credit card as he bought drinks for a gaggle of fellows who could have been his clones. Surely Amanda or Justin would have warned her if they'd invited Rupert to the drinks party?

Justin must have seen what she was looking at, for he caught her eye and gave a little grimace and a shrug, as if to say it was nothing to do with him.

This was the pub they so often went to for post-work drinks. There was no way Rupert was going to chase her out of it, Lisa decided. She turned her back and hoped he hadn't noticed her. She could hear him commenting on the barmaid's cleavage. So could most of the rest of the people in the pub. She grimaced. How could she have stayed with him for two years?

She recalled the last time they'd gone on holiday together. It was the occasion when the scales had fallen from her eyes. Before then, she hadn't noticed, or had chosen not to notice, his bad behaviour. But on holiday, in Nice in the south of France, he'd refused to even attempt to speak French. When she pointed out that the French like to start all interactions with a greeting – a simple *Bonjour* or *Bonsoir* – and that if you did that you were much more likely to make a connection with them, he'd simply laughed. 'Why would I want to do that? They all speak English. They're just too lazy to bother sometimes.' And when the French hadn't understood him, he'd spoken louder and louder, leaning right into the poor person's face and treating them as though they were simple. On one occasion when he'd done this, a waiter threw his hands in the air and walked off, then refused to serve them. Lisa had been mortified. She'd realised then that she couldn't stay with a man who behaved like that. But he was paying for the holiday and there seemed to be no easy way to begin a break-up conversation. She'd been with him too long. He'd sapped her self-confidence.

Two weeks after returning from that holiday, when she'd still been trying to work out how best to end things with the least amount of hassle, they'd been invited to one of her colleague's leaving drinks party. On the way home they had passed a homeless man curled up in a shop doorway in a grubby sleeping bag. Rupert had kicked the man's feet. 'Oy, wake up, tosser! You're making the place untidy!' he'd said.

'For God's sake, Rupert. Leave the poor bloke alone.' Lisa had pulled at Rupert's arm.

'Nah. I wanted to take a piss in that doorway and he's in the way. Maybe I'll take a piss anyway.' To her utter disgust he'd then started opening his flies.

'No, you bloody well won't,' Lisa said, dragging Rupert away. 'That's disgusting and despicable.'

'Only joking, Lees.' He shrugged her off. 'I don't even need a piss.'

She turned and walked away, wanting to lead him away from the man in the doorway but also wanting to get away from him.

'Don't walk off! Lees, for God's sake, I said I was joking.'

'You can't even joke about it, Rupert. It's a horrible thing to say.'

'He didn't even hear me. Too drunk, I think. Look.' It was true that the man seemed to have slept through it all, but that didn't excuse Rupert's behaviour.

And suddenly, that was it. The last straw, that somehow helped her find her confidence and find the strength to do what she ought to have done long before.

'Rupert, we are over. I'm going home. I'll drop round tomorrow with the things you've left at my flat.'

'What do you mean, we're over? Over? I'm the one who'll make that decision, Lees. Not you.'

She stared at him. 'Oh, no you're not. I've made the decision. We're finished. I can't be with someone who . . . who . . .'

'Who what?' He took a step towards her. His fists were clenched, she noticed. There was no one else in the street and suddenly she felt scared.

'I'll bring your things tomorrow.' And she turned and walked away quickly, hurrying around the corner onto a busier road and then into the nearest tube station entrance. Not the line she usually used but she'd just wanted to get away from him, get herself into a crowd where he couldn't hurt her.

As soon as she was safely on a tube train, she'd leaned against the closed door, breathing heavily, half appalled by what she'd done and half delighted. A woman had touched her arm, asking, 'You all right, love?' and Lisa had nodded.

'Yes, I think I will be.'

And that had been it. She'd gone to his flat at a time when she knew he'd be out at the gym and dropped off the few belongings he'd left at her flat. She'd let herself in with the key he'd given her, picked up a few of her own possessions and left the key in the kitchen. She'd felt shaky being in his place, terrified he might suddenly turn up. Her first anxiety attack. Thankfully, she'd never given him a key to her own place.

Within a week she'd heard that he'd already been seen out with a new girlfriend. Good luck to her, she'd thought. And then Gaby had suggested the Chamonix holiday. It was short notice but came at a perfect time for her.

Now, it was the first time she'd set eyes on him since that night. And she really wasn't certain she wanted to speak to him. She wasn't sure she had the strength to deal with him. She kept her back to the bar and prayed he wouldn't notice her.

But he'd noticed Amanda. 'Mandy! How good to see you! How's things? How's your little Justin?'

'I'm good, thanks,' Lisa heard Justin reply, in a slightly frosty tone. Being called 'little' would have irked him. He was shorter than Rupert but average height for a man.

'Ah, bloody hell, Lisa's here too. Hey, Lees. How are things? Missing me, are you?'

There was no choice but to acknowledge him at least. She turned slightly so she could see him. 'Hello, Rupert.'

'I asked if you were missing me?' There was a confrontational look in his eye. Justin moved so that he was partly between her and Rupert and she felt grateful for the quiet support.

'No, not really.' Not at all, she wanted to say, but there was no point in antagonising him. Her voice had emerged as a squeak.

'Hey, Rupert, mate. We're here on a kind of private party, you know? If you wouldn't mind . . .' Justin tried to usher Rupert away from their corner of the pub.

Oh, no, Lisa thought. Worst thing to do. And indeed, Rupert prodded Justin in the chest with a finger. 'Who are you to tell me which part of this pub I can be in? It's a *pub*, right? Public bar. And I want to sit in this corner. With my old friend, Lees.'

'Rupert . . .' Lisa began, not quite knowing what he was going to say. But he'd prodded Justin one too many times, and Justin caught his arm.

'Stop doing that.'

'Or what? I'm twice your size, bud. I could knock you out with one punch.'

'Right, mate, that's enough. You're out.' The landlord had made his way over, accompanied by the bouncer who usually was at the door. Right behind them was the barmaid Rupert had been harassing, and Lisa guessed she'd made a complaint.

'What? What've I done?' Rupert threw his hands up but clearly thought better of taking on the landlord and the burly bouncer.

'You're causing trouble. You're out.'

'Fuck you. Shithole of a pub anyway.' Rupert left, grumbling, escorted by the bouncer.

'He'd abused Shania. I was considering chucking him out anyway. Then I saw him angling for a fight with you. Don't need that sort of trouble.' The landlord nodded at Justin.

'Thanks, mate.'

'Know him, do you?'

Lisa grimaced. 'I used to date him. Not anymore.' Her heart was pounding after the confrontation.

'You're well out of it, I reckon.' The landlord turned away and went back to the bar. He was right, she thought. She certainly was better off without him.

'Well. That was a bit of excitement,' Justin said.

'Yes. Thanks for sticking up for me. I'll get you a drink.'

She went to the bar to buy him and Amanda a drink but

decided against another one for herself. Truth be told, she didn't want to stay much longer. Just fifteen minutes or so, to make sure Rupert was well away from the pub, then she'd make her excuses and leave. There was still more research she could do relating to the briefcase and its contents, and Rupert's appearance at the pub had made her feel sick.

Chapter 6

Wilfred, March 1947

It was beginning to get hot, and yet still only March. Wilfred was sweating by the time he left the railway station. Sanjit was there to meet him with the car, which had been parked in full sun and was stiflingly hot inside. Wilfred mopped his brow with a handkerchief as he eased himself into the back seat. London had been cool, with a bit of drizzle, and he had not seen the sun the entire time he'd been there. Not that you could really see the sun here either, now that there was so much dust in the air. But by Jove you could feel it. He'd be glad when the time came to leave India for good. Even though he'd lived almost all his life in the country, he was heartily sick of it.

'Welcome home, *sahib*,' Sanjit said, grinning at him in the rear-view mirror. 'I hope your trip went well.'

'Yes, I did all that I needed to.' He'd made arrangements at his bank to rent a safe deposit box, and had picked up property details for several houses which might be suitable for himself and Celia, when the time came. And he'd seen his brother Cyril, albeit very briefly. There was still work to be done in that regard. But at least they'd met, and Cyril knew he and Celia would soon be returning to England to live. The next time he flew to London would be the last; Celia would be alongside him and they'd be returning to England forever.

'Good, that is good, *sahib*.' Sanjit navigated the car through the streets of Agra towards the bungalow. Wilfred sat back and relaxed. It had been a long, long journey. He'd taken a train to Heathrow, then flights with BOAC from Heathrow to Milan, Beirut and finally Delhi, and then a train from Delhi to Agra. He was tired, hot and sticky, and wanted nothing more than to sit in his living room for the evening, with the ceiling fans turning and a glass of Scotch in his hand. Not long now. Though he would need to see Celia first, before she retired to bed.

'I assume everything has been all right while I've been away? Is Celia well?'

Sanjit waggled his head from side to side, in that curiously Indian gesture that signified agreement. 'Yes, *sahib*, she is well. Everything is fine.'

'Any trouble in the town?'

'There was a little trouble one day. But Celia and Sita returned safely from the bazaar.'

'Returned safely? Were they caught up in the trouble?' Wilfred widened his eyes and tried to catch Sanjit's gaze in the rear-view mirror, but Sanjit was concentrating on the traffic ahead. He steered around a cluster of rickshaws that were gathered at the side of the road before answering.

'They had to run away from the mob, I believe, but *sahib*, do not worry, they are safe.'

Wilfred shook his head, annoyed to hear that Celia had been in town during a riot. As they made their way through the city he could see evidence of recent violence – a burnt-out car, boarded-up windows, broken remains of market stalls. Sanjit was watching him nervously in the mirror, as though he'd realised that perhaps he should have said nothing about it. But he knew Wilfred would be angry if he'd lied or kept quiet, and was subsequently found out.

Wilfred made a mental note to quiz Celia on exactly what had happened. If necessary, he would forbid her from ever leaving the bungalow and its grounds until things settled down and the violence blew over. But he had no idea when that was likely to be. Quite possibly not until after independence, and by that time he and Celia should be safely back in England. And anyway, he thought wryly, it was quite possible that independence would be the start of even more violence, perhaps even civil war. He shuddered. Yes, the sooner he could take Celia out of this godforsaken country the better.

He'd read articles in the papers while he was in London about Lord Louis Mountbatten who'd recently been appointed viceroy of India, tasked with overseeing the route to independence. There was speculation it would happen next year, in the summer of 1948. Why wait, Wilfred thought. Maybe Mountbatten would bring it forward. In a few days Mountbatten would be sworn in as viceroy, an event Wilfred was due to attend. It meant journeying back to Delhi, but that couldn't be helped.

They reached his bungalow. Sanjit briefly got out of the car to open the gates then expertly steered up the driveway that led through the grounds, and pulled in beside the front door. Wilfred climbed out while Sanjit retrieved his suitcase and briefcase from the boot and took them inside, placing them neatly in the hallway. 'I'll put the car away and lock the gates, *sahib*, then I will unpack your case.'

'Thank you.' Wilfred nodded, and looked around expectantly for Celia. In times past, when he'd returned from business trips or visits to England, she'd have come running, squealing, to meet him, flinging her little arms around him and kissing his cheek. But in the last year or so, she'd grown up and now seemed to think it was too childish to be excited by his return. He missed those old days. Even more, he missed the days when dearest Alice would have been here to meet him, a glass of his favourite Scotch already poured and awaiting him on a silver tray, his pipe laid neatly beside it. He sighed. He'd been happy in India then. So very happy. He'd have hated the idea of moving home to England. How times changed.

He wandered through to the sitting room and rang the bell for service. One of the kitchen boys answered, and he ordered a supper of cold meats and fruit to be served to him on a tray, then poured his own whisky. Just as he sat down with it, Celia finally arrived. She was dressed in *salwar kameez* again, he saw to his annoyance. And her hair was plaited like an Indian girl's. It should be pinned up on her head in a style more befitting her age and nationality. Something else he should talk to her about.

'Papa!' She crossed the room to him and bent over to kiss his cheek. 'I'm glad you're safely back. I hate it when you're away. Did you have a good trip? Did you do everything you needed to?'

'Yes, and yes. Good evening, Celia. How have you passed the time while I've been away?' He'd give her the opportunity to tell him what had happened in the riot herself. It would be interesting to see if she decided to tell him or not.

'I've done *nothing*, Papa. Well, Sita and I went to the bazaar but we bought nothing of interest. And since then, Sanjit said I should stay home. I haven't even seen Vijay.'

'Why did Sanjit want you to stay home?' Wilfred watched her carefully as she answered.

She shrugged. 'He said he couldn't be certain of my safety. Just because some fellows went running through the streets and knocked over a few stalls. Sita and I were fine. We went into an old house and hid up on the roof until the men had passed through.'

'What men were they?'

'I don't know. Stupid men.' She pouted and flung herself down onto a sofa, lounging back, legs outstretched.

'Sanjit said it was a little more than a few stalls knocked over. And I saw the aftermath of it myself as we drove from the station.

He was right to keep you home after that. In fact, I don't want you going out either. Vijay can come here if you want company – you can sit with him in the grounds or on the veranda.'

'Papa! I don't want to hang around here all day. It's so . . . stifling!'

'That's just the hot weather. It won't be too long before you and Sita are off to the hills anyway.'

'I don't mean stifling like . . .' Celia waved her arms vaguely around as if to indicate the atmosphere. 'I mean . . . I need to go out. I can't just stay here! It's not all that dangerous out there. I know the hiding places, I know how to—'

Wilfred held up a hand to stop her. He was tired and now was not the time for this argument. 'You'll stay home if I tell you to, my girl, and you won't argue about it. Otherwise, you'll be confined to the house and won't even be allowed in the garden. Or perhaps just your room.' He glared at her then picked up his whisky and took a sip. 'Now, if you don't mind. I'm tired. I need to unwind from the journey.'

'I'm dismissed then. Fine.' Celia turned on her heel and flounced out of the room.

Wilfred sighed. Alice would have handled this so much better than he had. Sometimes he wondered if it was always like this between fifteen-year-old girls and their fathers, or if Celia was particularly difficult, or if he was simply bad at parenting.

Perhaps he'd been too hard on her. He could understand her wish to go out, to have the freedom he'd always let her enjoy. But she needed to understand that all he wanted was to keep her safe. He supposed he'd gone about it all in the wrong way. Again.

Maybe it would all be easier in England. At the very least, if he mended bridges with his brother, he'd have Cyril and his wife Winnie on hand nearby, to help and advise. Although they only had a son, no daughters, and the son – James – was quite a bit younger than Celia. Younger children were easier to deal with.

He retired to bed with a heavy heart. They had a long way to go to reach the kind of father–daughter relationship he'd like to think they'd have when she was fully grown.

Wilfred had debated bringing Celia with him to the swearing-in of Lord Mountbatten as viceroy of India. Mountbatten would be the last ever viceroy, barring anything dramatic and unforeseen happening, and would oversee the transition to an independent India. But Wilfred decided in the end that Celia was too young, and it was a long way for her to travel to Delhi in this country that no longer felt safe. Besides, he couldn't be certain she'd behave well enough. It was better that she should stay at home with Sita. Sanjit had strict instructions to keep her in the bungalow and its grounds. Vijay would visit to keep her amused – Wilfred had arranged this.

Thankfully, he only needed to be away for one night. He was travelling by train to Delhi, where the swearing-in was to be held at the viceroy's residence. It would be a grand, historic occasion, and all the higher-ranked members of the Indian Civil Service, together with senior members of the Indian Congress and various heads of the princely states across the country were due to be there. Vijay's father – Devraj Kaur, their local maharajah – was also invited but he would be travelling separately.

It wasn't the first viceroy swearing-in Wilfred had attended. As he stared out of the train at the parched countryside from his first-class compartment, he considered the previous ones he'd attended – was it three or four? Or five? As soon as he'd been senior enough, he'd found himself on the guest list. And the governorship of India changed hands rapidly. It didn't seem to be a job anyone wanted to keep for very long.

To think Lord Mountbatten would be the last Englishman to manage the subcontinent! India had formally been a part of the British Empire for a hundred years. And before that, the country had been largely run by the British East India Company. Mountbatten was considered a safe pair of hands, a diplomat, good at understanding and following the correct protocol in all situations. He was the right person to negotiate the terms of independence with all the various factions within India – Nehru for the Hindus, Jinnah for the Muslims, countless princes and nabobs and maharajahs who had been figurehead rulers in their own small states and now wanted their say in shaping the independent India. And also, of course, Gandhi, who was an old man now but still highly influential. Keeping all of them onside, keeping them all focused on the endgame of peaceful independence while ensuring they all got what they wanted, or at least thought they did, was no easy task, but it was this that Mountbatten had been chosen to do.

'Rather him than me,' Wilfred muttered to himself. He was glad that he'd risen through the ranks to a respectable level in the Indian Civil Service, but only to the point of being vice-governor in one city. That was enough. He briefly wondered what job he would do when they were back in England, but then brushed the thought away. There was enough on his mind already. He'd worry about that when the time came.

The train arrived in Delhi in the midafternoon, and Wilfred took a taxi to his hotel where he changed into his tailcoat and white tie. At the hotel desk he ordered another taxi to take him to the viceroy's residence. It wasn't far, but he had no intention of walking in the heat and arriving damp and sweating.

The ceremony was a glitzy affair. Dignitaries from all across India took their seats in the marble-clad Durbar Hall; their wives, whether dressed in Indian or western clothing, looking like birds of paradise beside them in their gowns or saris, with their showiest jewels on display. Everyone looked their best, everyone knew this was the last time, the end of an era. There were photographers and cinematographers present, recording the event for posterity. It would be shown on Pathé newsreels back home, Wilfred guessed. Alice would have loved every moment of it. She'd have been the most beautiful woman there, and she'd have worn the most impressive jewel – the diamond brooch. Oh, how he missed her, even after all these years! Everything seemed dull and pointless without her at his side.

The conversation in the room fell silent as Lord Mountbatten, in his splendid white dress uniform complete with a row of medals, entered the hall together with his wife Edwina, who shimmered in a white and gold full-length gown. The pair walked slowly up the aisle as though it was a wedding. Or a coronation – which actually, Wilfred supposed, it was in a way. They reached the raised platform where two ornate thrones had been placed, turned and sat in them.

'Like the King and Queen of India,' Wilfred muttered to himself, and was told to shush by his neighbour, an Indian woman in a bright blue and silver sari.

There were various, mercifully short, speeches and then Lord Mountbatten stood to take the oath of allegiance from the Lord Chief Justice of India, who was decked out in red robes trimmed with ermine and topped with a full powdered wig. Wilfred considered whether he really liked all this pomp and ceremony. It felt, today, like a relic of a bygone era. Which it was, or very soon would be. He supposed that India would soon modernise itself, after independence. It would throw off all the trappings of empire along with British rule. How well it managed as an independent state remained to be seen.

And then the ceremony was over, and the congregation stood in homage as the Mountbattens walked back along the aisle, nodding and smiling at people they recognised as they passed. Everyone followed them out of the hall, through the main entrance of the residence and down the magnificent steps into the grounds, which had been smartened up for the occasion. There were bougainvillea and hibiscus bushes providing a riot of colour to compete with the Indian women's saris, jasmine and honeysuckle providing scent and carefully tended roses reminding everyone of England. Wilfred ambled through the grounds with everyone else, glancing around for people he recognised, yet not really wanting to strike up any conversations.

It was the last swearing-in and he was glad. He hoped Mountbatten would get on quickly with the job so that he, Wilfred, could finish his time here in India and go back to England. Back home. While the war had raged in Europe, he'd felt they were safer in India, but not now. Not now that Hitler was defeated and Europe was at peace again. Not with the looming prospect of a potentially divided India ahead of them, and the possible civil war that would ensue.

And he was tired. Tired of everything – of the politics; the cultural differences; the dust and the heat; the various religions that would never agree; the petty, pampered local rulers who were rich beyond measure while their people were dirt poor, living lives that had barely changed since the Stone Age. He was heartily sick of it all.

He was tired too of trying and failing to deal with his spirited daughter. She'd embraced Indian culture far too much, and yet not the part of it that included children being obedient. She needed a new influence in her life. A female role model other than Sita, who indulged her far too much. Some discipline, of the type to be found in the better class of English girls' schools, back home. None of the various governesses and tutors he'd employed to teach her had been strict enough, in Wilfred's opinion. And the result was a headstrong girl he loved dearly but was frequently exasperated by.

'Please, God, let independence come quickly,' he muttered. As soon as a date was set, he'd be counting down the days; he knew it.

Chapter 7

Lisa, 2023

Back home after the aborted party in the pub, Lisa made herself a cup of tea and sat on the sofa, opening the briefcase once more. She was still feeling stressed by the encounter with Rupert and it was the best way she could think of to calm herself down before bed. Otherwise, she'd never sleep.

The newspaper in the case was still waiting to be read. But on the top was the letter – that sealed cream-coloured envelope. She picked it up and turned it over in her hands, noting the feel of the quality paper, the ink that looked like it was from an old-fashioned fountain pen and the subtle scent of it. This was the next item she wanted to research.

It felt wrong to be opening a sealed envelope that was not addressed to her. But, in all likelihood, the intended recipient, the 'Celia' on the envelope, was long dead. The writer too. Lisa realised she'd been assuming that Mr Fforbes-Whyte had written the letter and that the briefcase had belonged to him. It was possible, though, that he might have been carrying the letter for someone else to deliver it to Celia. Or perhaps it was someone else travelling with that case. Maybe even 'Celia', whoever she was. She might have put the unopened letter in her case, intending to read it later, and then not had a chance before the plane crashed.

'Well, Celia, I'm sorry. But the only way to find out more about who you were, who Mr Fforbes-Whyte was, is to read this letter. It might hold some clues that will help me reunite this case and all its contents with descendants or relatives of its owner.' Somehow, offering a little apology to the empty room before she opened the letter made it easier.

She carefully eased open the envelope without tearing it, and extracted the single piece of thick, cream-coloured writing paper that was inside – clearly a page taken from the pad of paper that had also been in the briefcase – and unfolded it.

She read it slowly, carefully, letting the words sink in as she read. It was from a father to his daughter – Celia – and it was the most heartbreaking letter Lisa had ever read. By the time she reached the end, tears were streaming down her cheeks. Especially, as seemed to be most likely, because Celia had never received the letter. She'd never read these words, never known what her father wanted to say to her. It was the kind of letter you would keep forever, and reread over and over again. An important yet undelivered, unread letter . . .

Disappointingly, the letter contained no more clues about the owner of the case. It was addressed simply to 'Celia' and signed 'Papa'. Behind the words, Lisa thought she detected some sort of crisis. Something had happened, which made the writer take hasty action, and somehow the letter was a part of this.

She glanced at the date at the top of the letter. It rang a bell. She grabbed the notebook where she'd jotted down the definite facts she'd discovered to check. Yes, the letter was dated the same day that the plane had crashed.

'Did you even write it while you were on the plane, Celia's dad?' She pictured a man sitting in the plane, pulling out paper and an envelope from his briefcase, perhaps even resting on the case to write it. Using the dead time while he was on his journey to explain himself to his daughter.

Another thought occurred to her. Maybe Celia had been on the same flight as her father, sitting across the aisle. Perhaps there'd been a frosty atmosphere on the plane and they hadn't been able to find the words they desperately needed to say to each other. And so the father had taken up his pen and paper and decided to write instead, so he could hand her the letter later, or leave it somewhere she'd find it, when they reached their destination.

'How can I find out exactly who was on the plane?' Lisa pondered. She wondered if there would be records somewhere? Or was it too long ago? BOAC no longer existed as an airline. Perhaps British Airways had kept their records? If she contacted them, would they give her a list of names of who was on board? These days, of course, airlines knew who'd bought tickets for a flight and who had been checked in. Back then, in the 1940s, was security as strict? Were such records kept at all?

The other thing she really wanted to do was try to find descendants of the family. Fforbes-Whyte – it was an unusual surname. On a whim she put it into the search bar on Facebook. But there were no matches. No one with that surname used Facebook. 'That would have been far too easy, Lisa,' she told herself. 'Finding someone with that name, sending them a message, and hearing the family's side of the story. Nope. You'll have to work a bit harder than that.'

She was about to do a Google search for the name, but then she glanced at the clock. It was late, it had been a long day, there was work tomorrow, and she really ought to get to bed. She put the letter back in its envelope, placed it back in the briefcase and closed the lid. Further research would have to wait.

'Did you and Amanda enjoy the rest of the evening?' Lisa asked Justin the next day in the office, as she settled down at her desk.

'I'm sorry I left early. Still a bit tired from the holiday and . . . well, you know.'

'That little spat with Rupert. Yeah, I know. Yes, we did, thanks. Most people stayed for a couple of drinks then we and four others went for a Thai meal.'

'Was it good?' Lisa felt a pang of regret. She'd have enjoyed going out for Thai food with everyone. Bloody Rupert, spoiling it all for her!

'Yeah, it was. Amanda loves Thai. By the way, she wanted me to let you know she hadn't invited Rupert or even told him we were going to the pub. Actually, neither of us ever see him now. It must have been sheer coincidence he turned up like that. I hope it didn't upset you too much.'

'No, don't worry. It didn't. Thanks again for sticking up for me.' Justin was a good work colleague but not a close friend – he didn't need to hear the details of just how shaken she'd felt when she left the pub. She'd never shared much about her personal relationships with him.

'No problem.' Justin gave her a little smile and she had the impression he was proud of his actions the previous night.

'I can't believe I went out with him for two years.'

'I did think you weren't very well matched,' Justin said, looking a little embarrassed to be saying such a thing.

'You're right, we weren't. Anyway, it's all over now, and hopefully, I'll never run into him again.'

'Future drinks after work will not be in the King's Arms, I promise.'

'Cheers.' Lisa turned back to her work. She had to complete a weekly report by lunchtime and there was still much number crunching to do before she could fill in that week's details.

To her right, a TV screen was showing the BBC News channel, muted but with subtitles on. Working in the Civil Service, you always had to keep abreast of any breaking news. They could never be sure when a minister would call for facts and figures to support whatever it was they wanted to say in response to a news event. Lisa angled her chair so that the TV screen was not in her eyeline, to allow her to concentrate on her work.

Even so, every now and again she'd glance up to see what was showing on the screen. It was good to refocus on something a little further off, in any case. And when she did glance up, to see a junior minister on the TV pontificating about the latest economic predictions from the Bank of England and what they meant for his department, she frowned, taking in the caption at the bottom: *David Fforbes-Whyte, Minister for Science and Research.*

'That's where I'd seen the name!' she said, thumping her desk in excitement.

'What name?' Justin looked up at her then twisted round to take in the TV screen. 'Oh, him. Just another dodgy minister. They're all as bad as each other. I know we're not meant to say that about our lords and masters but hey. Why were you wondering about his name?'

'Oh, I just came across... someone else with the same surname recently.' Lisa didn't want to go into the detail of the briefcase and the brooch. She wasn't yet sure what the right thing to do was, if she couldn't track down the rightful heirs to it. Until she'd exhausted all avenues of enquiry she wanted to keep it a secret – just between herself and Gaby.

'Must be a relative of his, then. Can't be many Fforbes-Whytes around.'

'That's what I thought.'

Justin leaned back in his chair. 'Bit of a poncy name, isn't it? Double-barrelled and the double "f". I mean, what's the point of that?'

'I suppose that's how it's always been spelt,' she replied.

So, that gave her a job for the evening. Find an email address for David Fforbes-Whyte and ask him... what? If the name Celia meant anything to him? If he had a relative, a father perhaps, named W Fforbes-Whyte who'd died in a plane crash in 1947?

How should she phrase it? She did some quick mental maths. If W Fforbes-Whyte was David's father that would mean David would have to be more than seventy-six years old and he didn't look it. Perhaps he was his grandfather, then. That was more likely.

The good thing, she thought, about him being an MP is that he should be easy to contact via his constituency office. Whether he'd reply or think she was some sort of crank and ignore her, remained to be seen. But at least she had a new lead that she could follow up on. Since reading that heartbreaking letter she felt it was even more important to do all that she could to track down W Fforbes-Whyte's descendants and the rightful owner of the diamond. It felt as though she owed it to Celia.

She quickly typed 'David Fforbes-Whyte' into Google and found the link for his MP's web page. She was right – it listed an email address to allow constituents to get in touch with him.

For much of the rest of the day it was a struggle to keep her mind on her job. Half of it was focused on how to word the email that she'd decided to send that very evening. By the time she arrived home she had the whole thing composed in her head, so it was a quick job to type it up and check it carefully.

She didn't mention the brooch; only that she'd found an old briefcase of papers belonging to a Mr W Fforbes-Whyte in a glacier in the French Alps, and that she wondered if it was anyone related to him. Often, MPs' emails were screened by people working in their offices, so it was quite possible her question wouldn't even reach him. She didn't live in his constituency (which was somewhere in Surrey, not too far out of London) so he was not obliged to answer. All she could do was wait and see what happened next.

Meanwhile, she could update Gaby on progress, and also tell her about the run-in with Rupert.

'Oh, mate,' Gaby said, when Lisa confided in her about how bad she'd felt after seeing him. 'You were doing well while we were away, I thought. And now . . .'

'I know. It's just . . . I had this horrible feeling he would suck me back in somehow, and I'd be trapped. You know how long it took me to find the courage to drop him.' To her shame Lisa found herself crying.

'I do know. Look, I'm always here for you. I wish I lived nearer . . . but I'm only ever a phone call away.'

'Thanks, Gaby. And you know, I feel better whenever I'm thinking about the mystery of this case and the diamond.'

'So, keep on researching it, girl!'

'I will.'

Chapter 8

Celia, March 1947

It was no use. No matter how much Celia pleaded with Sanjit, he would not let her leave the grounds. 'The *sahib* said no,' is all he would say, and in the end, Celia simply had to accept it. At least Papa was only away for a day this time. When he came back, she'd decided to ask him to take her out. A drive out of the city, a visit to the maharajah's palace perhaps. Anything for a change of scenery. If she was with Papa then he couldn't say it was too dangerous, could he?

She was wandering around the grounds for what felt like the hundredth time that day, looking at the same old shrubs and flowers, treading the same old paths alongside the flower beds and under the pergolas, looking back at the bungalow, which felt like a prison. And then as she began crossing the lawn yet again, or what was left of it after the long dry spell, she noticed someone walking towards her, a broad grin on his face.

'Vijay! Oh, thank goodness. I am beside myself with boredom! I didn't even have any lessons today. I've had *nothing* whatsoever to do!' she called, running across the grass towards him.

'Celia! Your father sent a message to say I should come today to entertain you. So here I am. At your disposal.' Vijay performed an ornate bow, which sent her dissolving into fits of giggles.

'You lunatic! But I am so glad you are here.'

'Making the most of it,' he said. 'You know my father is considering whether to send me to England to school in September? Maybe I am to finish my education there. School for two years and then university, assuming they'll have me. So I have to make the most of this summer with you.'

Celia was dismayed. Vijay had mentioned being sent away to school before, and had indeed been at boarding schools in India at times. But she'd always refused to think about the possibility of him going far away, to England, for long periods. 'Do you have to go?'

He nodded. 'I know. It's crazy. *Pitaji* wants India to be independent of British rule and yet he wants me to have an English education. But it's not for months yet. Six months. Anything could happen between now and then, so let's not worry about it. He'll probably change his mind two or three times. Hey, race you to the end of the garden!' With that he took off, running full pelt across the lawn.

Celia laughed and ran too, her baggy trousers flapping around her legs. She was catching him up, as she always did. Not because she was faster than him, but it had been an unwritten rule since they were small children that he would let her win – not all the time, but most of it. She was a year younger than him, smaller than him and not as strong. So it was only fair that he made allowances.

She reached the high wall that marked the boundary of the bungalow's grounds a split second before him and touched it, laughing and panting. 'Beat you!'

'You always do,' Vijay replied with a smile. Annoyingly, Celia thought, he was barely out of breath.

She wiped sweat from her brow and leaned back against the

wall. They were under a banyan tree in pleasant shade. 'Getting hot.'

'We've months yet until the monsoon, when I suppose you'll go to the hills?'

She nodded. 'Suppose so. Papa's at the new viceroy's swearing-in today.'

'I know, so's my father. And then he's going to host a formal dinner to celebrate, next week. I'm persuading him to invite both you and your father.'

'Formal dinner?' Celia pulled a face.

Vijay laughed. 'You're nearly grown-up now. You'll need to learn your manners and etiquette for these things.'

Celia punched him on the arm. 'Beast. I know my manners.'

'All right, I deserved that,' Vijay said, rubbing his arm. 'But please, please, when the invitation comes, tell your father you'll be delighted to attend. Because otherwise I'll be there all trussed up in my best white suit with no one to talk to.'

She tipped her head to one side and regarded him – his dark brown eyes she knew so well, his face that was changing now that he was almost an adult: his jawline becoming more defined, a wispy moustache taking shape on his upper lip. 'All right. I will. Vijay, can I ask you something?'

'Of course, Cee.'

'Do you sometimes wish everything could go back to how it was? I mean – forget independence, forget Gandhi and Nehru and Congress, forget us growing up. I wish we could be like we were a few years ago. Young, free, innocent, chasing each other around the garden like we always did . . .'

'But we have to grow up, Cee. You have to become a beautiful woman and marry a handsome rich Englishman. I have to sit at my father's right hand and make sure our people are looked after and cared for, no matter what government is in place.'

'I don't want to marry anyone.' Least of all an Englishman, she thought.

Vijay smiled. 'You used to say you did. You used to say you couldn't wait to wear the *Chamakta Sitara* on your wedding day.'

'I couldn't wear that now anyway. It's not here anymore.'

'Not here? Where is it then?'

Celia shrugged. 'Not sure. Perhaps in our house in Simla. Papa's been moving everything of value to safe places away from here in case there are more riots and they come looking for valuables. I swear he loves that diamond more than me!'

'I'm sure he doesn't, Cee.'

She pouted. 'Anyway, I don't care where it is or what happens to it. It's just a piece of rock. Not even all that pretty. I always thought it'd be better set into a necklace rather than a brooch.'

'It should be a turban pin.'

'Whatever. Bet you can't beat me climbing the fig tree!' Celia darted off across the grounds to the tree that had low branches worn shiny from the hundreds of times they'd clambered up on them. Within minutes she was high up in the enormous tree. There was a kind of hollow a little way up its trunk where two people could just about fit, hidden from view. It was one of her favourite places since she'd been about five years old. Back then, Vijay used to help her up onto the first branch. She could still remember how Mama had tutted about the stains she'd got on her clothes that first time they'd climbed it. After a while Mama had given up complaining, and just asked that she wear old clothes if she insisted on climbing trees and rolling around in the dirt of the garden. And then Mama had died, and Papa had different things to chastise her about, and Sita had always just smiled indulgently and quietly taken soiled clothes away to the *dhobi wallah* for washing.

But today Vijay did beat her to the tree, and went up it and was settled into the best spot before she even began climbing. 'Not fair. Your legs are longer than mine,' she said, when she reached the hollow and tucked herself in beside him.

'I know.' He stretched them out and she gazed at them. He was wearing long beige trousers and a dark green shirt, European style. These days he was more often in European dress than she was.

'Funny how you wear those clothes and I wear these,' she said.

Vijay looked at her as though only now noticing what she was wearing. 'Those clothes suit you. Especially that colour.' She was in her favourite turquoise *salwar kameez*.

She opened her mouth to answer but couldn't think of anything to say, and to her horror realised she was blushing. This was Vijay, her childhood friend, paying her a compliment. Somehow it didn't seem right. He should tease her, like he always had, not compliment her. And yet it felt good.

There'd been a boy, an English one, the son of someone Papa worked with, who'd been at a garden party she'd attended. The boy – his name was Harold or Arnold or something – had followed her around like a puppy, looking insanely pleased if she said anything to him. And then when they'd been out of sight of the grown-ups, he'd tried to kiss her and it had been awful. His lips were wet and sloppy – it was like kissing a fish, she'd thought. At the time she'd decided she never wanted to kiss a boy again, as long as she lived.

But now, contemplating Vijay's well-shaped mouth with that enticing beginning of a moustache, she found herself wondering what it would be like to kiss him. Much better than kissing Arnold or Harold, but perhaps too much like kissing a brother? Maybe one day she'd find out. The idea was strangely appealing.

He was looking at her with his head slightly on one side, as though he was thinking exactly the same thing. It was Celia who broke the spell first, looking away from him in confusion and across the garden towards the tennis court.

'Let's play tennis! Bet I can beat you six games to love!' Vijay pushed himself forward and jumped down from the tree. Celia felt oddly disappointed yet at the same time relieved. She needed to turn around to climb down, and by the time she was down Vijay had already sprinted across the lawn to the tennis court and was retrieving racquets and balls from the lidded box where they were stored.

'Heads or tails?' he said, pulling a coin from his pocket and tossing it expertly in the air. He caught it and slapped it onto the back of his other hand.

'Heads.'

'Heads it is,' he said, revealing it.

'So I'll serve first.' She took her place at the end of the court nearest the house, two balls in her hand. She was a pretty decent tennis player, but so was Vijay, and he usually beat her. If she could win one or two games, she'd be pleased.

They played for twenty minutes, completing a set. The score was six–two to Vijay, but Celia had won two of her service games and was happy with that. 'It's too hot to play another set,' she said, and he nodded in agreement. 'Let's get some lemonade.'

They trooped into the kitchen, just like they'd done on so many other hot days for so many years, and helped themselves to a glass of lemonade each from the refrigerator. Sita passed through and greeted Vijay, but then went to sit outside her own room. She usually left them alone when Vijay visited. Celia knew Sita felt she stifled them if she stayed too close.

They took their lemonades outside and went to sit on the veranda, on wicker sofas strewn with cushions. It was a shady spot, where Celia often liked to sit and read if there was no one else around and nothing to do.

'Wonder how things will change in India under the new viceroy,' Vijay mused.

Celia shrugged. 'We'll find out soon enough. I suppose he'll want to make his mark. Something to be remembered for.'

'He'll be remembered anyway, as the last ever viceroy. The one overseeing the end of the British Empire in India.'

Celia looked across at Vijay, who was staring across the garden. 'Are you looking forward to independence?'

He twisted his mouth before answering. 'Yes and no. I think

it's right that we run our own country. Empire is a thing of the past, not the modern times. But I'm concerned, too, about how it'll be achieved. These riots we've already seen – I fear things can only get worse. Especially if the country ends up partitioned.'

'Papa said no one wants partition.'

'No one wants it, but it might yet happen. But look, let's make the most of the next few months, before I have to go away to school and you have to—'

'Leave for the hills?'

'Yes, and after that . . .'

'If you mean go to live in England, well I'm not thinking about that.'

'I'd be there.' Vijay turned to look at her, a half-smile playing around his lips.

She smiled back, and nodded. Yes, that was one thing that might make a return to England easier to bear, if it meant she could still see Vijay. He and Sita were the two people she knew she could never bear to be parted from. She'd almost rather lose her father than either of them. That thought shocked her, yet she had to acknowledge to herself it was the truth.

'What will you do after?' she asked.

'After what?'

'School and university, and all that. Will you stay in England?'

Vijay shook his head. 'No. I suppose I'll come back here and help my father.'

Something about his tone made Celia turn to stare at him. 'Don't you want that?'

'No. I'd like to become a doctor. I could do some good for the poor of our country. But *Pitaji* says I have duties as the son of a maharajah, and that I must fulfil them. Independence will change all that, though. India must modernise and I don't see why I can't . . .' He broke off, as though fearful he'd say too much, say something he shouldn't.

'Vijay, you can do anything you like. You're a man . . . nearly. He can't stop you. It's different for me as a girl. Papa controls me.'

'Tries to. And fails.' Vijay's teasing tone was back.

Celia smiled at him acknowledging the tease, but she wasn't ready to give up the conversation yet. She wanted . . . needed . . . to know whether her relationship with her father was normal or not.

'Vijay, do you get on with your father?'

'Get on with him?' Vijay stared at her, then looked away, across the garden, as if he'd never been asked such a question before. She supposed that perhaps he hadn't. In Indian culture, fathers were the masters of their family. The maharajah was no different. In fact, as royalty, he was probably worse.

'Well,' Vijay said, 'I respect him. Of course. Every child must respect their father.'

'But do you *like* him? Do you think he likes you – as a person?'

'He loves me, of that I'm sure. I'm all he has. My mother died giving birth to me, as you know. I don't know why he never married again. He always said all he needed was a son, and he had me, so he needed no one else.'

Celia put a hand on Vijay's arm. 'You didn't answer me. Do you like him?'

Vijay was quiet for a moment before he answered, in a whisper. 'Not always, no. He can be . . . severe. Ruthless in getting what he wants. It's sometimes hard to deal with. Cee, what's brought this on?'

She shrugged. 'Just . . . as time goes on, I find my papa harder and harder to deal with, too. We spend too much time arguing. I think he wishes I was still a small child who worships him. He doesn't seem to realise that as I've got older, I've . . . Well, I've become my own person. I don't always agree with what he says or does. And he can't accept that.' To her shame she felt tears prickling at the corners of her eyes.

Vijay squeezed her hand. 'That's hard. But you must still respect him, Cee. I respect my father, even when I don't agree with him or don't like what he's done.'

Celia leaned back in her chair and stared at the veranda's ceiling. 'That's the problem. Sometimes, when we're completely at odds with each other, I find I don't respect him anymore. And anyway, why should I respect him when he doesn't show any respect towards me? I'm not a child anymore!'

'A short while ago you were wishing you still were, wishing we could go back a few years to when we were young and innocent . . .' Vijay's tone was gentle, not mocking.

'I know. And yes, that would be good. Or, if I was a proper grown-up and Papa treated me as one. It's this—' she kicked against the legs of her chair '—this horrible in-between state that I hate. Neither one thing nor the other. And surrounded by people who just don't understand me.'

'Cee, I understand you. I always have. We're like this, right?' Vijay held up a hand with his index and middle fingers crossed. It was an old sign they'd used since they were small, to show each other how close their friendship was.

Celia held up her own hand, fingers crossed, in response. 'Yes, like this. Always. Vijay, if you have to go to England this September, and Indian independence doesn't happen until next year or the year after, how on earth will I manage without you around?'

'You'll have Sita. And I'll come home for visits. We'll be all right.'

But Celia noticed there were worry lines between his brows, and his words held no conviction. He didn't like the prospect of a separation any more than she did, she realised. And that realisation made her heart swell with feelings for him. Feelings that she was too scared to call 'love', even while understanding that that's exactly what they were.

Chapter 9

Lisa, 2023

By the end of the week Lisa had almost given up on hearing back from the MP. She met up with Gaby on Friday night for a Greek meal and a catch-up. 'I reckon as I'm not in his constituency his office staff will have just binned my email,' she said, as she finished her story of emailing David Fforbes-Whyte.

'They'd have read it first.'

'Possibly not. You're supposed to put your postal address in emails to MPs so they can quickly determine if you are a constituent or not. Anyway, I tried.'

'What will you do next?' Gaby asked.

'I don't know. I suppose I'll take the brooch to a jeweller and determine if it's real. Because if it's not, then there's no point wasting so much energy tracking down the owner's family.'

Gaby looked at her shrewdly. 'I bet you still would, though.'

Lisa smiled. 'Yeah. I hate an unsolved mystery. And that letter to Celia, I guess it really got to me.'

'Me too. So you need to solve it, eh? Anyway, here's our *meze* at last. Mmm, looks good!'

Conversation moved on to other things as they tucked into the food. But Lisa kept half a mind on the briefcase and its contents. Gaby was right, she wouldn't rest until she'd found the descendants or relatives of W Fforbes-Whyte. Maybe she could find some other way to contact the MP. Perhaps he used social media (other than Facebook, where she'd already searched for the name) and she could reach him that way. But she was well aware the chances were that any social media in his name was also run by his parliamentary staff. In a weird way, concentrating on the research was helping her reclaim her sense of self-worth. This was something only she could do, something she enjoyed doing and might succeed at and which Rupert would never have understood. He'd have mocked her obsession with it to the point of making her give it up.

The following day, Saturday, she took the brooch to a jeweller not far from her flat, who offered free valuations. He was a serious-looking man in his fifties, who showed her into a back room where she sat on an uncomfortable chair and took out the brooch. She had already decided not to tell him where she'd found it. 'So, this is the item. Can you tell me anything about it?'

The jeweller took it from her and considered it, turning it over several times, then fitted an eyeglass to his eye to take a closer look. His eyes widened as he peered at the diamond. 'This is quite a magnificent stone. Has it been in your possession long?'

'Erm, kind of . . . It was, um, mislaid for some years and has recently been recovered. So are you saying it's definitely real? Only we weren't sure . . .'

'Not sure? So you have no provenance for the piece?'

'Not really . . .' Lisa felt deeply uncomfortable at the questions. She half expected him to accuse her there and then of stealing the brooch and call the police. All she could do was deflect. 'I was wondering if you could give me a rough valuation for insurance purposes?'

He looked at her over the tops of his glasses. 'Well, now, I'll weigh it, and then I can give you a figure for how much that quantity of diamond would fetch on the open market, if cut into smaller gems. But frankly, if it went to auction as a single piece, at the right auction it could fetch—' He sighed and shook his head. 'I don't want to give a figure. I don't think I've ever seen such a stone before in this shop. It's . . . priceless. And that's not a word I use lightly. You say you don't have any provenance for it?'

'I'm working on that,' Lisa replied.

'Hmm.' The jeweller made some notes on the numbers of emeralds set around the diamond, measured it, weighed it, and then named an enormous sum that the brooch would fetch if was broken up. 'And that's all I can really tell you. If you need advice regarding what to do with it, please do come back to me.'

'Thank you. I will.'

She shook his hand, but he didn't smile. She had the impression he would immediately be checking some sort of register of stolen jewellery to see if anything matching the brooch's description had been reported stolen. If he did, she mused, he'd be extremely unlikely to find anything, given that the brooch had spent seventy-five years in an Alpine glacier.

Lisa left the shop and went straight into Battersea Park where she sat on a bench and called Gaby. 'It's real,' she said, as soon as Gaby answered. 'It's priceless, he said. Even if broken up and the diamond was cut into smaller gems, it's worth a fortune.'

'Wow. Not surprised, though. I thought it was real. Something about the way it sparkled . . . So now you really do have to find out who it should belong to!'

'I'm going to give myself two weeks. If no joy at the end of that, I'm going to . . . talk to someone . . .'

'Who?'

Lisa shrugged. 'I haven't a clue. See, that's another job. Find out what I ought to be doing with this. It's a kind of treasure trove – there must be some guidelines somewhere online.' Privately, she was still praying she might get a response from the MP, or find some other way to contact him.

As if the cosmos heard her prayers, that very evening an email pinged into her inbox from the MP's office. It was written not by David Fforbes-Whyte but by a member of his staff. Lisa's heart was pounding as she read the response.

Dear Lisa,

I work in Mr Fforbes-Whyte's constituency office and was most intrigued to read your email. I agree it is very likely that the briefcase you found belonged to a relative of David Fforbes-Whyte. His great-uncle, in fact, who was believed lost in a plane crash in the 1940s. His name was Wilfred Fforbes-Whyte. I wonder if it would be possible to meet to discuss this and perhaps to take a look at the briefcase and its contents? I could then tell you as much as I know about him. I see that you live in London – I can easily travel and am free most weekends if that suits.

Please let me know where and when is convenient, and I'll be there. I love a mystery!
Ben Forbes

Lisa hadn't mentioned the plane crash in her initial email, so she had no doubt that this was genuine and she really had found the right family. His name was Wilfred! She jotted that down in her notebook. And this Ben sounded approachable. She definitely wanted to meet him and hear what he had to tell. If everything still added up, she would arrange to pass the diamond over to David Fforbes-Whyte.

She called Gaby, who squealed with excitement at the development. 'Well done, Lisa! Knew you'd stick at it until you found the answer!'

'So where should we meet him?'

'We?' Gaby groaned. 'Sorry, mate. Think it'll have to be just you. I'm away on a conference with work starting Monday and I need to spend tomorrow prepping for it. I will be with you in spirit, though. Make sure you meet in a public place in case he turns out to be a nutter.'

'Will do.' Lisa felt disappointed Gaby wouldn't be there with her but, on the other hand, it might be easier on her own. She'd be more interested in hearing everything Ben had to say, whereas Gaby would probably get impatient and want to hurry the stories along.

She pondered where to meet, and finally settled on a central London pub that had several snugs where they'd be able to find a spot to talk privately. She suggested they meet the next day, on Sunday afternoon.

And almost as soon as she'd sent the email, to Ben's personal email address that he'd given her rather than the constituency office, she received a reply agreeing to the time and place. He'd included his mobile phone number too, so she saved that in her phone but didn't give him hers. Not yet. Just in case.

Lisa reached the pub that was close to Oxford Circus early, so she could nab a good table and get herself organised before she met Ben. She'd brought the briefcase with her, but had left the brooch at home. She didn't want to travel through London carrying something so valuable. She'd barely sat down with a cup of coffee when a pleasant-faced man of around her own age walked in, running fingers through his hair as he looked around the bar. He approached her with a smile.

'Lisa Statton? I'm Ben Forbes.' He held out a hand, which she took. His grip was warm and firm.

'Good to meet you, Ben.'

'Can I get you anything?' He gestured towards the bar.

'No, thanks, I'm good.' She picked up her still-full coffee cup. He went over to order himself a pint of real ale, then settled himself opposite her. 'Well, Lisa, I must admit I was astonished to read your email. I should explain – David Fforbes-Whyte is my father. I help him with some of his constituency work at the weekends, and one of the things I do is take a first pass through his emails. I showed him yours, but he asked me to deal with it.'

Ben smiled. 'He knows I like a bit of family history, and he's right. I was absolutely intrigued by what you said. So tell me, how did you find the briefcase? Is that it?' He glanced down at where the briefcase lay on a bench seat beside Lisa.

'Yes, that's the one.' She told him then about how she and Gaby had been walking in the mountains above Chamonix and had pulled it from the ice at the edge of a glacier. 'I believe it's not the only relic from that plane crash that's been brought down by the movement of the ice.'

'Amazing, isn't it?' He was looking longingly at the case.

'So, look, I'll show you the papers inside it, which led me to you.' She opened it and pulled out the sheaf of documents including the hotel receipt and letter from the bank. 'Fforbes-Whyte is an unusual name. Then I saw your father on the TV and wondered if he was part of the same family.'

'Yes, it's unusual all right.' Ben grimaced. 'I prefer just plain Forbes for myself, though officially I'm a Fforbes-Whyte as well, according to my birth certificate and passport.'

'Well, if Wilfred had been simply a Forbes, I probably wouldn't have found you.' Lisa smiled, and Ben smiled back at her. He had nice eyes, she thought.

He cleared his throat. 'Anyway, let me tell you the family story, as it was passed down to Dad and me. Wilfred had a brother, Cyril, who was my great-grandfather. Both of them were born in India, but went to boarding schools and then university in England. They fell out over something – an argument to do with a girl is what I remember my grandfather telling me. Wilfred then went back to India where he worked for the Indian Civil Service.' Ben took a sip of his beer.

'I thought there was an Indian connection,' Lisa said, nodding. The newspaper was a bit of a giveaway.

'Wilfred had a daughter, Celia, but he was widowed quite early. With Indian independence looming, he was looking to relocate back to England and had tried to mend his relationship with Cyril. Cyril had agreed to put them up when they came back to England until they found a home of their own. Wilfred was bringing Celia to England when the plane they were in crashed in the Alps and they were both killed.'

'That's so sad. How old was Celia?'

'Not sure. Just a child, quite young, I think. Anyway, that was the end of the Fforbes-Whytes in India. Cyril and his family were the only ones in England. Cyril had one son – James, my grandfather – who in turn had one son, my father David. And he's kept the tradition going. I'm an only child.'

'Up to you to keep the name going then!' Though by his use of the simplified name, Forbes, it looked as though the Fforbes-Whyte name would die out with Ben anyway.

'Hmm.' Ben stared into his pint.

Lisa looked at him and frowned. There was something else going on. Something Ben wasn't telling her. Perhaps, like her, he'd been scarred by previous relationships so wasn't sure he'd ever have a child himself. What was she thinking? She'd only just met the man. For all she knew he could be happily married and a father of three.

'I'm sorry,' she said. 'That was perhaps a bit personal. Look, let me give you this case and the documents. You can go through them all, see if there's anything of interest to you in there. It's all good family history stuff, anyway. There's a letter among the papers – I'm sorry but I opened it, looking for more clues as to who it had all belonged to. It's a letter from Wilfred to Celia.' As she spoke the names, she realised what had niggled her about Ben's story. 'I'd wondered whether Celia was on the plane with Wilfred, but had the impression she wasn't – the letter sounds like he wrote it on the flight, intending to give to her or send to her when he landed.'

'Or perhaps he wrote it before the flight . . . I guess we'll never know.'

'Was he flying from England to India or the other way?' she asked.

'Other way. The family story is that Wilfred and Celia were on their way here to relocate.'

Lisa stared at him. Now was the time to mention the brooch. 'There was one other thing in the case that I need to tell you about. I haven't brought it here because . . . well . . . I was afraid of it being stolen. It's rather valuable.'

'Go on . . .' Ben suddenly looked a little pale.

'It's a piece of jewellery. A brooch. It's set with a large diamond and has emeralds around the edge. It's in a velvet box that was tucked into a pocket in the briefcase. I have it at home and, of course, I'll pass it on to you – I just didn't want to carry it through London.'

'The *Chamakta Sitara*.' Ben spoke in a whisper. He was definitely pale now.

'The what now?'

'The diamond. That's its name. So it has resurfaced after all these years. Oh, my God.' He clapped a hand to his mouth and stared at her in what she could only describe as utter horror.

Chapter 10

Wilfred, April 1947

Wilfred gazed at his reflection in the full-length mirror in his room and adjusted his cuffs. He looked smart. He had always suited a dinner jacket, he thought. He had the right figure for it, tall and lean. At least Alice had always told him so. He poked his head out into the corridor and called out, 'Are you ready, Celia?' They needed to leave in a few minutes. It was a formal dinner, and would be the first that Celia had attended as his companion rather than as his child. She'd be sitting at the maharajah's long dining table along with all the other local dignitaries. She'd gone with him on numerous other visits to the maharajah's palace, of course. They were near neighbours and she and Vijay, the maharajah's son, had been friends since they were very young. But usually, she and Vijay would have been sent off to play and then have a nursery tea in another part of the palace, while the adults ate their meal.

But Celia was fifteen now, and it was time she learned how to behave in company. She might as well learn here, in India, and then refine her social skills when they were back in England, when the hunt for a suitable husband would begin in earnest.

'Just about,' Celia shouted back to him from her room along the passage. Sita was with her, helping her to dress. Wilfred had insisted she wear European clothing this evening, and had paid over the odds for a dressmaker to make her a suitable evening dress. Full length, pale pink, with a demure neckline. Perfect for a young woman making her debut in society. He might have even let her wear the diamond brooch, if he hadn't hidden it away for safekeeping. The emeralds would have looked striking against the pink silk.

He gave his Brylcreemed hair a last comb through and stepped out into the passageway to wait for her. The doors to the courtyard were open and a warm breeze was blowing in. Wind should be cooling, he thought. The heat of this damned country was not something he'd miss when they returned home. Agra was pleasant in winter, just about bearable after the monsoon but from April through to post-monsoon it was horrible. How he'd stuck it this long he didn't know. He hoped that Mountbatten would hurry things along and announce a date for independence, so that he, Wilfred, could start counting down the days.

Celia emerged from her room. 'Well, how do I look?'

For a moment Wilfred was speechless. She looked beautiful. So grown-up in that pink gown, and more like Alice than ever before. Her hair was pinned up – a change from the usual long plait over one shoulder she seemed to favour. Sita had fastened a pink hibiscus flower in her hair that matched the dress perfectly. A long string of pearls was around her neck – Alice used to wear those back in the early days of their marriage. She had a smudge of lipstick on, not too much but just a little. He hadn't even known she possessed any. Perhaps it was one she'd kept out of Alice's things. And she was wearing shoes with a small heel that made her almost as tall as him. His little girl was gone, and in her place was this beautiful young woman. His heart swelled with pride for his daughter.

He smiled at her. 'You look stunning. When we're back in England you will break so many hearts.'

He'd meant it as a compliment but somehow his words made her scowl. 'Well, are we going now or not?'

'Yes. Sanjit should have the car ready for us at the front.'

'All right. I just need to . . .' Celia waved a hand vaguely in the direction of her room and walked off. Wilfred was left wondering whether to wait for her there or go out to the car to wait. It was a little thing but so typical, he thought, of their relationship these days. They never seemed to be quite in tune with each other. At least, he never seemed to know quite what to do or say around Celia that wouldn't annoy her. It was ridiculous. He was the adult, she was still a child, and he should be able to tell her what to do and how to behave. And yet, he was aware that somehow they needed to progress their relationship from parent/child to adult/adult. How one was supposed to manage that he had no idea. He sighed heavily and decided to go out to the car to wait rather than linger outside her room.

At the palace, Wilfred kept Celia in his sight while they and the other guests milled around on the terrace before dinner was announced. Fountains played into pools, carefully trimmed rose bushes were in neat rows and the scent of jacaranda was everywhere. Tiny lights had been strung up through the trees. Celia declared it was like a fairy palace and Wilfred had to agree the place looked beautiful.

Wilfred accepted a glass of champagne from a passing waiter but discreetly shook his head at Celia when she reached for one from the tray. 'You're fifteen. No alcohol for you,' he muttered to her, and received a brief scowl in return. He spotted glasses of mango juice being brought round by another servant and picked up one of those for her. She liked mango, he knew. She'd miss it when they went home to England.

One moment Celia was a child and the next she was acting

as though she couldn't wait to grow up. It was so difficult. As he watched her, making sure she didn't take a glass of champagne behind his back, Vijay came over to her and said something that made her laugh. Her whole face lit up when she was with him. He'd been a good friend to her and a good influence during her childhood. But now – as he watched her smile at him, standing close as Vijay leaned over to speak in her ear, then laugh at something he said – now he was beginning to wonder if he shouldn't put a stop to it. Vijay was Indian; Celia was English. They were both almost adults. Their friendship was perhaps no longer appropriate. Although personal relationships, even marriages, between people of the two cultures weren't unheard of it was not what he wanted for Celia. He'd always assumed she'd find herself a nice upstanding Englishman to marry. She needed to, so that she would settle in England, alongside him, of course. And he wanted her with him, rather than thousands of miles away in India.

Wilfred stared at them, debating whether he should speak to Celia about their friendship. There was probably no point. It wouldn't be too long, at most another year, before they'd be going back to England for good. Celia would be sixteen – still very young. There was no danger she'd get herself too involved with Vijay before then. And frankly, he couldn't face the backlash he'd get from her if he laid down the law and forbade her spending time with Vijay. The sooner they left this country the better. Not just for the sake of Celia's future but for himself too. Although he'd lived here for most of his life, the damned place reminded him too much of Alice. He'd been at his happiest with her by his side, but since her death it had been a struggle. Only his sense of duty, of wanting to see the job through to its end, had kept him – and Celia – here. He hoped that back in England he'd be able to move on, at last, and build himself and his daughter a new and better life.

'What is it, Papa? Why are you staring at me?' She'd approached and was frowning at him.

He shook his head. 'Sorry, my dear. I was miles away and thinking of nothing in particular. Well, there's the dinner gong. You'll accompany me in? Take my arm.'

She did as he asked and he was pleased to see she did it graciously. They went through to the marble-clad dining hall and found their seats at the immense sandalwood table. Overhead, huge gilded ceiling fans slowly turned, keeping the air moving and providing a slight but welcome breeze. Celia was placed beside Wilfred; Vijay sat opposite them. The maharajah was at the end of the table. An Indian woman Wilfred didn't recognise but who seemed to know who he was sat between him and Wilfred.

He glanced at his daughter who'd settled in her chair. 'Elbows off the table,' he hissed at her, and she quickly removed them, placing her hands demurely in her lap.

'Vijay, when do you think the monsoon will arrive this year? Will it be early or late, I wonder?' she asked in a light, airy tone. Vijay looked surprised at the banality of the question but then smiled before answering in a similar vein. It was as though, Wilfred thought, the two of them were speaking some secret code where the words they uttered bore no relation to what they actually meant. And indeed, Vijay's reply – muttering something about the monsoon arriving exactly when it was needed, neither before nor after; his raised eyebrow as he spoke – and the way Celia spluttered with laughter behind a napkin held to her face, confirmed his suspicions. But there was nothing he could do about it. The Indian woman to his right began joining in the discussion, oblivious to the subtext. Wilfred had no choice but to reply to her.

'I hope we will be able to go to the hills in good time before the rains come,' he said. 'I must admit I find Simla a very pleasant place to live. Do you leave Agra in the summer months too?'

'No, no, I am staying here, where my home and family are,' she replied, and then thankfully, the first course was served and the conversation moved on to discussing the food. Even then, Wilfred suspected that Vijay and Celia were sharing some private joke. Every time Vijay spoke, Celia's eyes would sparkle with merriment.

When they were half-way through the dessert course, something odd happened. Just as Wilfred was about to pass a comment to his neighbour on the deliciousness of the mango ice cream, music suddenly blared out across the room. 'God Save the King' was being played at high volume. Everyone looked stunned for a moment, then quickly put down their spoons and napkins and stood to attention, as of course one always must do for the national anthem. Wilfred did the same, standing tall, looking straight ahead. Beside him, Celia also stood up but she was stifling laughter. Wilfred nudged her to make her quiet.

A few people were frowning at each other. It was an odd moment to play the anthem, while people were still eating rather than at the beginning or end of the meal, but Wilfred supposed the maharajah must have his reasons. He looked along the table to its head, where Devraj Kaur, the maharajah, was standing. He too was looking confused, staring at his son Vijay. Vijay, of all the people at the table, looked cool and composed, standing respectfully and looking straight ahead as the anthem played out. When it finished and everyone sat back down again to continue eating, the maharajah beckoned Vijay to his side and muttered something in his ear. Wilfred watched as Vijay shook his head and raised his hands as if denying something, but as the boy turned to return to his seat there was an unmistakable smirk on his face, matched by one on Celia's.

The impromptu national anthem was undoubtedly Vijay's doing, Wilfred guessed. He looked at Celia, questioningly.

She beckoned him close and whispered in his ear, suppressing giggles. 'There's a button under the table, near where Vijay is sitting. "God Save the King" is played automatically when the button is pressed. He only wanted to liven up proceedings.'

'Well, he achieved that,' Wilfred replied, thin-lipped. If Vijay was his son, he'd receive a severe dressing-down for that. But Devraj rarely chastised his son for anything. He'd let this pass. Possibly he'd even laugh about it on some future, less formal occasion.

Dinner was over and people were beginning to leave the table to move to the terrace where coffee and brandy were to be served. Wilfred waited to walk through with Celia but she'd darted ahead to join Vijay, so instead he escorted the Indian woman whose name he'd completely forgotten if ever he'd known it.

'Wilfred, my friend,' Maharajah Devraj said, as soon as he reached the sitting room. 'I could not easily talk to you at dinner. There is something we must discuss.'

'Of course.' Wilfred excused himself from the Indian woman and followed Devraj into his office. 'What can I do for you?' He wondered if Devraj was going to comment on the relationship between Vijay and Celia. Perhaps he too had noticed how they seemed to have a secret unspoken code, how that now they were nearly adults their closeness was not quite as acceptable as it used to be.

But it was not that. 'Independence is coming soon, I think, now that Lord Mountbatten is here to manage it,' Devraj began, after he gestured to an armchair by the open patio doors of the office.

'Yes, a year, or perhaps a little more, I should think.' Wilfred took the seat that Devraj had indicated.

Devraj perched on the corner of his desk. 'And you will then be returning to England with Celia?'

'Yes.' Where was he going with this, Wilfred wondered. He'd known Devraj for so many years, since boyhood really, and yet he still often found he could not read the man.

'You will be taking all your possessions, everything your family has accumulated in your long history in India?'

'Well, I expect I will sell or leave behind a lot of the furniture, which won't be suitable for an English house, but otherwise—'

The maharajah held up a hand to cut him off. 'I am thinking of one particular item your family acquired, a long time ago. A very precious item.'

The diamond, Wilfred realised. He was talking about the diamond brooch.

'The *Chamakta Sitara*,' Devraj confirmed. 'Acquired by your grandfather Albert Fforbes during the Rebellion of 1857, if I remember the story correctly.' Devraj smiled at Wilfred. The two men had always been friends, even playing together as children, though they'd never been as close as their respective offspring were now.

'The mutiny.'

'We prefer to call it the First War of Independence,' Devraj said, raising an eyebrow. 'You know you can never take the diamond out of India? It is bad enough that it's been out of the possession of its original Indian owners. But to take it out of its home country . . .' He shook his head sadly. 'Well, the curse would simply become more potent. Hasn't it been bad enough for your family already? Your mother, your wife . . .'

Wilfred laughed. 'Devraj, you know I don't believe in any of that mumbo-jumbo. My mother and wife died young not because they weren't Indian and yet had worn the diamond, but from diseases – dysentery in the case of my mother and cancer in the case of my dear Alice. That's what killed them, not the diamond.'

The maharajah tipped his head to one side. 'And yet, your daughter does not wear the diamond tonight? I thought she would. I recall your wife wearing it to dinners here on several occasions.'

'She did, yes.' Wilfred could picture her now, the most beautiful woman in any room, the brooch pinned at her throat. 'But Celia is too young to wear it. She is still a child. I did not think it suitable.'

'Pity,' Devraj said. 'I should have liked to have seen it again. But mark my words, Wilfred. If you take that jewel out of India it will kill again. I suggest you leave it with me for safekeeping when you move back to England.'

Wilfred chuckled. The diamond had already been out of India

several times, when he and Alice had made trips home. He'd even lent it to Cyril's wife to wear on her wedding day. 'It is a lump of rock, Devraj. It cannot kill. And although I thank you for the offer, I must decline. My family has a long history associated with that diamond and I am not going to be the man who breaks with tradition.' The diamond had been worn by his grandmother, mother and wife and would, in turn, be worn by Celia and then her daughters or daughters-in-law. It would be their link to India once they'd returned, a reminder of their time here.

'Tradition – by which I assume you would include British rule in India – is about to be broken for good, Wilfred, whether we like it or not. Well, perhaps we should return now to my other guests.' Devraj gave him a tight smile as he held the door to his study open for Wilfred to pass through. Wilfred felt vaguely uneasy about the discussion – Devraj's claim about the diamond's curse wasn't the first time he'd heard such a story. But it was all a load of poppycock, of course. Still, his friend's words haunted him as he rejoined the other guests on the terrace and accepted a glass of brandy from one of the waiters.

Chapter 11

Lisa, 2023

Lisa had arranged with Ben that he should come to her flat on Wednesday evening to collect the brooch. She'd booked a temporary parking spot in her apartment block's underground garage for him, so he could drive in from Surrey rather than have to take such a valuable jewel on public transport. She'd had the impression that he didn't want to collect the brooch at all. His reaction, when he heard she'd found it in the briefcase, had been unnerving. 'But you *must* take it,' she'd insisted. 'It belongs to your family. If it had been Wilfred's, and he and his daughter died, then his next of kin would have been his brother – your great-grandfather. And, therefore, you, or rather your father, are the rightful owners now that it has been rediscovered.'

'I suppose so.' Ben had looked glum. 'I suppose it explains a lot.'

'What do you mean?'

But he'd shaken his head, drunk his pint, and refused to answer. 'I'll tell you more when I see the damned thing.' She'd got nothing more from him that Sunday afternoon. Indeed, he'd left her soon after, taking the briefcase with him.

Now, as she tidied her living room and arranged a tray of snacks – olives, crisps, slices of cheese and tiny squares of Melba toast – she pondered what more he might tell her. He'd heard of the diamond. It had a name. That must mean it had a story, a tale that was part of his family folklore, perhaps. From the fearful look on Ben's face when she told him how she and Gaby had discovered the brooch in the briefcase, its story wasn't a happy one. 'Explains a lot,' he'd said. Well, soon she'd find out what he meant by those words.

He arrived bang on time, ringing the doorbell to her building at precisely seven-thirty. She buzzed him in, and a minute later there he was, bringing with him a bunch of flowers. 'No idea if you like flowers, but anyway. Mum always used to say that everyone's happy to receive flowers.'

'She's right. They're beautiful, thank you.' Lisa took them – a mix of spray carnations in three shades of pink – and arranged them in a vase.

'*Was* right.'

'I'm sorry?'

'She died, when I was seventeen.'

'Oh. I'm very sorry to hear that. That's far too young to lose a parent.' Lisa looked away, feeling a little embarrassed that the conversation had taken such a sombre turn so soon. 'Can I get you a drink? I've zero-alcohol beer, as you're driving, or tea, coffee, sparkling elderflower . . .'

'The beer sounds great. Thank you.'

She poured two, one for each of them, then sat on the sofa. He took the other end of it, and perched on the edge, staring at the little velvet jewel box that she'd put ready on the middle of the coffee table.

'So, is that it?'

'Yes.' She reached for it, and he flinched. 'Are you all right? Shall I open it?'

'Er . . . yes. Go on. Let me see this blasted thing.'

She eased open the box and held it in front of him. He didn't reach to take it from her as she'd have expected. He just stared at it wordlessly, a look of hatred in his eyes.

'It's quite something, isn't it?' she said quietly, to break the tension. 'See how it catches the light.' She twisted the box this way and that, letting the diamond send its sparkles around the room.

'Yes.' He took a shuddering sigh. 'I need to tell you its story. And why it's affecting me like this.'

'Only if you want to,' she said gently.

He nodded. 'I do want to. You found it, you found me, and I want you to know what that diamond means to our family.' He picked up his beer and took a long swallow. 'It's called the *Chamakta Sitara*. It means Shining Star in Hindi.'

'A suitable name,' Lisa agreed. It certainly shone, almost as though it had a light source of its own embedded deep within.

'It belonged for years to an ancient Indian royal family. I don't know when or how it was originally found, but it had been passed down from one to the next for centuries. And then in 1857 there was the Indian Mutiny.'

'I've heard of that.'

'Indian *sepoys* – native soldiers who mostly were employed by the British East India Company – rebelled. They were using adapted Enfield rifles, and the cartridges came wrapped in greased paper. You had to bite the end off before using each one.'

Lisa frowned, not understanding the significance.

'The grease used came from either cows or pigs. It varied depending on the batch of cartridges, and there was no way of knowing which had been used on any particular batch. So using these cartridges offended both Hindus and Muslims.'

'Ah, I see.'

'And that, plus the *sepoys*' demands for better conditions and equal pay to the English soldiers, is what kicked off the mutiny. Until then, large parts of India had basically been administered by the British East India Company, which had its own army. The mutiny began in Delhi and spread across the country. The East India Company's forces and the British army fought back, and it all became pretty ugly. You know – rape and murder, villages burned, holy idols smashed. And treasures were looted from palaces and temples.'

'Among them this brooch?' Lisa guessed.

Ben nodded. 'Yes, though I believe at that time the diamond wasn't in its current setting.'

'Was it looted by your ancestor?' She frowned, trying to imagine it happening.

'No. A *sepoy* who worked for my ancestor – Albert Fforbes – took advantage of the mayhem and stole it. He then gave it to Albert in return for land and cash. At that time the diamond was set into a turban pin, but Albert's son Edward, the father of Wilfred, had it remodelled into this brooch when he married Victoria Whyte. As an aside, that's where our double-barrelled name came from.'

'And then the brooch stayed in your family until it was lost along with Wilfred and his daughter in the plane crash.'

'Yes.'

Lisa looked expectantly at him. This history was all very interesting, but it didn't explain why Ben seemed so glum about the diamond being returned to his family. She'd expected him to be excited about it. There was more to this story. He was holding something back. She said nothing, but kept her eyes on him, patiently waiting until he'd found the words.

He took a long, shuddering sigh. 'You're going to think I'm mad, when I tell you the next part. I don't want to believe it myself, but . . . Well, who knows.' He picked up his beer and took a long sip, clearly putting off the moment a little longer.

'Go on.' She was intrigued.

'The story I heard, that my grandfather used to tell me when I was a child, is that the diamond was cursed. That all the while it was out of the possession of its original owners, all the women in the family would die young.'

'A cursed diamond! Like the Koh-i-Noor!' Lisa stared at him, wide-eyed.

'I know, I know.' He waved a hand dismissively. 'Load of old baloney, you're thinking. But this is the family story that was passed down. Albert Fforbes' wife died soon after the mutiny. His son's wife Victoria Whyte died when she was only in her thirties. Wilfred married a woman called Alice, who died young; I'm not sure what from. Their daughter Celia was lost in the plane crash along with Wilfred. From then on, as you said, the diamond, even though it was lost, was effectively inherited by Wilfred's brother Cyril. Now then, Cyril's wife, Winnie, died young. Their only son, James, married a Frenchwoman named Hortense – my grandmother. I never knew her, because she died giving birth to my father David.' He paused, drawing breath. 'My grandfather used to tell me all this. As a child I lapped it up. I thought it was so cool that somewhere there was a cursed diamond still affecting our family, even though it was lost. All those women were unknown to me, dead long before I was born. But then my mother died when I was seventeen. She had a brain tumour. It didn't seem so cool then.' He looked away, staring across the room. 'Her death hit me hard. She was a lovely woman, warm and fun. And seventeen is a vulnerable age.'

He trailed off, lost in his memories of his mother. Lisa remained silent, giving him time to compose himself but also unable to think what to say.

He turned back to her. 'And now you're giving me the diamond back.'

'Because . . .' *Because it's yours*, she wanted to say. But it wasn't, really. It had been stolen, over a hundred and sixty years ago.

'I suppose it makes no difference,' Ben said, sadly. 'The curse has been working even though it hasn't been in our possession.'

'Your mother, grandmother, great-grandmother's deaths – those could be coincidental. I mean . . . a cursed diamond? *Really*?'

'I know. It's daft. I don't believe in magic or the supernatural, or cursed diamonds. But . . .' He shrugged, and drank the last of his beer.

'Let me get you another one of those,' she said, sensing he needed a moment alone to compose himself. He nodded gratefully and she went out to the kitchen. As she retrieved the beer from her fridge and opened it, she pondered what she'd heard. Did she believe in this curse? Well, no, generally, she didn't believe in magic or ghosts or the supernatural either. But in Ben's shoes, she understood that with so many women in his family meeting a premature end, it'd be only natural to wonder if perhaps there was some truth in this legend. No wonder he hadn't wanted to hold the brooch. Well, she didn't want to keep it either. She didn't want to risk the curse transferring to her, and her family . . . just in case. She put the opened bottle of beer on the tray along with the snacks she'd prepared earlier and carried it through.

'Here, just a few bits and pieces to eat, and another beer.' She placed it on the coffee table and handed him the drink.

He smiled at her gratefully, and she thought, not for the first time, how lovely his eyes were. That deep brown, like melted chocolate.

'Thanks, Lisa. This looks great.' He reached for a square of Melba toast and cheese. 'I didn't expect this.'

'No problem. I enjoyed preparing it all.' She blushed. He'd held her gaze a little longer than necessary when she'd brought in the tray. She took an olive and as she ate it, considered how to return to the subject of the diamond, without upsetting him.

'I suppose,' Ben said, pre-empting her, 'that now you've heard the story you're not going to want to keep the thing, are you?'

'I never wanted to,' she replied. 'It's not mine.'

'It's not my family's either, really.'

'Is your grandfather still alive?'

'No, he died a couple of years ago.'

'Then you must give the brooch to your father. Let him decide what to do.'

Ben nodded. 'Maybe there's a way to track down descendants of the original owner of the diamond. Perhaps if Dad returns it, the curse would be broken.'

'Yes! That's it, Ben. That's what has to be done.' Lisa expected that Ben would agree enthusiastically and that they'd move on to a discussion of how to find who the diamond had been stolen from back in the nineteenth century. But to her surprise he simply hung his head.

'That's not going to happen, though. I've already told Dad about our contact and mentioned that I was coming here tonight to fetch the diamond. I said to him we should try to return it to India. But he just laughed and said there's no way he'd do that. He's delighted it's been found. He said he'd like to get it reset into a necklace that he'd loan to whoever his current girlfriend is. He gets a new partner pretty regularly, you see. Since Mum died he's had several, but none have lasted long.'

'You mean they . . .' Lisa was horrified. Surely the diamond's curse didn't affect casual relationships too? She had visions of David Fforbes-Whyte's girlfriends dropping dead one after the other.

'What? Oh!' Ben gave a hollow laugh. 'No, they didn't die. My father just seems incapable of committing to anyone these days, but he always likes to have someone he can take along to parties and conferences and the like. Looks good, he says, for a minister to have a partner.'

'Oh, yes, I suppose so. Well, here it is.' She pushed the little velvet box towards him, then gave him a wry smile. 'I'm not going to let you leave without it.'

'Even though passing it on might mean endangering the lives of several poor ministerial aides and civil servants, whoever my dad fancies going out with next?' But Ben's tone was wry, amused, and she knew he didn't really think that.

'I suppose it'd be a quick way for your father to get rid of anyone he's tired of. "Here, darling, wear this diamond tonight, why don't you?" And next day, bam, she's gone.'

Ben chuckled. 'Dad wouldn't like that. Not good optics for government ministers' dates to drop dead.'

'No, I guess not.' Lisa laughed but then suddenly realised she was making jokes about the way his mother and grandmother had died. 'Ben, sorry. It's not a laughing matter, is it?'

'I dunno. Sometimes I think it's better to make a joke of it all. I mean, our family's been unfortunate and had more than its share of tragedy, but it can't really be down to possession of a diamond, a lump of compressed carbon that was dug out of the ground, can it?'

'No, Ben. It can't. And I'm really sorry about your mother and the others.'

'I didn't know the others. Only Mum. And she'd have been the one making the jokes, believe me. She had a wicked sense of humour.' He smiled wistfully, staring into space as though picturing his mother standing close by.

'Sounds like she was a wonderful woman.'

'She was. She had to be, to put up with Dad. He's not an easy man. Charming on the surface but can be a bit . . . well . . . controlling. Typical politician, I suppose. But Mum would never stand for his bossiness. She'd tell him, "Lighten up, David," and crack a joke, and he'd grumble but then give in and laugh with the rest of us. She was good for him. He's not really been happy since she died.'

He took a deep breath, once more fighting to get his emotions back under control. 'Look, I dug out some photos.' He reached into his jacket pocket and pulled out an envelope. Inside was a small bundle of photos. He sifted through and handed one to Lisa. 'That's Mum.'

Lisa looked carefully at the photo. It showed a laughing woman aged around forty, with her arm around a teenaged Ben. There was an obvious warmth between them, and Lisa was struck once more by how hard it must have been to lose a mother aged seventeen.

'And that's my grandmother,' Ben said, handing her another

photo. This one looked to date from the 1960s judging by the fashion and hairstyle, and showed an elegant young woman on a beach, gazing out to sea.

'She was pretty,' Lisa said.

'And my great-grandmother. Cyril's wife, Winnie. On their wedding day.'

This one, in black and white, showed a 1930s bride in a long white dress and veil. Lisa smiled and put it on the pile with the others. She wasn't sure why Ben was showing her all these pictures, unless it was to give faces to the women who'd died young. 'Nice.'

'Look closely. The brooch she's wearing.'

Lisa picked up the photo again and stared at it, recognising the brooch. 'Oh, yes!'

'She borrowed it for the wedding. And here is one of Wilfred and Cyril's mother, Victoria Whyte, at her home in India. My great-great-grandmother. She's wearing it too.'

This picture, sepia-coloured, showed a woman in late-Victorian-style dress, standing beside a huge potted palm. Behind her a row of arches revealed a veranda beyond. It was unmistakably colonial style, Lisa thought. And the brooch was pinned at the throat of the woman's high-necked gown.

'Last photo,' Ben said, handing her another black and white image. 'This is the only one I could find of Wilfred, his wife Alice and their daughter Celia. It must have been taken when they'd come to England for a visit. Possibly they'd come for Cyril and Winnie's wedding.'

The photo showed the little family group standing together on the Embankment in London, with the Houses of Parliament behind them. Lisa looked closely at the faces. Alice looked kind, Wilfred rather severe. And Celia, who couldn't have been more than about five in the photo, had a defiant, rather sulky look to her, as though she'd recently been reprimanded by a parent, most likely her father. 'Alice isn't wearing the brooch,' she said.

'No, it wouldn't have been an everyday piece of jewellery to wear. Special occasions only, I'd have thought. Or when there was a need to impress someone with their wealth and status.'

Lisa looked quickly at him. He'd almost spat out those last words. 'Did a lot of your ancestors live in India?'

'Yes, starting with Albert Fforbes who was with the East India Company, and then after the mutiny, when Britain took direct control of India and it became officially part of the British Empire, he joined the Indian Civil Service. His son Edward and grandson Wilfred followed in his footsteps. Cyril was supposed to as well, but he never went back to India after his university days in England. There was some falling-out between him and Wilfred, so the family story goes. Other than Cyril's wedding I think they hardly saw each other. Apparently, they were on the point of making up, Granddad told me, as Wilfred was planning to move to England after independence, but then he and Celia died in that plane crash before that happened.'

'That's tragic.'

'Yes.'

Ben looked so sad that now Lisa wanted to change the subject. She'd learned the history, she'd heard about the diamond's curse and what had happened to Ben's family. He was going to take the brooch away, and that was the end of the story, for her.

She felt unexpectedly disappointed about this. There was no reason for her to contact Ben again after today. No need to see him. And yet . . .

As if he'd read her thoughts, he looked up at her and smiled. 'You know, I really would like to try to track down the descendants of the Indian family who originally owned the diamond. And if you're interested, I wonder if . . . you'd like to help? We could . . . put our heads together? Or not, if you feel you've had enough of this diamond and its story . . .' He trailed off as Lisa grinned at him.

'Ben, I'd love to.'

He looked genuinely delighted by her enthusiastic response.

'Right then – I'll start by going through my family's archive, there are lots of old letters and stuff that might contain some clues. Might not be able to get to it immediately but I'll do it as soon as I've got time. Then I'll be in touch and we can continue researching together, at the British Library perhaps.'

'Perfect!'

When he left, with the diamond brooch safely zipped into a pocket of his fleece jacket, Lisa couldn't stop smiling. She'd enjoyed the evening and was very much looking forward to doing some more research alongside him.

Chapter 12

Celia, April 1947

'When will I get to wear Mama's brooch?' Celia asked, as they left the maharajah's palace after the dinner. 'I rather thought you might want me to wear it tonight.'

'When you're a little older, and we're in England, my dear. There will be plenty of occasions, probably starting soon after we move there. I'm hoping you'll be presented to the king when you are eighteen, and therefore be a debutante, three years from now.'

Celia laughed. What was he talking about? 'What do you mean, presented to the king, Papa?'

'All young ladies from decent families are presented to the king and queen, at court,' Wilfred said, sounding exasperated. 'You already know this. It will be your launch into society.'

'You're assuming we'll be in England before I'm eighteen, then.' She frowned. This was not part of her personal plan for the rest of her life.

'Yes. We will be. Independence for India is not much more than a year away, perhaps even less. And as I've told you before, when it happens, we shall immediately return home.'

She did know this. She just wanted to never miss an opportunity to impress on him how much she would prefer to stay in India, one way or another.

They'd reached the motorcar, where Sanjit was sitting in the driver's seat waiting for them. Celia began to reply to Papa but he shushed her. 'Not in front of the servants. We can talk later.'

And so she spent the journey home – her real home, the house where she'd been born and grew up, not cold damp England – staring out of the car's windows at the passing night-time traffic. Beggars sleeping on the pavements. A few ox-carts plodding their way through the city. One or two smart motorcars like their own, probably people who'd also been at the maharajah's dinner. A police car slowly patrolling. Rickshaws at the side of the road, their drivers curled up asleep across the passenger seats. A drunken man on a bicycle wobbling along on the wrong side of the street. It was all much quieter than the teeming masses of people one would see during the day but it was still there – all Indian life from the rich to the poor, the privileged to the deprived, the righteous to the criminal.

Celia loved it all. She would not allow herself to be taken to England. Not by Papa nor anyone. She hoped independence would take rather longer than Papa had suggested. If it didn't happen until she was of age, then he couldn't make her go with him. She could stay in India, by herself. Not by herself – Sita would stay with her. She'd surely be able to stay in the house because it had belonged to her grandparents and, somehow, she'd persuade Papa not to sell it but to let her stay on and take care of it. And she'd find ways of making money. Vijay would help. He'd be there for her always. She crossed her fingers on her lap in their secret sign. She and Vijay, close as that.

When they arrived home Papa went straight to his room without continuing the conversation they'd started. Celia stared after him, her mouth hanging open. So he wasn't even giving her a chance to reply to him this evening. She considered following him, banging on his door until he let her in, and telling him exactly what she thought of the idea of him dragging her against her will back to England. It'd be practically kidnapping – even though she was his daughter she had rights, didn't she? And this presenting at court – the whole point of it, she knew, was to start the process of finding a husband. People like her father might sneer at the Indians and their system of arranged marriages but really, was it so much different in England, at least for the upper classes? Young ladies went to court and met the king, then attended a host of parties and balls and soirees and met lots of eligible young men. Sooner or later, there'd be one the parents approved of, someone from the right sort of family, with an adequate amount of money, and he'd be encouraged to woo the girl, and she'd be told to accept him.

But there was no point trying to confront Papa now about it all, she knew. Better to wait until tomorrow and have it out with him then. Tomorrow was Sunday, Papa would not be working and there would be plenty of time to talk to him. Before or after church. Probably before, she thought, and with any luck the row would be intense enough that she'd be sent to her room for the morning and would have to miss going to church. At this time of year, it was always far too hot and stuffy to be singing hymns and kneeling for prayers among all the other English people.

So it was over breakfast, after Sanjit had served them and left the room and Sita was occupied elsewhere, that Celia raised the subject.

'Papa. About this idea of us going to England when India gains independence,' she began. He looked up at her over the top of his glasses, and put down his coffee cup with a sigh.

'Celia, I do hope you are not going to be difficult about it.'

'I'm not being difficult. I just want to know why you think we must leave. Surely the new Indian government would allow you to stay and get a job – they will still need civil servants and people of your experience? I should think they'd be delighted for you to stay and work for them.'

'They will want to employ Indians. Not the English. The new government will want to distance itself as much as possible from India's colonial rule. Putting Englishmen in top jobs would send out the wrong message. No, there is no chance of a job for me. Besides, Celia, I do not wish to stay. I am English – *we* are English – and we will return to our home nation. I don't want to live in an India that is not British.'

'I was born here, I have lived here all my life. You were also born here and lived all your life here.'

'I was at school and university in England. I loved those years. You also would have gone to school in England had your dear mother not died when she did.'

'But I didn't. I don't know England. I've only been there for short trips, what . . . about three or four times? And most of those were when I was very young. Last year's visit was awful. You and Uncle Cyril sniping at each other all the time. And I missed Sita so very much.' To her horror she felt tears welling up as she imagined leaving Sita . . . and Vijay behind. Tears didn't work on Papa. 'I'm not English, Papa. Not really.'

He stood up sharply, in the way she knew meant he was frustrated by her, and slapped the table with the flat of his hand.

'You *are* English, my girl. It makes no difference where you were born or lived. It's who your parents are that counts. You are fully English.'

She tried another tactic. 'Must we go immediately? If independence happens next year, couldn't we stay here a few more years before going to England?'

'You mean until you're of age and can decide to stay here against my wishes? That's your plan, is it? I see right through it. No, Celia. We will leave as soon as independence takes place. We'll be on the first aeroplane flight to leave post-independence, on the very day it happens.' He sat down again and picked up a slice of toast, buttering it angrily. 'I'll hear no more of it. Be ready for church in twenty minutes.'

Celia glared at him but there was no point continuing the discussion now. She'd had an idea, though. An idea that might help him see just how Indian she really felt.

As soon as breakfast was over, Celia ran to find Sita, who was sitting outside her room with some sewing, as she so often did in the quiet part of the morning before Celia demanded her time.

'Sita, can you help me?'

'Of course, *meri jaan*. What do you need?' Sita put her sewing away into a cloth bag and looked up at Celia expectantly.

'I need some help dressing this morning.'

Sita frowned, but Celia didn't wait for her to ask why she needed help. She turned and walked back across the courtyard to the family's side of the house. Sita would follow her. She always had. The *ayah* was devoted to her and would do anything she asked. She'd been there for her since she was a baby – and that was just it, wasn't it? How could Papa think she could leave Sita? It wasn't that she needed Sita anymore, now that she was grown. It was that she liked Sita's presence. She was a friend. No, it was more than that. She'd been like a mother to her, since Mama's death. She loved Sita with all her heart and couldn't imagine life without having her nearby. And Sita had already told her she wouldn't leave her family in India to move to England. In any case, it would be unfair to expect her to do that. So Celia would just have to remain in India, wouldn't she? One way or another.

Celia reached her room with Sita close behind. Once inside she firmly closed the door. 'Now then, I want to wear something really special to church this morning.'

'Is it a special occasion?' Sita asked as she opened the wardrobe doors.

'No. I just want to show off my newest outfit.'

'Your newest . . .' Celia watched Sita as the penny dropped and Sita realised what she was referring to. 'You don't mean . . .'

'My sari. Yes. Can you help? I only have fifteen minutes before it's time to leave, and I have no idea how to put it on.' Celia pulled the sari and blouse out of the drawer she'd stored them in and laid them on her bed. She quickly slipped out of the dress she'd originally put on and stood in her underwear.

'Your father will not like it.'

'No, he won't, and that's kind of the point,' Celia said, making her tone firm so that Sita knew there'd be no use trying to talk her out of it.

Still the Indian woman didn't make a move. '*Meri jaan*, are you sure? I don't want you to get in trouble.'

'I won't tell him you helped me.'

'It's not me I'm worried about. It's you.'

'Let me worry about that. Come on, will you help me?' Celia had already tugged on the tight blouse that fastened with a row of tiny hooks at the back. She turned so that Sita could fasten them and then held out the length of fabric.

Sita sighed. 'You need an underskirt. I will fetch one of mine.'

'Be quick.'

Sita hurried from the room and was back a moment later with a dark green underskirt that Celia stepped into. 'Now, hold out your arms,' Sita instructed. She wound the fabric around Celia's waist, tucking it into the waistband of the underskirt. Celia watched as she expertly made pleats to tuck into the waistband, then pleated the end, known as the *pallu*, to drape over Celia's left shoulder.

'You'll have to teach me this one day,' Celia said.

'Yes. There. You look beautiful.' Sita stepped back so that Celia could admire herself in the full-length mirror on the outside of her wardrobe door. She smiled at her reflection. Yes, she looked good. Add a *bindi* and maybe a jewel in her belly button and she could most definitely pass for Indian with her dark colouring.

She should learn more Hindi, she thought. And other dialects. Vijay would teach her.

'Celia! The car is outside waiting for us!' Papa's shout made Sita stare at her wide-eyed.

'You wait here. Leave the room after we've gone so he doesn't suspect you helped.' Celia kissed Sita's cheeks as a thank you and left the room. The sari swished around her ankles in a satisfying way, and the *pallu* flared out behind her as she walked. It was a lovely garment. So elegant. Really beautiful. She felt more of a woman than she ever had in her Western-style dresses, even the long evening dress she'd worn at the maharajah's dinner the previous night.

Papa had his back to her as she approached the car. He was leaning over to speak to Sanjit through the side window. 'Here I am, Papa,' she said.

He turned with a smile, which quickly vanished when he registered what she was wearing. 'What the blazes? What are you wearing?'

'A sari, Papa. I bought it in the market a couple of weeks ago. It is rather beautiful, don't you think? The colour suits me and look at this embroidery!' She indicated the ornate golden edging that swooped up over her shoulder.

'I can see it's a sari. Why are you wearing it?'

'Because I like it and I look good in it.'

'And you choose to wear it to church, where we will see all our friends and acquaintances? And they will all point and say, "Look at that Fforbes-Whyte girl; she's gone full native." And they will wonder why I allow it, and mutter about how the lack of an Englishwoman in your life has ruined you.'

'And yet, I am wearing it today.' Celia raised her chin defiantly.

'What next, I wonder? A loincloth like Gandhi?'

'*Dhoti*, Papa. It's called a *dhoti*.'

'I don't care what it's called. And you—' he gestured angrily to the sari '—you have no place wearing that. Granted it looks elegant enough on a native woman but not on you. It's all wrong. Go and change at once.'

'Papa, there's no time.' Celia walked past him and climbed into the back seat of the car, gathering up the skirts of her sari as she did. Her father stared at her, then threw his hands in the air in exasperation and climbed in to the front passenger seat.

'Quick as you can, Sanjit. We're already late.'

Celia smiled triumphantly to herself in the back seat. She was making a point, in the strongest way she could, and it had worked. Only time would tell whether she'd be able to change his mind about leaving India, but she would do all that she could to ensure she, at least, could stay.

As Sanjit drove them away from the bungalow she looked back and saw Sita standing by the door, watching after them anxiously. Celia gave her a triumphant little wave.

Chapter 13

Lisa, 2023

A couple of weeks passed after Ben's visit to collect the diamond, during which Lisa had just one brief message from him thanking her for her hospitality. *No problem*, she'd replied. *Let me know when you want me to help with the research.* She'd had a thumbs up to that but nothing more. She felt oddly disappointed. She'd looked forward to trying to find out more about the diamond. The project had helped her so much already and she wanted more. She also thought it might be rather nice to spend a bit more time in Ben's company.

On a Friday, when she began to wonder if she'd ever hear from Ben again, she had a reply. *Sorry for delay. Work, yada yada. Had no time yet to look at family papers. I know it's short notice, but I wondered if you'd like to come out to Surrey tomorrow if you're free – lunch out plus meet my father and we can ask him together about returning the diamond. It's as much your story as mine now.*

She sent a quick reply confirming that yes, she was free and would like to come. A second message came from Ben almost immediately naming a time and place to meet.

And so on Saturday morning Lisa took a tube to Waterloo station and a train to Woking, and then a taxi to the village pub Ben had named. It was near his father's house, he'd said, and also near Ben's flat.

Ben was already there, sitting at a table by the window. He stood up smiling as she approached, looking genuinely pleased to see her. She felt an odd flutter in her stomach as he greeted her. Just nerves at the prospect of meeting his government-minister father, she told herself.

'I thought we'd eat first, then go to see Dad this afternoon. They do a fabulous chicken pie here. Or if you want something lighter, the Caesar salad is good too,' he told her.

'The salad would be great.'

'And a bottle of wine to go with it? Or is it too early?'

She smiled. 'Just a glass for me, thanks.'

A waitress took their order. As they waited for the food and then ate, they chatted nonstop. Lisa found herself thoroughly enjoying the lunch. Ben was easy, charming, and delightful company. She couldn't help but compare him with Rupert. Ben's charms were less superficial; he gave the impression of having hidden depths that Lisa thought she'd rather like to explore.

Ben was a writer, penning his third novel while trying to get the other ones published. 'I'm close, I think, with one of them. A publisher has asked for the full manuscript, so I'm hopeful.'

'Ooh, that's exciting!' Lisa said. Much more exciting than her own boring job, anyway.

'So to make ends meet, while I wait in hope for the big book deal, I have part-time jobs in a pub and a shop, and I work for Dad at the weekends helping with his admin. Occasionally I manage to sell articles or short stories to magazines. All rather bitty, and no actual career, which is a bone of contention between me and Dad.' He pulled a face.

'Your writing could become your career. You just need that first little break.'

'Yes. One day, hopefully.' He gave a little shrug. 'You know how I said Dad could be rather controlling? He thinks I should become an accountant. We have a lot of, shall we say, "discussions" about it.' He made quote marks in the air, and she understood that they'd rowed about it. 'Mum would have supported my writing. She'd have been so proud. If ever I'm published, I am going to dedicate my first book to her memory.' He looked away and once more she was struck by how hard he'd taken the loss of his mother.

'That's a lovely thought. What sort of books do you write?'

'Historical mystery. Sometimes with a dash of romance.'

She grinned. 'The mystery of the lost diamond, perhaps? Could be a future title for you?'

He laughed. 'Well, who knows? Depends what happens next, doesn't it?'

All too soon it was time to go to his father's house. Ben had driven his car to the pub – a battered old Ford Focus – and drove her there. Lisa felt strangely nervous about meeting David Fforbes-Whyte. She'd seen him on TV often enough – being interviewed on political chat shows or on the news – but this would be the first time she'd meet a government minister, even though he was a junior one, in the flesh. Something about her nervousness must have shown on her face, for Ben turned to her as he steered the car into a wide driveway. 'He doesn't bite, you know. He's a normal bloke, just happens to have a rather public job. And he's only bossy and controlling towards me, or people who work for him. Everyone else, he charms.'

'Of course.' She flashed him a smile that she hoped showed she wasn't worried by the prospect of meeting him, despite what Ben had told her about his own relationship with him.

Ben parked in front of a large, modern house set in neatly tended gardens that suggested a gardener was regularly employed. Every rose bush was tidily pruned and there wasn't a single dandelion in the lawn. He led her to a side door that was unlocked, and showed her into a small lobby area where Barbour jackets and Wellington boots were stored. It looked like a scene from *Country Life* magazine. 'Go on through,' he told her, ushering her into a large, bright kitchen and from there into the main hallway of the house.

'Dad? You in here?' he said, pushing open a door that led into a living room. It was furnished tastefully in what Lisa thought of as 'John Lewis style' – decent quality, relatively expensive, not too showy.

'Hello, Ben. Ah, you must be Lisa Statton. Pleased to meet you.' David Fforbes-Whyte stood up from where he'd been sitting on a large cream-coloured sofa and shook her hand. 'And let me immediately thank you for contacting Ben and returning that diamond brooch to our family. It's an important piece, as you understand, and I am very glad to have it back in our possession.'

'No problem. It turned out to be easy to find you and Ben, thanks to the documents inside the case.'

'Yes. You must relate to me the full story of how you found it. Ben's told me some of it, of course, but I would love to hear it directly from you. But first, would you like tea? Or something stronger – there's whisky or I could open a bottle of wine?'

'Tea, thank you.'

David nodded and went out to the kitchen to make it. Ben smiled at Lisa. 'See, he's not an ogre,' he whispered, which made her want to giggle. He was right, though. David was charming and, on the surface, seemed as easy-going as his son. The only difference was that David's charm came across as slightly false, somewhat put on. He was a politician after all, a man used to manipulating people's opinions of him. Lisa's instinct was that he was a man that she wouldn't trust one hundred per cent. He put her in mind of an older Rupert. A charmer who was very used to having his own way.

David was back a few minutes later, carrying a tray holding

a teapot, cups and saucers, and a plate of posh-looking biscuits. No custard creams in this house.

'Now, then. I'd love to hear the full story of the finding of the brooch,' David said.

Lisa obliged, and both men listened with interest. She told too, the story of how she'd researched the Fforbes-Whyte name, and wondered if Wilfred had been a relation of David, and how she'd then sent an email to which Ben had responded. Ben took up the narrative then, reminding his father about the family tales of how the diamond had come into their possession. 'I want to do some research, see if I can find out who the original owners were, and see if I can find any descendants . . .'

Lisa watched David, as the implications of what Ben was saying sunk in. He frowned at his son, then lifted a hand to stop Ben saying any more. 'Are you suggesting what I think you're suggesting?'

'That we do the research and, if possible, return the diamond, yes. It was stolen back in 1857.'

'Not by our family. Our ancestor legally swapped land and money for it.'

'But the diamond should never have been traded. I think we should repatriate it, now that it has turned up again after all these years. And if we can't find out who it should belong to, we should at least return it to India, to a museum perhaps.'

'Humph.' David snorted. 'Next, you'll be saying Britain should return the Koh-i-Noor. And the Elgin Marbles. And everything else we've ever brought back from other countries.'

'Well . . .' Lisa began, thinking that yes, perhaps there was a strong case for the Elgin Marbles to be returned. The Greek government was constantly asking for them back. But out of the corner of her eye she caught a glance from Ben and a tiny shake of his head, which she took to mean David wouldn't respond well to that argument. She'd be better off staying quiet, and let Ben talk his father round. After all, it wasn't her decision to make.

'We're not talking about anything other than the *Chamakta Sitara*, Dad. We know a bit about its provenance, we know how and when it was acquired. It's not even been in our hands for the last seventy-five years, so we surely don't need it now.'

'But we have it now. It's been returned to us – and I must thank you again for that, Lisa. Not everyone would have tried to find the rightful owners.'

'We're *not* the rightful owners, Dad, not if you go back—'

'Well, nobody owns anything if you go back far enough, Ben. That's a poor argument. We *do* own it. Probably somewhere among the family archives I'll have documentation relating to its purchase.'

'It was stolen goods. Our ancestor bought stolen property.'

David waved a hand as if dismissing that statement. 'We don't know how the man who sold it to Albert Fforbes acquired it.'

'We do. He stole it during the chaos of the Indian Mutiny in 1857.'

'Such was the tale your grandfather told you. Have you ever stopped to think, Benedict, that perhaps he might have embellished it a little? Or even a lot? Bear in mind he was telling you stories he'd heard himself from his own father or grandfather. We're going back very many years.' David's tone was hectoring now, as though he was standing in the House of Commons answering a challenge from the opposition. Lisa glanced over at Ben, who seemed to be cowering slightly. She hoped to catch his eye, to send him silent support, but he didn't look her way.

'Yes, but his story never changed. Don't you think we should at least try?'

'And how on earth would you go about it? It's impossible, son. Even if you did find who you thought were the right people and make contact, what would you tell them? *Look, here's a priceless jewel, might it be yours?* Ridiculous. Of course they'd agree and say yes, it is, and that they're happy to take it off your hands. And then they'll get it cut up and sell it off, and that's the end of it. No, the diamond is best kept with us. I have put it in my safe, and it'll only come out on special occasions. In time, Ben, you'll find someone special and then it'll be yours to give to your wife.'

Ben blanched. 'I don't want it, Dad. Not ever. Certainly not to give to someone I care for.' He threw a glance in Lisa's direction as he said that. She pretended not to notice, though she felt a wave of warmth surge through her.

David laughed. 'You think there's something in your grandfather's old stories of a curse? Ha! He filled your head with far too much rubbish. Now, come on. We're neglecting our guest. Lisa, more tea?' Now he was dismissive, drawing a line under the subject. He was certainly a man who considered his word was final.

'Er, no, I'm all right, thanks.'

Ben sighed, then looked at her. 'I thought we'd go for a walk, since it's a nice day. We could go over to Horsell Common. Unless you need to get back to London soon?'

'No, I have all day,' she replied. 'A walk would be lovely.'

He smiled at her with what looked like relief, then he began collecting up teacups to reload the tray. 'Great. I'll just take this out to the kitchen, then we'll get going. I'm sure Dad needs to be left in peace now.'

'Well . . . I do have plenty of constituency correspondence to deal with.'

'I'll be available to help with that tomorrow,' Ben said, and David nodded.

A few minutes later they were back in Ben's car, driving through narrow Surrey lanes to a car park on the edge of Horsell Common. They parked up and set off, walking on trails through woodland and across open common land. It was clearly a favourite place for locals to bring dogs and children at the weekends, and for Lisa, it was bliss to be out in the countryside.

'Well, I'm sorry about Dad's attitude,' Ben said, as they walked. 'I thought he'd at least consider the idea of sending the diamond back, and give his blessing to me doing some research. But it doesn't look as though he's going to be easily persuaded.'

'Maybe give him time to think about it.'

'Yes, I think that's all I can do. He's head of the family so I suppose he needs to agree to it.'

'You . . . or we . . . could do the research anyway? He can't stop you. Just do it out of interest, if nothing else. It might come to nothing but you never know.'

Ben looked at her with an expression of curiosity. 'Why are you so interested?'

She shrugged. 'Well, I guess . . . it's been a bit of a tonic for me – going through that case, searching for you and your father, having something to think about. I needed the distraction after—'

'After? I'm not prying, Lisa, but if you need to talk . . .'

She regarded him, his wide brown eyes inviting her to confide in him. 'After a break-up.'

'Oh, I'm sorry. Them, or you?'

'Me. And I'm better off without him, I know. But I'm having to . . . rebuild myself, I suppose. He knocked my self-confidence over the years I was with him.'

'Hmm. I know all about needing more self-confidence,' Ben said.

'You had a bad relationship too?'

Ben took his time answering and then shook his head. 'No. Tell the truth, I've never had a serious girlfriend, just dates.'

That surprised her. He was so easy-going, nice-looking, and kind. Why had no one snapped him up?

'You'll find someone one day,' she said gently.

He gave her an odd, sideways look that she couldn't quite interpret. 'Maybe. Anyway. Think I might just do that. The research, I mean, starting with the family archives. Thanks, Lisa.'

'Glad to have helped a bit.'

'You have. You really have. I'm so pleased to have met you, Lisa.'

She smiled but didn't answer. She was glad to have met him too, and the more time she spent with him the more she liked him.

Chapter 14

Celia, June 1947

It was June already, and temperatures were becoming unbearable. Even so, Celia was telling her father daily that she was happy enough staying in Agra. 'No need to send me to the hills, Papa. If the Indians can bear to stay here all year, then so can I. Even when the monsoon comes.' She'd have to, she privately thought, if she intended staying in India after independence or at least returning here as soon as she could, when she was old enough to do what she wanted. Might as well get used to it now, if Papa would allow it. One day, she thought, she'd be independent of him, making her own choices. She smiled. Just like India would be independent of Britain, governing itself.

But everything changed with the news that Papa passed on to her one evening over dinner. He looked tired but delighted, his eyes sparkling.

'Lord Mountbatten has brought forward the date for independence. It is to be *this year*, Celia. August! Only two months away!'

'What? So soon!' The last Celia had heard was that it was scheduled for the following summer.

'Yes! At last we have a date that we can work towards. Mountbatten has somehow managed to convince all factions that an earlier severance is better. What he's promised Nehru and Jinnah and Gandhi to achieve this God only knows, but it's to be done, and that's a good thing for us, my dear. I suppose it'll mean partitioning the country, which is a shame, but that will be their problem, not ours any longer. We'll be gone from here.'

Celia stared at her father, working through the implications of this news in her head. She couldn't believe it was coming round so quickly. August – before the monsoon had even ended. Her favourite time in India was the period after the rains when everything was fresh and clean and cool. She'd be missing that. All she could remember of English autumn weather, from her few visits, was heavy grey clouds covering the sky, yet without releasing their rain. But on the other hand – in September, Vijay was due to go to England to finish his schooling, and then go to university. Now it looked as though she'd be there before him, in August. If they lived close enough to each other, so that they could continue to see each other once a week or perhaps more, then being in England would be bearable. When Vijay finished his studies and returned to India, she'd have to find some way to come back with him. But that was years down the line. All in all, perhaps the earlier date for Indian independence might prove to be a good thing, for her personally, even though it was a shock to know it was happening so soon.

But then she remembered Sita. She couldn't leave Sita.

Papa must have noticed her worried expression. 'Ah, my dear, don't fret. Just think, two more months and we'll be going back home to a late English summer. Trust me, Celia, you will love it. Warm but not sweltering. No monsoon. Tea on the lawn, cricket on the green, ice cream on the prom. Just perfect.' He sighed and smiled wistfully.

She shook her head. It might be a vision of England he remembered from his school days but it didn't chime with her experiences. 'It's not my home,' she couldn't help herself saying. It would have to be her home for a few years, but not forever. No, she could not bear to think that she would stay forever.

Wilfred's expression softened. 'It'll be all right, my dear. It's a big change for you, I understand that. But you are young and you will soon adapt and quickly settle among our own people. I shall write to my brother and ask him to find us a house we can rent as a starting point. And we'll find a suitable school for you – where there are lots of girls of your own age and nationality. No more tutors and governesses. It'll be so much more fun for you. It's time you had some friends.'

'I have friends here. Sita. Vijay.'

He smiled at her and reached a hand across the table to pat her arm. 'Yes, of course, and you'll be able to write to them to stay in touch, but it will be good to have friends who are girls your own age, won't it? I shall find a good school, near our home, where you can be a day pupil. You won't need to board. Dear, you will love it when you get used to it. Just give it a chance, please?'

She nodded slowly. For now, there was no point arguing. He seemed pleased she was agreeing, and squeezed her hand across the table.

'That's my girl. And as for going to the hills, I think you might as well go soon with Sita. In a fortnight, perhaps. Of course, we'll need to close up the Simla house as well. There are valuable items there I don't want to leave behind. Perhaps you can be in charge of packing it all up? And then you can return to Agra a week before we leave for England, which will allow you time to pack up here and say your goodbyes.'

Celia stared at him. The thought of saying goodbye to Sita, even if she had plans to return when she was old enough to come alone, was too awful.

'Can we ask Sita to come with us? I need her!' She could not imagine life without her *ayah* nearby.

'Celia, you need to learn that it does not do to rely too much on other people. You must be more self-sufficient when you are a grown-up. Besides, I don't think it is fair to ask Sita to come with us. She has family here, Celia. She won't want to leave them and you can't expect her to.'

Celia couldn't argue with that. It was exactly what Sita had said when Celia had broached the subject with her once before. Sita adored her brother's children; Celia knew that. And although it was wrong, Celia couldn't help but be jealous that Sita put them above her, that Sita would prefer to stay in India rather than remain with Celia. On one occasion that Celia remembered, Sita had left their house to go and stay with her brother's family, to help look after a sick niece. Celia had thrown a tantrum on Sita's return, screaming at her that she loved her niece more than she loved Celia, and that was wrong. Her *ayah* should love her most and best of all.

Now, looking back on that time, Celia was embarrassed by her outburst. She'd been young then and rather self-centred. If it happened again, she'd be more understanding. She knew she couldn't expect Sita to leave behind all her family to come to England. Not permanently, anyway. Perhaps she could persuade her to come in the short term, for a few years, returning to England when Celia was of age? It might be worth a try.

The rest of dinnertime passed quietly. Celia was lost in her own thoughts and no matter what Papa said to her she could not summon up any lively conversation. He gave up after a while, but she noticed the smile never left his face, the sparkle in his eye remained. He was genuinely excited to be leaving India. She supposed that since Mama had died, he must have been lonely, and perhaps in England he'd find a new wife. If he did, that would be a good thing, as he would become less dependent on her for company – which might help free her to return to India in time. She made a mental note to encourage him to meet women and try to find himself someone new to love.

* * *

Celia telephoned Vijay the very next day, and asked him to come to see her. She wanted to talk things through with him, to try to find out where he was likely to be at school and work out how that related to where she'd be living. Not that she knew where she would be living yet, but she assumed it would be London or somewhere near to London. Her grasp of the geography of England was poor. Hopefully, Vijay knew more and they'd be able to work out whether they'd be near each other, or able to easily visit each other. Celia had dim memories of travelling by train during her visits to England. If the trains ran everywhere like they did in India, then surely visiting each other would be easy even if they lived at opposite ends of the country. One thing she was certain of was that England was a small place, nothing like the vast expanse of land that was India.

Vijay arrived in the late morning, after Papa had gone out for the day. Celia greeted him with a kiss on his cheek. Vijay blushed and rubbed at the spot.

'You're embarrassed. It was only a friendly greeting!' she teased him, linking her arm through his. His body felt warm against hers.

'I know, I know. Nice to see you, Cee. What did you want to talk to me about?'

'Let's go out on the veranda,' she said. She wanted to speak to him with no fear of being overheard by Sanjit or Sita or any of the other servants. It was too hot to be in the open parts of the garden, but the veranda was shady.

'All right.' Vijay followed her out. He was wondering, she guessed, why she was being so serious. Usually, they'd run outside and joke and laugh and play, but not today.

They sat down and Celia poured them each a glass of lemonade, from a jug she'd put there in readiness. She took a sip and waited for Vijay to drink some too, before she began to talk.

'Vijay, it's this independence thing. You heard that it's to happen in August this year? I can't believe it is going to happen so soon!'

He smiled at her and nodded. 'Yes, it is very soon. I am happy for India. It will be good not to be under the control of another country.'

'It will, yes. And for us – you and me, Vijay – it is working out very well. Papa says that he and I will go to England as soon as independence happens. In August. We're to be on the first flight out, he said.'

'For how long?' Vijay's expression was one of worry.

'For*ever*, he says. But I'm not thinking about the long term right now. I'm just considering the next few years.' She smiled as she said this, waiting for the penny to drop with him that she'd be in England by the time he was sent there to school, and that they'd still be able to see each other.

But Vijay continued to frown. Something was wrong. 'I suppose . . . your father will need a new job. Is that why you're going immediately?'

'Yes . . . and he can't wait to go. And I . . . well, I don't mind too much for the first few years . . .' She looked at him expectantly.

'I'll miss you, Cee,' he said, sadly.

'But . . . you'll be there too! You're going in September, to school then university! Oxford, you said. As soon as we both know exactly where we'll be living, we'll be able to still meet up! There are trains . . .'

Vijay stared at her and shook his head. He was biting the corner of his mouth, and Celia knew that meant he had bad news and was working out how best to tell her. 'What is it, Vijay?'

'Cee, my father's changed his plans. Now he knows independence is coming so soon, he wants me to stay here for school and then go to a university here in India. He says we should cut all ties with England and support our own country. He thinks—'

'What? But he was all for you getting a British education!' She couldn't believe it. Just as she'd begun to think that going to England would be all right because Vijay would be there, now everything was changing again.

'I know, Cee, I know. But you know my father. He can be

impulsive at times. And I have to do what he says, whether I like it or not. For all we know he'll change his mind again before September.'

'Do you think that's likely?' She turned to him, hoping to see optimism in his expression.

But Vijay pulled a face. 'Not really, no. I think I'm here to stay.'

'And I'll be over there.' Celia felt tears prickling at the corners of her eyes. 'Papa can't wait to go. I don't understand it. He's like me – he was born here and he's lived here all his life, other than school days and a few years at university in England. But he sees himself as English and says he's had enough of it here.' She sniffed. 'I think India reminds him too much of Mama. He's never got over losing her, you know. It . . . changed him. He used to be happy, easy-going and fun. At least that's how I remember him back then. And then she died and he became stricter and grumpier.'

Vijay nodded. 'It's to be expected.'

'Yes, but it's been seven years now.'

'Perhaps he'll change when he's in England. No wonder he wants to go so badly. And you?'

'Me – I feel as Indian as you are. I don't want to go, not now I know you're not going to be there!'

'You'll have to go with him.'

'I know! But I don't want to.' Celia dashed away the tears that were running down her cheek. 'I really don't want to, Vijay! What can I do?'

Vijay put a hand on her shoulder and patted it awkwardly. 'Cee, I don't know what you can do. I'll miss you . . .'

'Your father . . .' She'd had a vague idea.

'What about him?'

'If you spoke to him, would he perhaps . . . I don't know . . . let me come and live at the palace? I could . . . work somehow. Teach English to the children of his servants. I could learn to type and do secretarial work for him. In return for board and lodging? Just till I'm of age . . .'

'Come and live with me?'

'Yes. And bring Sita too, of course.'

Vijay stared at her, open-mouthed.

'Well? What do you think? Would he agree?'

'I don't know . . . Your father wouldn't allow it though.'

'Maybe . . . I wouldn't even tell him. Perhaps on the day we're due to leave, I could slip away, hide with you . . . and he'd have to go on his own.'

Vijay gave a chuckle and shook his head. 'That wouldn't work. He wouldn't leave without you; he'd search high and low for you.'

'Would he? Or would he be happy to be rid of me?' Celia struggled to keep a bitter tone out of her voice.

'Don't be silly. He loves you. He wouldn't go without you.'

'Then maybe we'd get your father's agreement and I could move sooner, and refuse to leave with Papa. He couldn't drag me out of the palace, not if your father had agreed to let me stay.'

'I still don't think—' Vijay began.

'But you'll ask him? Please? Because I really, really don't want to go and live in England and leave you and Sita. I don't know the place. I've only been a few times. It's grey and cold and wet and horrible.' She lifted her head and looked at him, letting him see the tears running down her cheeks, showing him how much she wanted this.

Vijay's expression softened. 'Of course I will. I will do all that I can to help you. But I am not sure whether it will do any good.'

'We've got to try, Vijay.'

'Yes. And we will.' He smiled at her and reached out a hand. She took it and held it against her cheek for a moment, liking the feel of his soft palm against her skin, until he pulled it away, looking embarrassed.

'Shall we play tennis or is it too hot?' she said, to lighten the mood.

'We'll play. Maybe only for quarter of an hour. And then we could swim in the river.'

'Yes!' Celia leapt up and ran inside to change into her tennis things. She felt better about the future now. Even if her plan didn't work, she'd have tried. She owed it to herself, her Indian self, to do all that she could to stay here, near to Vijay. She knew she'd never forgive herself if she didn't at least try. And now it was up to Vijay and his father. Who knew, maybe the maharajah would jump at the chance to have her stay in the palace, teaching or typing or whatever was necessary. If it came to it, she'd even clean rooms for him. Anything rather than go to a stuffy school in England, be presented to the king and made to marry a boring, sallow English youth.

Chapter 15

Lisa, 2023

A few days after Lisa's visit to Surrey, Ben called her. 'No real news, I'm afraid. I got as far as finding the boxes of old family papers in the loft but haven't had a chance to go through them yet.'

'No worries,' she replied, feeling disappointed that he hadn't had time. She knew he had a busy life, between his two jobs, helping his father and writing novels.

'And I need some time for fun things – speaking of which, there's a new exhibition on at the Tate Modern. Wondered if you fancied going there? Maybe Saturday? We could grab some lunch, perhaps somewhere on the South Bank . . .'

'Sounds lovely. Yes, I'd love to go. Thanks for inviting me.'

'There's no one I'd rather go with. The exhibition is on the theme of mountains, and their influence on human activity and human nature. Made me think of you in the Alps, finding that briefcase.'

'Now I really want to go!'

'It's a date, then.'

A *date*? Or just a date. She wasn't sure. But it was something to look forward to, and Lisa was pleased he'd asked her.

Despite telling herself all week that it did not matter in the slightest what clothes she chose to wear on Saturday, Lisa still spent half an hour choosing her outfit before ending up in a colourful cotton dress with a pair of red Converse. It was a summery but not too dressy look. She grabbed a light cardigan, just in case the weather, which promised to be glorious, turned chilly. It was the kind of day when you wanted to be sitting in a park, not going round an art gallery, but it didn't matter. Perhaps they'd find somewhere outside to sit for lunch afterwards. And the company would be good.

Lisa met Ben as planned, outside the main entrance to the Tate Modern. She arrived first, having caught the tube to Waterloo station then walked along the South Bank enjoying the late summer sunshine. She loved this gallery. It was such an inspired use of an old power station: its Art Deco brickwork soaring into the sky above her. She lived within sight of another of London's old, iconic power stations – Battersea – that was now a shopping and entertainment complex.

Ben arrived a few minutes after her, casually dressed in a faded blue T-shirt and shorts. He was carrying a rucksack that looked as though it contained a bit more than a jumper in case of chilly weather.

'Hi! What've you got in there?' she asked, as he approached and kissed her on the cheek.

'I had a brainwave, given how good the weather is. After we've been round the exhibition, I thought we could have a picnic, sitting on a bench out here. So—' he tapped the shoulder strap of his rucksack '—that's what's in here. Grub. All shop-bought; I'm not very good at cooking. Hope you're hungry.'

'Wow. That sounds perfect. Brilliant thinking!' What had

promised to be a good day now looked as though it'd be even better.

'Ah, I'm not just a pretty face,' Ben said, grinning. 'I'll leave this rucksack in a locker and we'll pick it up later. Ready to go in?'

'Sure!' As they crossed over to the entrance, Lisa had an almost overwhelming urge to hold Ben's hand. But no, she couldn't do such a thing. Not until she knew what his feelings for her were.

'You all right?' Ben asked. He must have noticed her slightly strained expression.

'Yes, just . . . a stone in my shoe,' she lied, stopping at a bench to dig a finger down the side of her Converse and hook out an imaginary piece of grit.

They wandered around the exhibition together, commenting on pieces, discussing how each piece made them feel.

'I adore mountains,' Ben said, as they looked at a photo montage of tiny black and white portraits of mountaineers that when you stood back, became an image of Mount Everest. 'Something about gazing at distant horizons makes my soul sing. You can do that from the tops of mountains. You can't do it in a city where you're too hemmed in on all sides by tall buildings.'

She stared at him. 'That's exactly how I feel.' There it was again. More evidence that they just might be perfect for each other.

'I'm envious of your hiking trip in the Alps. I've always wanted to do that. There's a hiking route that goes all the way around Mont Blanc I'd love to try.'

'You should definitely do it!'

'I've never found anyone to go with.'

'You could come with me and Gaby. We'll probably go to Chamonix again next spring.'

He turned to her and smiled in response, his wide, sunny smile that she was beginning to love. 'I might well take you up on that offer, if your friend's OK with me tagging along.'

'I'm sure she would be.'

Ben looked at his watch. 'Well, if you're ready, we could go for our picnic now. We could pretend we're half-way up a mountain and not sitting on the banks of the Thames in central London.'

Lisa laughed. 'That's going to take quite a bit of imagination! Yes, let's eat. I'm starving, actually. What've you brought?'

'Ah, wait and see.' He grinned and waggled his eyebrows at her. She followed him out of the art gallery and through the streets to a small park. There he put his rucksack down on a patch of grass, opened it and began pulling out containers of food.

It turned out to be quite a spread. He'd bought three types of sandwiches – cheese, pâté and chicken salad. There were tubs of olives and sweet peppers, and a packet of crumbly feta cheese to spread onto crackers. A packet of vegetable crisps, and little pots of shop-bought tiramisu for dessert completed the feast. And to go with it all, two small bottles of cava, along with a couple of plastic champagne flutes.

As Ben spread it out on a chequered tablecloth on the grass, Lisa sat down happily on the ground, tucking her feet underneath her. 'Wow. You went to a lot of trouble.' It was so far removed from the type of 'eating out' she'd done with Rupert. And very much more to her liking.

'It's all shop-bought, as I said, so it was no trouble. I love picnics.'

'So do I!'

'Well, cheers to that!' He passed her a glass of cava and clinked his own against hers.

The picnic tasted as good as it looked. By the time they'd finished, and Ben was packing the empty containers back into his rucksack and sharing out the last of the cava, Lisa felt full, relaxed and contented. She lay back on the grass and gazed up at the fragments of blue sky showing between branches of trees. 'That was glorious. Thank you so much. I could happily do this every weekend. At least while the weather's so good.'

'It's been fun, hasn't it?'

As they left the South Bank and parted at the entrance to a tube station, Lisa wondered whether he'd make a move to kiss her, or ask her out again. But he said nothing, just gave her a chaste hug and promised to get started on going through his family's archives.

Lisa went home feeling a little confused. She'd had a wonderful day and she really liked Ben. What did he feel about her? But anyway, wasn't it too soon after Rupert to even think of dating anyone else? Maybe that was why Ben was holding back, thinking she wasn't ready? She needed to talk it all through with someone. With Gaby.

'So you see, I just don't know what to do now.' Lisa picked up her glass and looked across the table at Gaby. They had met up for drinks after work a few days after Lisa's 'date' with Ben. Luckily Gaby was in London for a couple of days for a conference, which gave Lisa the perfect opportunity to ask her for advice. She'd already updated her on everything that had happened – handing over the diamond, meeting his father, the visit to the art gallery.

'You like him, yes?'

'I do, but he's keeping me at arm's length. And he hasn't been in touch since Saturday.'

'Is there another woman? Or even another man?'

'No. He said he's never had a serious girlfriend, just dates.'

'A confidence issue?'

Lisa nodded. 'I think so, though he doesn't come across as lacking in confidence. It's more like he's holding back. I wondered if it's because he knows it's not long since . . . since Rupert.' She took a sip of her drink. 'And it isn't all that long, is it? Should I even be thinking of dating another man?'

Gaby gave her a stern look. 'If you like him, don't let him get away. A new relationship with a decent bloke might be exactly what you need to complete the healing process. Seriously, mate, I know the whole diamond mystery has helped you heal, but it sounds to me like Ben might help finish the job. If he's as nice as you say he is, he'll help you realise that not all men are like Rupert.'

'He's very definitely nothing like Rupert. But he hasn't been in touch since Saturday, so . . .'

'So, *you* ask *him* out!' Gaby grinned triumphantly. 'This is 2023. It's OK for women to ask men on dates; OK for women to make the first move. So, go for it! And if perchance it doesn't work out, there's a friend of a friend I think might be suitable for you . . . I could set you up on a blind date. His name's Ryan. I met him once. He's lovely, very nice-looking. He's based in Wandsworth, I think.'

'That's not far from me,' Lisa pondered. Maybe Gaby was right, and dating would be good for her. 'All right. I'll give Ben a call.'

'And you'll let me know what happens?'

'Of course I will! I'd take you along in my back pocket if I could, Gabs.'

'Hmm, that might be a bit *too* close, if things work out with him,' Gaby quipped in reply, waggling her eyebrows, and sending Lisa into spasms of laughter.

'Well, on that note, do you fancy another glass of wine? My round.' Lisa went to the bar, still chuckling at what Gaby had said.

Lisa lost no time after her night out with Gaby. She messaged Ben late that same evening, suggesting they meet up the following weekend. There was an open-air concert on in Battersea Park that they could go to in the afternoon, and then perhaps they might eat out somewhere afterwards. To her delight he responded almost immediately with an enthusiastic yes. She hadn't been sure he'd want to go to the concert – it was a line-up of Irish musicians playing a mix of traditional music and Irish rock – but he said he loved that kind of music. *Huge fan of The Pogues, The Dubliners, and everything in between*, he messaged. *Mum played it all the time, so this will be right up my street.*

Of course, she remembered, he'd told her his mother was Irish.

And so she'd bought the tickets, arranged a meeting place with him, and then treated herself to a new cotton summer dress and sandals that would be perfect for an afternoon in the park. 'Bought for me, not him,' she told herself, but she couldn't deny she wanted to look her best. Give herself the best chance. Though she already knew that if Ben was interested it would be because he liked her personality, not because of her looks or clothes. That was the kind of guy he was.

She met him at one of the park entrances as they'd agreed. It was a sunny day with only a few wisps of cloud around, but thankfully it was not too hot. She'd brought a denim jacket to slip over her dress if it was too cool, and she had a small rucksack containing bottles of water thrown over her shoulder. Ben was already there, speaking to a homeless man who was sitting on a tatty sleeping bag beside the park gate. As she approached, she saw the man laugh at something Ben said. Then Ben reached into his pocket and pulled out a note – it looked like a tenner – and passed it to the man who took it gratefully but with surprise. How very different to the way Rupert had treated homeless people!

Ben turned then and saw her, hurrying over. He pulled her into a brief hug, kissing her cheek, as she greeted him.

'Hi, Lisa. Good to see you again. I've been looking forward to this ever since you suggested it!'

'Hi, Ben. Yes, me too.' What to read into the hug and cheek-kiss, she wondered. Was it how he'd greet any friend? The kiss and hug had been brief, no lingering of lips on her skin, but they were warm and clearly heartfelt. 'Kind of you to give that man something. So, look, the stage is over there, but we've a bit of time before it all kicks off. Want to get a cold drink from the café?'

'I'd love to.'

'Great, follow me.' She led the way to the café, where they ordered a couple of bottles of sparkling water.

'It's good to be well hydrated before this starts,' Ben said.

'Yes. Though I've brought bottles of water in my bag anyway.'

He smiled. 'That's what I love about you. I was too disorganised to think of bringing anything.'

'Ah well, you were the organised one bringing the picnic last time,' she said, picking up on the words *love about you*. Here was her chance. 'We can take it in turns, if we're likely to see a lot of each other, as time goes on?' She made it a question and watched him carefully to see how he responded.

He blinked at her. 'Um, yes . . . I think I'd . . . well, that is . . . yes, of course we'll see each other. That research . . .'

It wasn't quite the response Lisa had been hoping for. But there were hours ahead and who knew what might happen. She changed the subject, talking about the bands they were about to see and the type of music they played. Soon she felt they were back on an even keel, chatting and laughing as they had on previous occasions. They finished their drinks then found a spot not far from the stage. It was a wonderful afternoon, with bands playing plenty of lively Irish music that had them singing along – 'The Wild Rover', 'The Black Velvet Band', 'Irish Rover'. Another group switched to gentler, more lyrical tunes – 'On Raglan Road', 'Grace', 'The Fields of Athenry'.

As 'The Fields of Athenry' finished, Ben turned to Lisa. 'That's given me an idea. Next weekend—'

'Yep. I'm up for it,' Lisa interrupted, and Ben laughed.

'You haven't heard what I was about to suggest. Lisa, do you like . . . rugby?'

'Rugby?' She widened her eyes. 'Well, yes, kind of. Better than football, I think. My dad's a big fan and has taken me to a couple of international matches. Are you a fan?'

'Absolutely. I support Munster. My mum was from Limerick, so Dad and I became Munster fans because she was obsessed by it. So, this is going to sound mad, but . . .'

'Go on.' She was intrigued now.

'So, Dad bought two tickets for him and me to go to a Munster game next Friday. But now he can't go. There's an important vote in Parliament, and it's a three-line whip, so he absolutely has to be there. He's said I can have both tickets and take someone else.'

'And you're asking me?'

'I am.'

'What time's the match? Do I need to get Friday afternoon off?'

'Er, yes. You'd need the day off, if you can manage it? The match is in Dublin. Munster are playing Leinster.'

'Dublin!' She'd assumed the match would be somewhere close to London, a train journey away. But Dublin meant taking a plane, staying a night in a hotel, perhaps spending a full weekend in Ben's company . . .

'Yes. Don't worry, Dad had already booked flights and I can transfer one ticket into your name for a small fee. There's a hotel already booked too for one night. We had a twin room reserved but I can easily book a second room. What do you say?'

'Well . . .' Lisa was still processing the idea. Rugby wasn't really her cup of tea. But the idea of going away for a short break . . . yes, it'd be amazing. And surely this meant he was definitely interested in her? 'Ben, I'd love to go. A twin room is fine. But let me pay you for the tickets and flights and everything.'

He held up a hand. 'Not at all. They're all paid for courtesy of my father. He'd feel aggrieved if you tried to pay him. He'll be delighted they're not going to waste.'

'Well . . . all right, then! Yes, let's do it!'

'Yee-haw!' Ben whooped, and they high-fived. 'Wow. I'm so glad you agreed! The flight's from Stansted at midday, so it should be a fairly relaxed start to the day. And the match is at seven in the evening. We'll have plenty of time to settle into the hotel and then get public transport out to the ground. We can get an early dinner somewhere in the city.'

Lisa laughed. 'You've got it all planned out!'

'Yes. Tell the truth, I've been working out the details, praying you'd say yes, ever since Dad told me he couldn't come.'

The band started playing a noisy rendition of 'Seven Drunken

Nights' so they had to stop talking but Lisa couldn't stop herself grinning. She had another fabulous weekend ahead to look forward to.

The concert went on all afternoon and into the evening, finishing just after sunset. Lisa and Ben bought hot dogs from a stall and a couple of pints of lager to keep them going.

'I'll walk you home if you like,' Ben said, as the last round of applause died away and people began gathering their belongings.

'I don't live far away, but yes, you certainly can. Shall we go via the river bank?' It was either that or along busy roads.

'Definitely.' He took her hand as they left the park, using an exit that led them onto the promenade that ran along the south side of the Thames. It was a beautiful evening, still warm, and reflections of the lights of buildings on the opposite bank twinkled in the river water below. As they got further from the park the crowds thinned out. Lisa found she didn't want the evening to end, so when she spotted a bench overlooking the river she gestured towards it and he nodded.

They sat for a moment, enjoying the peace of the evening, watching ripples from occasional rivercraft lap against the embankment. 'It's lovely here,' Ben said.

'It is. London at its best.' Lisa shifted position, moving a little closer to him, and Ben laid his arm along the back of the bench, his fingers on her shoulder. In response she rested her head lightly against him, and they stayed like that for a few minutes, not talking, just sitting. Just *being*, she thought, and she imagined a future where they shared many moments like this.

And then he turned, facing her, and there was a question in his eyes. She gave a small smile that she hoped would give him confidence that yes, this was what she wanted. He leaned in, and her eyes dropped to his lips, and then they were kissing and for a moment it was wonderful, it was everything she'd hoped for, and it promised so much for their future.

Ben broke away first, before Lisa was ready to. He moved away from her and stared down at the ground in front of him. 'I'm sorry, I . . .'

'It's all right, Ben, I wanted to,' she said, gently. But he was shaking his head, running fingers through his hair as though frustrated.

He sighed, then muttered something under his breath. All Lisa caught sounded like, *get over yourself, man*, and then he turned back to her, took her in his arms and kissed her again.

It was the perfect end to a perfect day, Lisa thought later, when he'd seen her back to her flat but declined to come in, needing to be sure to catch the last train home. Still, she had next weekend in Dublin to look forward to, and a night away in a hotel with him. It'd be the true start to their relationship, and she couldn't wait.

Chapter 16

Sita, June 1947

Sita watched through the window of her room as Celia and Vijay walked across the garden towards the tennis court. They were close, their shoulders bumping occasionally as they went, and every now and again Celia would look up at Vijay smiling. He was making her laugh. The two had always been close. When they were children, there'd been many times when Sita had been charged with looking after both of them, keeping an eye on them as they played in the garden here or at the maharajah's palace. She was fond of Vijay. He was a good boy, and there'd been times when she'd wondered whether he and Celia might perhaps eventually marry. It was unusual but not unheard of for Englishwomen to marry Indian men. It was more usual the other way around: white men quite frequently married Indian women. But Celia was not like other English girls. She had often said she felt herself to be more Indian than English. Sita always smiled and indulged her when she said this, but privately thought that whatever she said, Celia was English through and through, whether she liked it or not.

But marriage to Vijay, or any other Indian man, would never happen now for Celia. Not now that she'd be leaving for England so soon.

Sita turned away from the window and picked up her sewing. She always did a little in the mornings, sitting outside her room. It was her time for thinking, for mulling over what was happening in her life, in Agra, in India.

She knew, of course, of the revised date for Indian independence. It had surprised her that it was going to be so soon. It was almost as though the British now couldn't wait to be finished with India, couldn't wait to return to their green and grey country. It worried her that it was being brought forward. The chances of unrest, especially in the Punjab, were high. She knew the politicians were still hoping there'd be a way of reaching independence without partitioning India, despite Mountbatten's announcement that a separate Muslim state – Pakistan – was to be formed, but it seemed unlikely. All those people, the Muslims in the east who'd be forced to move west, the Hindus in the west who'd have to move east. It didn't bear thinking about. She was glad that she and her family, her aged parents, her brother and his wife, their son and their dear little daughters, would not be displaced.

What life would be like for her personally after independence she had no idea. She had worked almost all her adult life for the Fforbes-Whytes. Mr Fforbes-Whyte would of course go back to England and he'd take Celia with him. She would miss Celia, so much. So very much. The girl was like a daughter to her. Sita had been employed by Mrs Fforbes-Whyte when Celia was just a week old, to take care of her and let her mother rest after a long and difficult labour. And since then, there had been a total of just sixty-seven days when Celia had gone on visits to England that Sita had not been with her. Sixty-seven days out of the fifteen, almost sixteen, years of Celia's life.

There was no possibility of Sita going to England with them. The *sahib* hadn't asked her, and even if he did, she would have to say no. She was needed here, in Agra. Her brother Bhavik and his wife had looked after her parents for much of the last fifteen years but now it was her turn. Her parents were becoming more and more frail and needed round-the-clock care. Her sister-in-law had been providing this, but she also needed to care for her children. The eldest one, their son, was nearly grown, soon to be married but there were three girls at school and another girl who was still only a baby. When independence came, Sita would move in with her brother and parents, and become her parents' carer, and her sister-in-law would then be free to spend time with her children as was only right.

Thankfully, Bhavik earned enough money to keep them all, and he'd already insisted that she should come to live with them when Celia no longer needed her. Sita had always imagined that would happen when Celia was a grown woman, getting married, setting up a home of her own. And she'd dared to dream that Celia would want her to stay with her, caring for Celia's own children in time. Of course she'd dreamed of all this taking place in India, in Agra, under British rule. She'd imagined nothing changing in her life, and yet here they all were, with everything about to be thrown up in the air and who knew where it would all land?

She sighed as she stitched the hem of a new pink blouse to wear with her favourite sari. Everything was changing. She'd enjoyed looking after Celia, watching the pretty baby turn into a delightful sunny-natured child, even if she was a little too strong-willed. And now Celia had grown into a beautiful young woman. Sita was proud of the girl, as proud as she would have been of a child of her own. She was only sad she would now never see her wed, never meet the children she'd bear in time.

There was a tap on her door, and Sanjit entered, holding out an envelope. 'Sita, there is a message for you. It was delivered by a boy.'

'Thank you.' She took it and frowned. It was unusual to get written messages. She supposed it must be from her brother or sister-in-law and her stomach gave a lurch. It would be bad news if either of them were writing to her. Was her mother sick? Her father? Or one of the children?

Sanjit was still hovering nearby, looking as though he wanted to know what was in the note. She raised her eyes to his and glared, and he lifted a hand in apology and moved away. Sita tore open the envelope and scanned the note inside. It was written in English.

> *Mr Willfred Forbes-White requests you come to the market to pick up a parsel he has bought. The mango-seller on the corner on Poiya Ghat Road has the parsel and is giving it to you.*

She frowned again. This was not good English. It looked like English written by an Indian, and she supposed it must be. The *sahib* must have told a servant what to write. Why did he not write it himself? Why did he want her to collect a parcel? It was the sort of job Sanjit would normally do. But he'd asked her, so she had better do it.

She glanced across the lawns towards the tennis court. Celia and Vijay were still playing, despite the heat. She'd heard them talk about going for a swim in the river later. Celia would not be needing her, so she could run this errand now, and be back before Vijay left.

Sita put away her sewing, checked her appearance in the mirror and draped the end of her *pallu* over her head to keep the sun off. She fetched her basket to carry the parcel back in, and left the house, following the familiar streets through the city to the market area, and then to Poiya Ghat Road.

The mango seller's stall was in its usual place on a corner part way along. It wasn't a stall Sita often frequented as she preferred the mangoes from a stall in the bazaar, and she wasn't sure why the master's parcel would be left there, of all places, for her to collect. It was a street corner where there were often beggars squatting, their hands outstretched, their eyes pleading, and she so rarely had much she could give them. But the note was clear and she had no reason to question it, so she approached the stall and spoke to the seller.

'I am to collect a parcel for Mr Fforbes-Whyte.'

The mango seller nodded and pointed behind him, to an open door that led into a derelict shop. 'In there.'

Sita began to say something more but the seller had turned away to serve a customer, so she shrugged and went into the shop, blinking as her eyes adjusted to the dim light inside.

Behind her the door suddenly slammed shut and she turned, gasping. A man stood there, and as she dithered, wondering whether to push past him back out into the street, another man emerged from a back room. The two of them stepped towards her and took an arm each. 'What are you doing? Let go of me!' Sita was frightened now. What could they possibly want?

'Come, we will not hurt you,' one of the men said in Hindi, his voice gruff. He was holding her tightly and she could smell the stale, foul stench of unwashed clothes.

'What do you want?' she said, this time in Hindi, her voice sounding shrill and scared.

'To talk, is all. In here.' The men pushed her into a back room and made her sit down on a rickety old wooden chair. The room had no windows but was lit by a single bare light bulb dangling from the sagging ceiling. Opposite her on a similar chair placed behind a ramshackle table was a third man, aged around forty, bearded with wisps of grey at his temples. He was wearing a clean *kurti* and was well groomed. He looked vaguely familiar but Sita couldn't think where she'd seen him before. The two men who'd dragged her into the room stood either side of her. The implication was clear – she would not be allowed to leave until the bearded man had said whatever he needed to say. She pulled herself upright and stared at him defiantly.

'Sita Thakur?' This man spoke in English.

'Yes.'

'You work for Mr Wilfred Fforbes-Whyte?'

'You know I do.'

'You have a brother Bhavik Thakur?'

'What of him?' Her stomach lurched. Was something wrong with Bhavik or his family after all?

'And he has those lovely little girls and the baby.' The bearded man smiled and leaned forward onto his elbows. Sita was reminded of a cobra about to strike. She did not answer him, but pressed her lips together.

'I saw them, playing in your brother's yard. And your parents, the doting grandparents, watching over them. A delightful family.'

Again, there was no response Sita wished to give him. His tone was scaring her, even though his words were innocent enough, on the surface.

'You are wondering why you are here?'

'To pick up a parcel. Or so it said on the note I received.'

He smiled again. 'Ah. There is no parcel, I am sorry. It was all I could think of writing to ensure you came immediately, as I cannot spend all day here.'

Then get to the point, she thought, but said nothing. She kept her eyes on his, waiting for him to say something more.

He leaned back and steepled his fingers under his chin, regarding her. 'Now then, Sita Thakur, I have a commission for you. One you will want to accept and carry out fully without question. So that nothing ... *untoward* shall we say ... happens to your little nieces. Or to your frail, vulnerable parents. I'm wondering, you see, just how safe the children are when their parents go out and the old, weak people are left to guard them.'

And there it was, the threat, if she didn't do whatever it was he wanted. Sita swallowed, picturing her little nieces playing together while her parents sat in the yard watching them, picturing – what? Men with guns and knives storming the house, snatching the children, cutting down her parents as they feebly tried to defend their grandchildren . . . She felt sweat run down her neck and her heart was racing.

'Who would want to hurt them?' she asked, her voice emerging as not much more than a whisper.

'Oh, no one at all, I'm sure.' The man waved a hand dismissively. 'But to keep them all safe and well, this is what I need you to do.' He outlined a plan that made her gasp, horrifying her beyond belief.

Sita stared at the man. What he was asking her to do was unconscionable. But if she didn't, he'd do something bad . . . he'd hurt her nieces, or her parents, or both. He, and the two thugs who stood either side of her, and the dozen more men he'd assured her he could call upon if necessary.

'But I—I . . .' she began, not knowing what she wanted to say. Why oh why had she followed the instructions on the note? She should have stayed home and none of this would have happened. She could have given the note to Sanjit, or checked it with the *sahib*.

At least, none of it would have happened today. But this man, these men, were organised and determined, and she had no doubt that they would have found some other way to get to her, to tell her their instructions.

She had no choice; she realised that. She had to go along with what they wanted her to do, or they would bring harm on her family.

She nodded, slowly. 'But sir, you must promise me . . .'

He twisted his mouth into a cruel, amused smile. 'What must *I* promise *you*? You are not in a position to make demands.'

'You must promise me, that if I do what you want, she will come to no harm. She is like my own child. I love her very much. You cannot hurt her!'

'That is out of my hands, Sita Thakur. I can assure you that I personally will not hurt her, and if all goes to plan and everyone does what they are told, she will not be harmed by anyone. That is as much as I can say. The rest is up to your employer. But you must not tell him, or anyone else at all, of our meeting. Otherwise, it will go badly for your small nieces. That I *can* promise you.'

Sita stared at him and nodded. She understood.

The man nodded back at her and stood up. The two thugs pulled Sita to her feet and pushed her out of the room. She hurried through the empty shop, not daring to look behind her in case they were coming after her again, and went out onto the street. The mango seller glanced at her as she passed him but said nothing.

As soon as she had rounded a corner onto a different street, out of sight of the stall and the shop, she stopped and leaned against a wall, clutching her chest and gasping for breath. What on earth had she agreed to? How could she do what the bearded man asked? How could she *bring herself* to do it? And yet . . . she *had* to. For the good of her family. There was no real choice. She loved Celia, but she loved her brother, his children, and her parents even more. They were her blood. And she'd been assured that Celia would be safe, if everyone did what they were told to do. Celia would be safe.

'Celia will be safe, Celia will be safe,' Sita muttered over and over as she walked home. If she said it often enough it would be true. It was all she could cling to, the only thing that could calm her racing heart and her ragged breathing as she made her way through the streets back to the British part of town.

Chapter 17

Lisa, 2023

On the Friday following that wonderful day at the concert, Lisa and Ben met at the airport before their flight to Dublin. It was a grey, blustery day, completely unlike the previous weekend. Summer was taking a break, it seemed. Lisa had put on jeans and a warm fleece, and she'd packed a puffer jacket, just in case. Dublin might well be colder than London, and sitting in a sports stadium for hours in the evening might be very chilly.

Ben was also in jeans and wearing a puffer jacket. 'Not quite the weather we had last week, is it?' he said, as he hugged her and kissed her cheek in greeting.

'No, but then rugby's a winter game so I suppose this is suitable weather for it. I'm looking forward to the match!' Even more, she was looking forward to the twenty-four hours in his company and the chance to progress their new relationship to the next level. She smiled at him, feeling suddenly shy. He smiled back, but there was something in his expression she couldn't quite read. Never mind. They had all weekend to get to know each other better.

'I'm looking forward to it too. Here – I brought you a scarf.

Dad and I have quite a collection of them.' He handed her a red and navy scarf, with the Munster emblem of three crowns and a stag on each end and the word Munster running along it.

'Ah, thanks! That looks cosy.' She wrapped it around her neck, although inside the airport it was a little too warm for it.

Their flight was on time. It was a basic, no-frills airline, but for the short one-hour flight to Dublin it was perfectly adequate. They settled into their seats, talking non-stop as the plane prepared for departure.

A few rows back from them was a man who'd clearly been drinking heavily. Lisa had noticed him stumble as he tried to stow his cabin baggage and take his seat. 'Bit early for that,' she'd muttered to Ben, who'd nodded agreement.

'Must admit, I have never liked flying,' Lisa confided in Ben after take-off, as the plane went through turbulent clouds to gain altitude. The 'fasten seatbelt' sign stayed switched on as they were jolted around for a few minutes.

'I don't much like it either,' Ben said. 'But it's kind of a necessary evil in today's world.'

As the plane gave a sudden lurch, buffeted sideways by the turbulence, Lisa instinctively grabbed hold of Ben's hand on the armrest between them. He squeezed it in response.

'It'll be all right. Don't worry.' He smiled at her, and she found it reassuring. Somehow with him by her side it felt as though nothing bad could happen to her. He rubbed his thumb over the back of her hand, and she loved the warmth and reassurance of the gesture.

The plane levelled out above the cloud at last, and the flight became smoother. But Ben kept hold of her hand. She'd have had to pull hers away, and she decided she rather liked him holding it. At least for a few minutes, until she needed both hands for something.

They were seated at the front of the plane, the first row behind the exit. Behind them, Lisa could hear the drunken man asking for a whisky; an air steward answering him in quiet, firm tones.

'We'll be first off,' Ben said, nodding towards the door.

'Great! I hate that part when you have to stand in the aisle with your bags as people fumble around in front of you, taking ages to get off.'

'Ooh, little miss impatient!'

Lisa laughed. 'I just hate flying. I can never wait to get off the plane once it's landed. This is the perfect seat for me. We'll land, they'll open the doors and I'll be off at a sprint.'

'I like the leg room you get in these seats,' Ben said, stretching his legs luxuriously in front of him. Lisa couldn't help but admire his long, slim legs, with clearly defined thigh muscles showing through his jeans. She turned away to gaze out of the window beside her, not daring to be caught staring at his legs. The thought of the twenty-four hours ahead of them, the time they'd spend together in the hotel room brought a flush to her face. She wanted to turn to him now and kiss him, and not care what other people thought of them, but it wasn't appropriate behaviour. She'd have to restrain herself.

He looked across at her as though he'd read her mind. 'I do really like you, you know,' he said quietly. 'I know it's early days, but I wanted you to know.'

'I feel the same,' she whispered. 'It's like we have some kind of connection. Funny to think how we were brought together by that diamond.'

His smile dropped and he stared at her, then turned to look out of the window beside him. She realised the mistake she'd made. She should never have mentioned the diamond. He'd said he didn't believe in its curse, but even so she knew something about it unnerved him. And here and now, at twenty-nine thousand feet up, was not the time or place to be reminding him of it.

She changed the subject. 'It's amazing up here, above the clouds. Look at that blue sky! The weather's so much better up here. And the clouds look so lovely from this side. It's as though you could hurl yourself out of the plane and just bounce around on them.'

'I don't recommend trying it,' Ben replied with a chuckle. 'We're somewhere over Wales, or perhaps the Irish Sea by now. You'd never be seen again.'

'Well, obviously I wouldn't actually try it!'

Shortly after, the plane began making its descent and once again there was turbulence as they went through the clouds. Lisa's ears popped as they lost altitude, and below them the coastline of Ireland became clear as they emerged beneath the clouds again. The air stewards were making their way through the cabin collecting rubbish in a plastic sack. The drunken man was out of his seat, squeezing past the stewards and muttering about needing the toilet, not being able to wait. He stopped beside Lisa and Ben's row, looking around anxiously.

'Toilet's just there, mate,' Ben said, pointing to where it was situated between the exit and the door to the cockpit.

'I gotta go,' the man said, staggering into Lisa.

'Hey, watch out!' she said, pushing him upright.

An air steward was approaching from behind but trapped behind a trolley. He called out, 'Sir, you need to return to your seat.'

'But I gotta piss,' the man said. 'And I wan' more whis . . . whishky. They won't bring me none,' he said to Lisa.

She was about to answer him when the man suddenly lunged for the exit door beside her, grabbing the emergency lever and yanking it upwards, into the open position.

'Oh, my God!' Lisa screamed, as the door's seal was broken and air began rushing through the cabin and out. The door hadn't fully opened – it had to be pulled inwards first – but she could feel the suck of the pressure differential pulling at her hair and her scarf as the cabin depressurised.

Everyone around them was screaming and the air crew were hurrying forwards along the aisle, fighting their way past the catering trolley. But Ben was there first, grabbing the man around his chest and pulling him back away from the door, and pinning his arms to his side.

'Ben!' Lisa screamed, but she was held in her seat by her seatbelt. It was becoming hard to breathe as air was sucked out through the gaps around the door. The emergency oxygen masks had dropped down and everyone was fumbling with them as they tried to put them on. Ben turned his head to her and shouted something she couldn't make out over the sound of rushing air and passengers screaming. A mask flapped against her face and she realised she should put it on, pulling the elastic around the back of her head and taking a deep breath. A member of the cabin crew had managed to reach them and helped Ben hold the man down, and then another one hurled herself against the door to push it back closed, and pulled the lever down into the locked position.

As soon as it was sealed the commotion in the cabin died down, though there was still a babble of anxious calls for help. Lisa pulled her mask off – she no longer needed it. With the man restrained now by two members of the cabin crew, Ben got up and came back to sit beside Lisa. He was panting heavily as he turned and took her in his arms, pulling her close.

'Oh, my God. That was . . .' Lisa tried to describe how she'd felt during those few awful moments but there were no words. 'If the door had opened fully . . .' She couldn't bring herself to imagine what might have happened. Ben hadn't had his seatbelt fastened, and as the nearest person to the door, other than the man who'd opened it, he might have been sucked out.

'It's all right. It couldn't have opened fully. The pressure inside is too great. That's why they have to be pulled inwards first – as a safety feature.' Ben's voice sounded shaky.

'Ladies and gentlemen, we've had a slight situation but it's all now under control and we will be continuing our descent to Dublin airport as planned,' the captain's voice came over the Tannoy. 'Please remain in your seats with your seatbelts fastened. If you need assistance or medical attention, please press the call button over your head and a member of cabin crew will come to you.'

Lisa twisted to look around the aeroplane behind her. There was some debris in the aisle – papers, plastic water bottles, pieces of rubbish that had blown towards the door. A few people were crying, one or two were shouting angrily at anyone who'd listen. One man had got out of his seat and was being persuaded back to it by a member of the crew. The drunk man had been pushed into a window seat a few rows back, with a male air steward beside him. He seemed subdued now, as though he realised what he'd done, in some part of his alcohol-befuddled mind.

'Bloody hell, Lisa. That was a bit . . .' Ben waved a hand vaguely as though he couldn't find the words. His face was a pasty white.

'Yes. Are you OK, Ben? I mean you . . . you were a hero . . .'

'I'm fine. I really am.'

He didn't look fine, she thought. He looked as though he'd seen his life flash before him, or whatever was supposed to happen with near-death experiences. *Had* it been near death? Ben had said there was no way the door could have flung right open. But it had opened enough to cause that roaring wind through the cabin, enough to pull papers and bottles towards it. It had frightened everyone on board, particularly those at the front. And especially the cabin crew. One female member of crew was holding a small ice pack to a bruise forming on her cheek. How she'd got that injury Lisa had no idea, but there'd been a few moments when everything was in chaos and she'd been picturing the worst, with the door flying open and Ben and the drunk being sucked out . . .

'Oh, God,' she groaned.

Ben looked at her with concern in his eyes. 'What? Are you all right?'

'I am . . . just . . . I suppose we'll get flashbacks for a while. I keep thinking of what might have happened, if that door . . .'

'I told you, the door couldn't have opened fully. I'm all right, Lisa. We're safe. Look, we're not far off landing now.' He pointed out of the window, where Lisa could see the coastline of Ireland, an island, a long sandy beach, fields beyond. 'We'll be down in a few minutes.'

'The sooner the better,' she said quietly. He nodded and once more, took her hand. She held his tightly for the rest of the flight, barely breathing as the aeroplane touched down at Dublin airport. Either side of the runway, fire engines and emergency vehicles were parked, ready to rush to the aircraft's aid if necessary. It was only when the captain had applied the brakes and the plane was taxiing slowly towards the terminal building, that Lisa felt she could breathe easily again.

The captain made another announcement. 'Ladies and gentlemen, we have arrived at Dublin airport. Please remain in your seats. The local police will be coming on board to escort a passenger off, and disembarking will occur after that. Thank you for your understanding.'

'So we won't be first off after all,' Ben said, with a wry smile.

Lisa looked behind her to where the drunken man was seated. He'd been quiet and calm during the landing, thank goodness. But now he looked agitated again and the air steward beside him was having a hard time keeping him in his seat.

Thankfully, it was only a few minutes before the cabin crew opened the door and a number of security guards and men in Garda uniform entered the plane. They escorted the drunk man off, in handcuffs, and still ranting about wanting more 'whishky'. A small cheer went up from the passengers as the man left the plane.

A moment later the captain's voice over the Tannoy invited everyone to disembark. There were mutterings of relief from all the passengers as bags were gathered, coats were put on, and the shuffle towards the exits began. Ben and Lisa were quickly out, and were soon making their way through the airport. They'd flown with hand luggage only so it wasn't long before they were on a bus heading into the city centre.

They'd hardly spoken since the incident. But Lisa instinctively knew this was because they were each needing time and space to process what had happened. They'd also barely let go of each other's hands. She felt comforted by the feel of Ben's warm, strong hand in hers. It was as though nothing bad could happen if he was within her reach.

It was a short walk from the bus stop, on the banks of the Liffey, to the hotel. 'It's only a Premier Inn,' Ben said, with a shrug. 'Dad's got shares in them so he always uses them. But it's a new one in a convenient part of town.'

'It's perfect,' Lisa said, as they approached the modern hotel, tucked away on a back street in among residential blocks and office buildings. All she wanted to do was collapse on a bed and try to unwind. She needed to put out of her mind the image of Ben wrestling the drunk to the floor beside an unsealed aeroplane exit while they were thousands of metres above the ground.

They checked in quickly and found their room, several floors up and along a twisting corridor. It was a standard Premier Inn twin room with a view of the building across the street, but never had a bed looked so inviting. Lisa dumped her rucksack on a chair and watched as Ben shrugged off his jacket and kicked off his shoes.

'Do you want to have a snooze before we go out?' Ben said. 'Might be a good idea to rest after . . . all that excitement. We need to leave here by about six-thirty. It's only two stops on the DART to Lansdowne Road. But we might want to eat first.'

'Dart?'

'Dublin's railway system.'

'Ah. I think I just need half an hour or so to relax, then we can head out.'

'Sure. I could do with some time too. I'm happy to go down to the bar if you want to be alone?'

'No, it's fine.' Actually, if she was being honest with herself, Lisa wanted Ben to stay. She wanted him there lying on the other bed, with his presence, his closeness keeping her safe. Just as he'd kept her safe on the plane, by putting himself at risk. He'd been a hero. The cabin crew had thanked him, but he deserved more. He deserved a medal.

'You know you were a hero, back there,' she said quietly. She was standing in front of him, and wrapped her arms around him.

He shrugged. 'All I could think of was that I had to keep you safe.'

There was no answer she could give to that, that wouldn't make her cry, so she just held him tightly a moment longer, nuzzling her face against his shoulder, then released him. He flopped onto one of the beds and turned away from her. She'd hoped . . . that perhaps they'd lie together for a bit, cuddling, calming each other after the ordeal. She lay on the other bed, pulled a pillow from under her and hugged it, as though it was a child's teddy bear, drawing comfort from the action. She gazed at Ben's broad shoulders, the little hairs on the back of his neck above his collar, his mismatched socks – one depicting a robot from *Star Wars*, the other showing Harry Potter.

How she wanted to lie there with him, comforting him! But she recognised that he needed time alone. There would be plenty of time later for them to get closer, she knew, once the adrenaline had ebbed away.

Chapter 18

Celia, July 1947

Celia was supposed to be packing, but she was not in the mood for it right now. She and Sita were due to go to the hill station the very next day. The heat in Agra had become unbearable. The monsoon would begin any day now, and usually she'd be happy to be going but this year things felt different. Because it was the last year, the last time she'd make this journey. And they wouldn't be there for the whole of the season – they'd return after only a month, just before independence, so that Celia could join her father for the journey to England.

She would prefer to stay in Agra and simply put up with the heat and the rains, Celia thought. She'd like to spend as much time as possible with Vijay, and try again to find a way in which she might be able to remain in India post-independence.

But it was impossible. Papa had booked train tickets for herself and Sita for the next day. And there was no chance of persuading him to let her stay. Celia sighed as she folded a blouse and put it in the bottom of her trunk. It was a long journey to Simla and she wasn't in the mood for it at all. At least, though, she would be going out. Papa had kept her largely confined to the bungalow and its grounds for ages.

Back when she was younger, she'd always loved this time of year. She'd relished escaping the heat of the plains for the cool mountain air, the chance to play outside again, the change of scenery, the break from her studies with her tutors. And the journey itself could be fun – the glimpses of India she spied through the carriage windows as the train hurtled past. The vast, fantastic country of her birth never ceased to enthral her.

It'd be different this year, knowing it was probably the last time. And Sita wasn't going to be very good company. She'd been acting strangely for the last couple of weeks. Distracted, aloof. Worried about something.

Celia had questioned her, asking what was wrong.

'Ah, nothing's wrong, *meri jaan*. Maybe I am thinking of how much I will miss you when you go to England; that is all.' Sita had smiled sadly, but to Celia the smile looked false. There was something else on her *ayah's* mind; she knew it. Something else was going on.

But as she remembered Mama saying, if a person didn't want to talk about their problems there was no use in pushing them. They'd talk when they were ready. In the meantime, all you could do was be there, ready to listen. Celia thought that perhaps at some point on the long train journey Sita might open up and tell her what was wrong.

It was unusual. Celia couldn't remember a time when Sita hadn't been cheerful and happy. Or maybe, she thought, she simply hadn't noticed Sita's mood changes. Maybe she was growing up and learning to spot when someone wasn't happy.

Or perhaps it was simply as Sita had said – that she was dreading the time when they would have to part. Who knew when, or even whether, they'd see each other again? Sita presumably wouldn't be able to afford to come to England. Celia would have to travel to India – and she would, as soon as she possibly could. But she couldn't guarantee when that would happen. It might not be possible until she was of age and no longer under Papa's control. That was years away.

She resolved to ask Papa one more time whether Sita could come with them in August, because Sita wasn't the only one feeling miserable about the forthcoming separation.

She picked up a skirt, folded it and put it in the trunk, then took it out again. 'I hate that damn thing,' she said to herself. If it was to be her last season in the hill station, she'd rather wear Indian clothes. There would be far too much time ahead of her when she would have to dress as an Englishwoman. She opened a drawer and tugged out a pile of *salwar kameez*, trousers and tunics, and smiled. Those were better. A few minutes later the trunk was full of them, along with her sari, blouse and underskirt. She added her tennis clothes – there was always someone who'd give her a game in Simla – and that was that. She was packed, more or less.

There was no chance to see Vijay again before she left for Simla so she would have to say her goodbyes to him on the telephone. And she would insist that they return from Simla in time to see him before leaving for England. Even Papa couldn't deny her that.

She went to the hallway where the house telephone sat on a small table, then changed her mind. Better to use the extension in Papa's study, where she was less likely to be overheard. Papa was at his office today, working long hours as he had ever since Lord Mountbatten had brought the date of independence forward. Sita was nowhere to be seen – she seemed to be keeping out of Celia's way today.

She went through to the study, sat on Papa's chair behind the desk and dialled the number for the palace. It was answered by Arun Gupta, one of the maharajah's most trusted servants. Celia knew him from her many visits to the palace.

'Arun, hello. It's Celia Fforbes-Whyte here. Is Vijay able to come to the phone right now?'

'Ah, Miss Celia. I will check. What do you need him for?'

Celia frowned. Usually, Arun would just fetch Vijay immediately and not question why she wanted him. 'Well, just to say goodbye really.'

'You are leaving?'

'For Simla. On the morning train tomorrow.'

'Of course. I shall look for Mr Vijay.'

There was the sound of the handset being placed on a table. Celia waited impatiently, drumming her fingers on Papa's desk. At last Vijay spoke.

'Cee-cee! So glad to hear from you. Arun says you are leaving tomorrow! So soon!'

'Just for Simla. Not for England. But there's no chance to see you today and when I come back it'll be to go straight off again, so I thought I'd telephone you to say goodbye today, and then catch you in August just before we leave for good.' To her shame her voice broke as she said the words 'for good'.

'Oh, Cee. I'm going to miss you.' He sounded resigned, but not as sad about their forthcoming separation as she had expected.

'Vijay, I don't suppose you've spoken to your father . . . about me staying here with you and not going to England at all?'

'I did. He says no.'

'Oh.' So that was that.

'Cee, it'll be all right living in England. Honestly. Look, I hadn't told you before as I wasn't sure of the timings. But *Pitaji* has changed his mind again, and says that although I must finish my schooling in India, I am to attend university in England, after all. And I have looked at a map, and Oxford, if I get into it, is not far from anywhere in England. It is such a small country. Wherever you are living, and I suppose it will be in London or near London, I will be able to visit you.'

Celia gasped. 'You're coming to live in England?'

'Yes, for at least three years, starting in two years' time. So we will not be apart for very long.'

'That's still two years!'

'I know, but then we'll be able to meet up as often as you like. Every weekend.'

Celia smiled. 'That makes me feel a little better, Vijay. I hate that I'm having to go away this summer. I'd rather stay here. But Papa says I have to go, and actually the only good thing about it is that I'll be away from *him*. He's being so strict, so grumpy about everything. Worse than ever. Sita's not much better. And the endless riots. It's not right, Vijay, none of it.'

'I know. But things will settle down after independence, *Pitaji* says. And you'll be in England and it won't be too long before I'm there too, and we'll be standing in the English light rain laughing about how cold it is.'

'Drizzle.'

'What?'

'That's what they call the English light rain. Drizzle. Not proper rain at all. And there's a lot of it, over there.'

'Well, we shall stand outside in the drizzle and laugh about it.'

She couldn't imagine laughing about being in England but it was comforting that Vijay would be there too, eventually. 'Will you leave England after getting your degree?'

'I expect so. But that's a long way off.'

'Perhaps you'll bring me back here with you, then.'

There was a moment's silence and Celia panicked a little, imagining Vijay screwing up his face trying to find a way to tell her no, he wouldn't bring her back, he wouldn't want to – theirs was a childhood friendship that had run its course . . .

'Perhaps I will,' he replied, with a tenderness to his tone, and Celia let out a breath.

'I hope—'

'What's that?' Vijay had turned away from the telephone to answer someone else. Celia could hear muttering but could not work out what the other person was saying.

'Vijay?'

'Yes, sorry. I'm still here. What time is your train tomorrow?'
'Eleven-thirty.'
'Is Sanjit driving you there?'
'I think so.'
'And Sita will be with you?'
'Yes.'
'Right.' There was a pause, some muffled sounds, and then Vijay was back again. 'So, I had better go. I have studying to do, so I can be sure of getting a place at Oxford. I'll see you in August then?'
'Yes. Goodbye, Vijay.'

Celia felt strangely flat when she put the phone down. Talking to Vijay hadn't cheered her up the way she'd hoped. Sure there'd been the good news about him coming to England for his degree course after all and the prospect of meeting up and spending time with him then. But before then . . . there would be so few opportunities to see him. She was missing him already. Sometimes it felt as though she was only really alive when she was with him. She wondered if he felt the same.

She tidied the papers on Papa's desk that she'd knocked aside when she'd sat down, and left the study, making sure no one could tell she'd been in there. Papa never liked her going in there, telling her that sometimes there were important and confidential documents on his desk that no one should touch. Well then, she thought, he shouldn't leave them out, should he? They should be locked away, the way he always kept the *Chamakta Sitara* safely out of reach.

'*Meri jaan*, have you finished packing?' Sita asked, intercepting her as she made her way to the veranda to sit with a book.

'More or less. I'll add the last few things in the morning. You?'

'Yes. My trunk is heavy. Sanjit will struggle to lift it into the car and onto the train.' Sita bit her lip.

'It's all right, Sita. He'll manage, I am sure. And we'll be met at Simla station by someone to help us there. Papa has it all arranged, even though he's not coming with us this time. We've done it so many times.'

'Yes. And this is to be the last.' There was a tear glistening in Sita's eye as she spoke. Celia's heart went out to her. She supposed that when they left for England, to Sita, it would feel like having a child leave home. She stepped forward and put her arms around Sita, feeling her familiar plump softness and realising how very much taller than her *ayah* she was these days. It always came as a surprise.

For a moment Sita hugged her back, her face nestled against Celia's shoulder but then she let go and pushed her away. 'Yes, *meri jaan*, it will be all right. I promise.'

'It's me promising you, you silly thing,' Celia said. She reached towards Sita to pull her back into her arms but the older woman turned away.

'I must go and see about lunch,' she muttered, bustling off along the veranda and back into the house.

Celia watched her leave and shrugged. Maybe the heat was getting to her too. That and the knowledge it was their last summer in Simla. She should make allowances for Sita. But it would be hard if she spent the whole of the time moping and sulking. They wouldn't have nearly as much fun as usual.

Maybe she'd cheer up once the journey was over and they could relax, away from the heat. Away from the riots and demonstrations too. From what she understood, there hadn't been so much trouble in Simla. There, life just went on as normal, in a cooler more forgiving climate.

Chapter 19

Lisa, 2023

The short sleep worked wonders for Lisa. She woke up feeling revived, and much calmer than when she'd got off the plane. Ben was still snoozing, so she crept into the bathroom, closing the door gently, to freshen up. It was only five o'clock; there was still plenty of time for them to get out to the stadium in time for the match. She was looking forward more to Ben's company in the evening after the match, than actually watching the rugby. She splashed some water on her face, brushed her hair and touched up her make-up. There were sounds that indicated Ben had woken up, so she went back out to the bedroom.

'Did you sleep well?' she asked.

'Yes. I'm surprised I did – I can't normally sleep in the daytime.'

'Must be the shock of what happened. I believe it's a common reaction to feel exhausted after something traumatic.'

'You could be right. At the time I didn't think anything of it. Just acted instinctively. But now . . .' He shook his head. 'I'm half thinking I must have been mad, and half thinking that I should have done more. Maybe I could have stopped him before he went for the door.'

'You couldn't have done anything more.' She gazed at him, feeling oddly proud of him.

He held her gaze for a moment. She expected him to step forward, take her in his arms and kiss her, but instead he nodded and turned away, biting his lip as though he'd been about to say something then changed his mind. 'Shall we go out soon?' he said.

'Yes. I'm ready whenever you are.'

He smiled and a few minutes later they left the hotel, walking through the streets to a DART station and then travelling the few stops to Lansdowne Road, near the rugby stadium. There were plenty of restaurants in the area and they browsed the menus posted outside a few before choosing a small, cosy place that offered an intriguing menu – a mix of traditional Irish and more modern cuisine. Ben checked the restaurant's ratings on Google before going in and pronounced it suitable. 'Overall 4.6 stars, so that's good. I don't go anywhere under 4.3, unless there's really no choice.'

'Ooh, you're fussy!' Lisa teased.

'Yep. And proud of it!' Ben said, and Lisa laughed.

The restaurant turned out to be a little gem, with superbly cooked food, good service and a convivial atmosphere. They shared a bottle of wine. Lisa wished they could stay there for the rest of the evening but there was a rugby match to go to. It was the reason they'd come to Dublin, after all.

The match was fun, even more so because Munster won by a good margin. There was a wonderful atmosphere in the stadium. Lisa enjoyed joining in with the singing of 'The Fields of Athenry' and the chants, jumping to her feet to cheer whenever Munster scored a try. They left the match tired but elated, and took the DART back to their hotel district.

'Let's go for a late-night drink,' Ben said, and Lisa agreed, not wanting the evening to end yet. They found a traditional Irish pub, dark and cosy. Ben ushered her into a snug and ordered drinks. As he brought them back and sat at a table opposite her, she noticed a sad, determined expression on his face.

'What's up, Ben?' She wondered if it was still the shock affecting him. He'd been all right at the match, but maybe now the events of the day were catching up with him. 'Are you all right? Would you rather go back to the hotel room?'

He shook his head. 'No. I'm all right. Just need to . . . talk.'

'What is it?' She whispered the words. On the plane he'd said he liked her, but now . . . this felt as though it was going to be a break-up conversation. 'Just tell me, whatever it is.'

He took a deep breath, and stared at a point across the bar somewhere over her right shoulder. 'All right then. Here we go. I do like you, Lisa. A lot. And in normal circumstances . . .' he changed his gaze so that he was focused on her '. . . I would very much like us to be together. Very much.' These last words emerged as a whisper.

'Normal circumstances?' Lisa frowned. What wasn't normal about this? Suddenly she had a horrible thought that perhaps he was going to tell her he had some terrible terminal illness or maybe he'd made a commitment to take a job on the other side of the world.

He sighed. 'Lisa, it's . . . it's just that . . .'

'What? Just say it, Ben. Please.'

'That bloody diamond. The curse. I know it's all rubbish. I don't really . . . I don't think I really believe in it, but what if there's something in it? *What if* it really does kill all women who get involved with a Fforbes-Whyte? I mean, you know my family history. So many, all of them for generations, dying far too young.' He slapped a hand down on the table. 'That's my problem, Lisa. I don't want to risk it happening to you. I can't let it.'

She listened to all this in silence, letting his words sink in, as she worked out how best to respond. Yes, the curse was all a load of superstitious nonsense. Of course it was. Wasn't it?

'Do you see?' He was pleading with her. 'Do you understand? I can't get into a relationship with someone who . . . I care about. Just in case . . .'

He reached across the table and lightly touched the back of her hand. Lisa looked down at his fingers on hers, then up at his face. His expression was anguished, tormented.

'Ben, it's all rubbish. It means nothing. You don't believe in magic, do you? There's nothing in it.'

'My family . . . my mother . . . And then what happened to us today, on the plane. That was far too close for comfort. You might have . . .' He shook his head, despairingly.

'I'm so sad all those women in your family died, but it's all a tragic coincidence. It's not because of some stupid diamond. How can it be?' She couldn't believe that he was holding back because of . . . because of a *fairy story*. 'And today – it was horrifying, very frightening and you were absolutely a hero, but it was because of that drunk man. Not because of a lump of rock.' She spoke firmly but kindly.

'I know, you're right . . . but even so. I can't risk it. I can't risk *you*.' His expression was strained, tortured.

'You're not risking anything. Except your own happiness.' *And mine*, she wanted to add, but maybe that would put too much pressure on him.

He looked miserable at this comment. He hung his head and sighed, and her heart went out to him. She sympathised, she really did, but he had to get over himself. He had to accept that there was no substance in the legend of the diamond's curse. He said he didn't believe it, and yet he did – at least enough to let it influence his behaviour. She supposed that having lost his mother and knowing the history of his grandmother, Wilfred's wife and daughter, and whoever else had died young, that made it hard for him. The incident on the flight over definitely hadn't helped.

'I know,' he said, lifting his eyes to hers. 'You're right. It's totally mad. Makes no sense at all. But I just can't seem to . . . I don't know. Can we, for now, just stay friends? Maybe in time . . . we'll see. If we can give the diamond back, to whoever.' He heaved a huge sigh. 'I'm sorry, Lisa. Really, I am. But I can't go into something feeling the way I do. I wouldn't be able to relax. I'm so . . . so *terrified* of what might happen. What so nearly did happen. I'd been telling myself not to be so stupid, that of course the legend of the curse is meaningless and that it'd be all right to get involved with you. But then . . . what happened today . . . I'm sorry. I just . . . can't.'

She regarded him quietly for a moment. 'It's all right. I'll hold on. I'll wait.'

'You shouldn't. You should date other people. I want you to. Because I can't promise I'll ever . . .' He sighed, and looked her straight in the eye. 'If we can't find the true owners of the diamond, I might never get over this.'

There was nothing she could say to that. They sat in silence finishing their drinks.

That night, with Ben lying in the next bed, Lisa found it hard to sleep. She had so much going through her mind, and Ben's presence – so close yet not close enough – didn't help. He was sleeping soundly; she could tell by the evenness of his breathing. She tried not to toss and turn too much, not wanting to make any noise that might wake him. But every time she tried to sleep, images of him diving onto the drunken man, while air rushed out of the plane's cabin, ran through her head. She'd briefly thought that she was going to lose him, in the most horrible way. She could recall in every detail the anguished look on his face as he held the man down and twisted towards her, as though he was terrified that she was in more danger than himself.

No wonder he couldn't help himself believing in the curse of the diamond.

She eventually slept, waking late, when Ben gently shook her shoulder. 'Lisa? It's ten past nine. We probably need to get going if you'd like to get some breakfast before we head to the airport.'

'Mmm?' She'd been in the middle of a vivid dream, in which she and Ben were walking hand in hand towards the Taj Mahal, which in her dream was set with enormous diamonds all over its many domes. Dream Ben was just about to say something to her that she knew was really important. Something she desperately needed to hear. But then real Ben was telling her the time and that she needed to get up. 'OK. Give me a minute.'

'No problem. You've got about forty minutes. An hour if you need it. Just thought you'd rather not have to rush, or miss breakfast.'

'Thanks.' She opened her eyes now and realised he wasn't dressed himself. He'd showered, but was wearing only a towel around his waist. She turned over, averting her gaze. Now that was a sight that she'd love to wake up to every day. But only if she was allowed to touch and not just look. That bloody diamond. She may not believe in its curse, but it *was* cursed – by her!

A couple of hours later they'd breakfasted and made their way to the airport. Once on the plane, thankfully seated far from any exit, Lisa looked across at Ben. His jaw was clenched and he was perspiring slightly. She took hold of his hand. 'Relax. We'll be fine. And any nutters on this flight are not your responsibility.'

He smiled at her and his features softened a little. 'Thanks. I'm very glad you're here with me.'

'I'm glad you invited me.' Despite everything, she meant it. She loved his company.

Soon, Lisa told herself, soon, somehow, they'd find the diamond's rightful owners and take the thing back to India. And then . . . and then . . . she'd take him in her arms and kiss him soundly. She'd never let him go. That had to happen, somehow. She wasn't ready to give up on him yet. She stole a glance at Ben. He looked tense as the plane accelerated down the runway for take-off. She took his hand and gave it a quick squeeze of reassurance, and received a grateful smile in return.

Chapter 20

Celia, July 1947

Celia looked across the breakfast table at Papa, who, as usual, had the *Times of India* spread beside him. He was spreading butter on a slice of toast, but his eyes and mind were obviously on the newspaper and the butter covered only half the slice. He was clearly paying far more attention to the paper than to what he was eating. She was exasperated with him. It was their last breakfast together for weeks, given that he wasn't coming to Simla this year. He'd told her he had too much to do in Agra, with all the work needed to prepare for independence, and handing over to the new Indian administration.

'Papa.' She stared at him, waiting for him to look up at her.

'Mmm?' He kept his eyes down, focused on the article he was reading.

'Papa!'

'What, dear?'

'It's my last morning here. You could at least pay me a little attention.'

He looked up at her then, his mouth set in a thin line. 'This—'

he jabbed at the paper with a finger '—is an important article. I need to read and absorb it. If you would do me the courtesy of remaining silent until I come to the end of it, I'd be grateful. I shall pay you attention then, so you may say whatever it is you want to say.'

She pouted. 'You've got weeks ahead of you when you can read the paper over breakfast in silence, when I won't even be in the house. Is this what it'll be like back in England too? Do they have the *Times of India* there?' She knew she sounded petulant but she could not help herself.

'They have the original *Times*, and yes, I will take that paper every day and read it in the mornings.'

'And I'll be ignored.'

'You'll learn how to behave. For a start, you *do not* talk to me like that. You will treat me with respect.'

'Certainly. And you can treat *me* with a little more respect, too. Like not reading at the meal tables.' Celia felt her blood boiling. If she stayed another moment, he'd say something more and she'd raise her voice and then he'd shout at her, and before they knew it, they'd be in a full-on fight. That was how it always went. And this was their last morning together for ages. This was not how it should be. They should part on good terms.

She pushed back her chair roughly and left the room, to give herself time to cool off, and to give Papa a moment to reflect on his behaviour. She smiled wryly to herself as she had that thought. It was as though she was the adult and he the child. But surely, now she was almost sixteen, respect ought to go both ways? She only wanted to be treated as he himself expected to be treated. That wasn't too much to ask, was it?

Celia returned to her bedroom to put the last few items in her trunk. She then found Sanjit and told him it was ready for him to put in the boot of the car. Sita was standing outside by the car already, biting her fingernails. 'We'll be off soon,' Celia told her, checking her watch. 'We need to leave in ten minutes to be sure to catch the train.'

Sita nodded. Her face looked drawn and anxious. She must be really dreading the journey, Celia thought. It was unusual. Normally Sita said she enjoyed long train journeys, relishing the chance to see a bit of her native country, and the chance to sit and chat to Celia without feeling there were tasks she ought to be getting on with.

Papa came out to say goodbye. But he did not say he was sorry. He embraced Celia stiffly for barely two seconds, then stood back, unsmiling. 'You will telephone me when you arrive at the Simla house?'

'Yes.'

'And you will obey Sita while you are on the journey? Remember, she is the adult; she is in charge.'

Celia couldn't help but roll her eyes at this. But now was not the time to have another argument about how grown-up she was. 'Of course, Papa.'

'Then I shall bid you farewell. I'll see you when you return in August.'

She opened her mouth to say goodbye to him but he'd already turned away to go back to his study. She stared after him for a moment then shrugged and climbed into the car. If that was how he wanted to leave it, when they wouldn't see each other again for ages, then so be it. If he wanted to be distant then so would she. Even so, she felt a prickling of tears behind her eyes and had to take a deep breath to stop them falling. Now was not the time, in front of everyone, to show how much Papa's coldness had hurt her.

Sanjit loaded her trunk, Sita got in the back of the car beside her and Sanjit climbed into the driving seat, then they set off for the short journey to Agra's railway station.

The journey passed in silence. Sita kept her head turned away from Celia, staring out of the side window as they drove through the streets into the town, passing all manner of rickshaws and bullock carts and bicycles. Sanjit rarely spoke while he was driving, unless he absolutely needed to. He kept his hands at ten to two on the steering wheel, driving slowly and carefully, focusing intently on the road ahead.

Sanjit parked the car at the front of the station building and went off to find a porter's trolley for their trunks, while Celia and Sita waited by the car. Sita was, Celia noticed, even more agitated than earlier. She'd pulled her *pallu* up to cover her head, and was twisting the end of it in her hands.

'What's wrong, Sita?'

She received a weak smile in response. 'Nothing, *meri jaan*. I will be glad when we get to Simla. This heat!' She wafted the end of her *pallu* in front of her face like a fan.

They were standing in full sun, and Celia could feel sweat trickling down her back. 'Hurry up, Sanjit,' she said. 'We'll die out here in this.' He'd gone into the station building and was out of sight.

Just then a van pulled up behind them, between their car and the station, blocking them in. Celia frowned. It was restricting her view of the station and would make it hard for Sanjit to get close to the car's boot with a trolley. She took a step towards the van to tell the driver to move and park properly. But Sita caught her arm and pulled her back. 'No, *meri jaan*, do not say anything.'

Celia was about to answer when three men exited from the back of the van and walked towards them. 'What are you—' she began, but two of them roughly grabbed her by the arms and pushed her to the open rear van doors, bundling her inside. She screamed and tried to fight them off but they were strong – she had no chance. The third man was pushing Sita in behind her.

'What's going on? Sanjit! SANJIT!' she yelled, as loudly as she could, but one of the men clamped his hand over her mouth. She tried to bite him, but he quickly tied a cloth around her face, gagging her. She kicked out, managing to land a kick on his thigh, making him yelp with pain.

'Stop it, little bitch,' one of the men said, as he forced her arms behind her and began tying her wrists.

'Don't fight them, *meri jaan*,' Sita said. 'It will only mean you get hurt.'

Sita, Celia noticed, seemed to be submitting to the men, sitting meekly in the back of the van while one of the men tied her hands. They hadn't gagged her. Why was she not calling out for help?

The van doors were slammed shut and a moment later the van roared away, its wheels spinning. It was dark in the back of it, with only a chink of light shining through from the front. Celia shuffled close to Sita and leaned against her. She worked her jaw, trying to loosen the gag. Beside her, Sita was sniffling, sobbing quietly. Celia wished she could say something to comfort her, but she could only grunt unintelligibly through the gag.

As her eyes became accustomed to the dark, she could see that there was a small opening between the back of the van and the cab area. This was where the limited light was shining in. The men must have all got into the cab, for there was only herself and Sita in the back, along with a few pieces of rope, an empty barrel and some tools. The van was probably normally used by some workman, for transporting materials perhaps.

What on earth did the men want with them? They'd been kidnapped, she supposed, but what did the men want? Papa wasn't rich. He was well-off, certainly by the standards of ordinary Indians, but not hugely rich. If you were going to abduct someone for the purposes of extorting money, you'd surely pick someone like Vijay, whose father was a maharajah. So why had she and Sita been taken?

They'd find out soon enough, she supposed. She snuggled against Sita, resting her cheek against the other woman's shoulder in an attempt to reassure her that they would be all right, that surely the men wouldn't hurt them.

But she was scared. Very scared. What if it wasn't a kidnapping? What if it was some gang who just wanted women for evil purposes? She'd heard of such things – she'd heard servants whispering; she'd seen newspaper articles. There were men who liked nothing more than young girls for their pleasure. But why then had Sita, a plump middle-aged woman, also been taken? Perhaps to stop her raising the alarm?

Sanjit might have seen the van. Celia could only hope that he had been on his way back with a luggage trolley and had seen what happened. Right now, he would be driving after them, taking care not to lose sight of the van and tracking where they were taken. He'd rescue them; he had to. Or at the very least he'd raise the alarm and send the police to rescue them. This horror would all be over soon and those thugs would be locked up. Celia mouthed a little prayer that that was what was happening.

She tried estimating how long they had been driving for, and in what direction they were going. Not long, she thought, probably ten minutes or so, but she had no clues as to the direction. They'd been thrown around a little in the back of the van, as though corners had been taken at speed, but she had no idea what route they'd taken, or even whether they'd left the city or not. And what would happen next – might they be driving for miles, out of the city, across the open plains? She already felt bruised from being bundled into the van and if it was a long journey she'd find it very uncomfortable, especially with her hands tied behind her, which meant she couldn't stop herself from rolling around.

But then, suddenly, the van came to a stop, the engine was switched off, and she heard the sound of the men getting out of the cab, speaking to each other. A moment later the van's back doors were flung open once more and sunlight flooded in. Celia blinked, temporarily blinded by the brightness. She was roughly grabbed by her upper arms and pulled out, stumbling as she hit the ground. As before, two men had a hold of her, while only one held Sita.

Celia looked about her, desperate to get some clues as to where they'd been brought. But it could have been anywhere on the edge of the city. The van had pulled into a courtyard behind some ramshackle buildings, that were partly stone and brick, partly corrugated iron. The ground was dried mud. There was a battered wooden door ahead, and she was being led towards it. It was covered by peeling blue paint – a detail she committed to memory. One man tugged the door open – it stuck a little against the ground as though it had dropped on its hinges, and the man had to pull hard.

She was pushed inside, into a dark room that had only one small window letting in light. And then they were shoved through another door into another room; this one also had only one window and to her dismay Celia saw that the window was barred. There was a single bed against one wall, with dirty-looking sheets on it. A lidded bucket stood in one corner next to a basin of water that was placed on a low stool. That corner was to function as their bathroom, she realised, with a grimace.

At last, one of the men removed her gag. 'Where are we and what do you want with us?' Celia said, as imperiously as she could manage, as soon as the gag was released.

He didn't answer. He just untied her hands and left the room. Sita too had been untied, but she'd kept quiet. Why hadn't Sita spoken to the men in Hindi? Celia couldn't understand. When the last of the men turned away Celia darted towards the door, but it was slammed closed in her face and there was the ominous sound of bolts being pushed across on the other side. She tried the handle but couldn't budge the door an inch. She pounded on it with her fists. 'Let us out! My father will be furious and there will be trouble for you!'

There was no response. It was as though the men had left the building. Indeed, listening carefully, she heard the van's engine start and the sound of it driving away. They were alone. They were locked in some ramshackle building in God knows what part of the city, and there was no one out there, no one to hear them shout, no one to help. She wanted to curl into a ball and cry, but that wasn't going to help them, was it? A stiff upper lip was needed, as Papa always said when things went wrong. And so she blinked back the tears and forced herself to keep calm and think logically.

She turned to see that Sita was sitting on the bed, her head in her hands, sobbing. Here was something she could do – comfort her *ayah*. She rushed over to sit beside Sita, wrapping an arm around her shoulders. 'Sita! Don't cry. It'll be all right. They won't hurt us. We'll work out what they want and we'll find a way out of here.'

But the older woman seemed inconsolable. Celia held her fast until the sobbing subsided, and Sita finally lifted her face away from her hands.

'Are you hurt, *meri jaan*? I will never forgive . . .'

'No, I'm all right. Maybe a few bruises from where they pushed me into the van. You?'

'I am not hurt.'

'What do you think they want?'

Somehow this question brought on a new bout of sobbing and Celia had to wait until Sita could compose herself again. But all she did was shrug in response.

'Money? Or do they think my father has political influence, perhaps? I wish they'd told us what they wanted.'

'They did not speak to us at all.'

'No.' Celia pondered. It was almost as though the three men who'd taken them had been told not to speak to them. Which must mean that someone else, someone who'd told them not to talk, was in charge. Those three men were, she realised, just the heavies who'd been tasked with abducting them and bringing them here. Sooner or later someone else would come, someone who might let them know what was going on. Until then, all they could do was wait and see who turned up.

She looked around the room again. At the end of the bed a jug of water and two chipped cups sat on a tray. She suddenly realised she was thirsty, very thirsty, and left Sita's side to pour them each a drink. The water was warm but it was clean. How often would it be replenished? Would they be brought any food? How long would they have to stay there, and what would happen next?

Her mind whirled with all the questions but she did not dare voice them to Sita. Her *ayah* seemed to be handling this very badly, much worse than she herself was. Celia supposed that was because Sita was supposed to be taking care of her, and perhaps felt responsible in a way. But it wasn't her fault. It wasn't Sanjit's, either. Maybe her father should have sent another servant, so that they would always have had a man with them. Maybe it was Papa's fault.

Well, it would serve him right for being so distant with her that morning.

Chapter 21

Lisa, 2023

Lisa had only been back home for a few hours when her phone rang. Her stomach gave a lurch as just for a brief moment she imagined it might be Ben, calling with a change of heart and a plan to meet up the next day. But it was Gaby.

'So, spill the beans! How was Dublin?'

'Great. Munster won.'

'Mate, I do not care in the slightest about the blinking rugby! I want to know how things went with Ben! Last I heard you'd snogged him on the Thames embankment and you were all misty-eyed about how gorgeous he was. And now you've had a night away together . . . and I want all the juicy details!'

Lisa had to laugh at Gaby's enthusiasm. But it was all a bit too complicated to tell her over the phone – the incident on the plane, Ben's reaction to it. 'It was an eventful little trip. I'm going to need to tell you it all in person, though. Are you in London this week at all?'

'You're going to keep me hanging, Lisa! No, I'm not in London this week. But if you're free next weekend, not seeing the delectable

Ben, Josh is away, and I thought we could go for a hike in the South Downs? You could get the train to Brighton on Saturday; I'll pick you up at the station and we'll walk in the Ditchling Beacon area. Dinner in Brighton and a girlie sleepover at mine.'

'Gaby, I can't think of anything I'd enjoy more.' And Lisa meant it.

'Right, it's a date. Message me when you know what train you'll be on.' Gaby's voice then softened. 'And from your instant agreement to spend a weekend with me I'm guessing you and Ben aren't an item.'

'We're not, no, but as I said . . .'

'Yeah, yeah. It's complex. Well, see you next week, then, and you can tell me all.'

'Will do.' Lisa ended the call with a smile on her face. Something to look forward to, and her best mate to confide in.

It was just what she needed, Lisa thought, as she sat on the train to Brighton the following Saturday. A good day out, a walk in the countryside, a meal in a pub and a sleepover with a mate. It would all help to take her mind off her troubles. The sun was out, there was a pleasant breeze and no forecast of rain. She had a small rucksack with her, containing a bottle of water and a few snacks, her sunglasses and a few things for overnight. Walking in the hills with Gaby – it'd be a little recreation of their Chamonix trip and she couldn't wait.

Gaby was waiting for her in her classic Mini outside Brighton station.

'Thanks for suggesting this,' Lisa said. 'I needed to get out of London.'

'We all need to get into the countryside now and again. Somewhere you can't hear any roads or see any buildings. South Downs, here we come!'

'Yee-haw!' Lisa whooped, and Gaby laughed.

Soon they'd parked in a gravel car park and were setting off to walk a length of the South Downs Way. 'It's an out-and-back route, I'm afraid,' Gaby said. 'One day I'd like to walk the whole thing, end to end. Takes a bit of logistical planning to work out places to stay, though. Or you can bring a tent and book into campsites.'

'I'll do it with you,' Lisa said. If she couldn't find a decent boyfriend, she'd make the most of time with her girlfriends.

'Would you? That'd be awesome! I don't have enough holiday to do it this year but maybe earmark for next year?'

'Along with the next Alpine walking trip?'

'We're going to be busy girls.'

Lisa laughed, feeling herself unwind as they strode up a chalky path leading onto the ridge of the Downs. 'We certainly will be.'

'So,' Gaby said, as they reached the crest from where the views stretched for miles, northwards down the escarpment to the small villages of Ditchling and Clayton, and southwards to the distant line of the English Channel. 'Tell me all. Ben, Dublin, even the rugby. I want all the updates, in all the detail.'

'OK, here we go.' Lisa took a deep breath and began to recount all that had happened the previous weekend, starting with the incident on the plane.

'Oh, my God!' Gaby gasped. 'I saw something about that on the news but didn't for a moment imagine it was the flight you were on.' She clutched Lisa's arm and pulled her close for a hug. 'So glad you're safe.'

'You've Ben to thank. He was a hero.'

Gaby tipped her head to one side and regarded her. 'You really do like him, don't you? It sounds like you've got what romance writers call "chemistry" with him. So why is he holding back? He has no girlfriend, no ties, lives close enough to you, gets on well with you . . .'

Lisa twisted her mouth, then told Gaby about the *Chamakta Sitara's* so-called curse.

'Ben says we can't be together because of the diamond. The

curse. He says he doesn't believe in it, and yet he doesn't want to risk it. Says he can't risk anything happening to someone he likes. Says that what happened on the plane is proof the curse is still potent.'

'But . . . but that's ridiculous. *You* don't believe that, do you?'

'Well, no, of course not. But he does. And so . . . we're at an impasse.'

'Hmm. Can I be frank?'

'Please.'

'Either he needs to get over himself or you need to get over him. One or the other. Remember, Lisa, there's more to life than men.'

Lisa stopped walking and stared for a moment at the view across the rolling hills between the escarpment they were on and the distant buildings of Brighton. It was stunning. 'I know. If you'd told me a few weeks ago, when we came back from Chamonix, that I'd be mooning over a fella like this I'd have laughed in your face. I'd gotten shot of Rupert and honestly thought I'd enjoy being on my own. And I was enjoying it, until I met Ben, and now he's all I can think about. That bloody diamond. I wish we'd never found it.'

Gaby came to stand beside her, rubbing her shoulder sympathetically. 'If we hadn't found it you wouldn't have met Ben. Maybe you need to look elsewhere? Try dating someone else? That Ryan I told you about – I'll set you up with him if you want. You never know. My mate Abi says he's a good bloke.'

'All right. Might as well. Any night this coming week would be good.' Gaby was right. Perhaps she needed to move on from Ben.

'Will do. And if Ryan doesn't work out, there's only one other answer.'

'What's that?'

'The diamond has to go.'

Lisa snorted. 'The diamond is in his father's safe. Ben suggested to his dad it should be repatriated to India, but his dad wouldn't hear of it. So we're stumped there too.'

'Oh, dear. Only one thing for it, then.'

'What?'

'Forget about it all for today, and simply enjoy this bee-yew-ti-ful day!' Gaby stretched out the word, spread her arms wide and spun around.

Lisa laughed and joined in, singing, *The hills are alive, with the sound of music.*

'Music, you call that?'

'Ha, best I can do, and if I recall correctly, you can't sing either,' Lisa retorted, and they both laughed. Yes, this weekend away was certainly doing her the power of good. The Ben problem wasn't solved but for a few hours she could forget about him and simply enjoy being with her friend, in the countryside.

Lisa had a marvellous weekend with Gaby. The walk on Saturday was long enough to tire her out but not so long that she was too exhausted to enjoy the evening. They had a huge pub dinner – chicken and bacon pie with mash, washed down with a pint of real ale. A proper walkers' meal. The end of the evening was spent at Gaby's house, watching a cheesy romcom movie while sipping a glass of wine. She had a long, deep sleep in Gaby's spare room, waking up to the sound of birdsong: something she never heard in Battersea. To top it all, Gaby had cooked a fry-up for breakfast, even though Lisa had still felt full from the pub dinner.

She'd caught a midday train back to London on Sunday. Both women had chores to do that afternoon. 'I'd have loved to stay the rest of the day,' Lisa said as they parted, 'but the flat's a mess, the washing basket is overflowing and apparently it's Monday tomorrow.'

'I know. Me too. Anyway, we'll do this again in a few weeks, yes?'

'While the summer weather holds, absolutely!'

It'd be fun, meeting up every few weeks for a walk and a catch-up. And with no boyfriend to get in her way, there was no reason not to do it. Gaby's boyfriend Josh was always busy with his own activities at the weekend, which left Gaby free too. Lisa found herself looking forward to the rest of the summer.

She let herself into her flat in the midafternoon, and gazed around at the signs of all the chores she really needed to do. She'd been out on Friday night with Justin and other workmates, then gone down to Brighton early on Saturday. It all meant she'd left washing-up in the sink, had an overflowing basket of ironing, and a mound of dirty clothes in front of the washing machine, to which she would now add, after the weekend away. Not to mention the fact the entire flat needed a good clean. She threw her rucksack onto the bed and sighed. She'd better get on with it. The flat wouldn't clean itself. Last time she'd had it properly tidy was the evening Ben had come round to collect the diamond.

Ben. Damn it, now she was thinking about him again. Being with Gaby had successfully taken her mind off him, but now, within five minutes of returning home he was at the forefront of her mind again. She sighed and began collecting dirty cups and plates from around the flat, taking them into the kitchen. While there she shoved a load of washing into the machine and turned it on. There, that was one job underway. She spent a few minutes loading the dishwasher and put that on, too. Two machines working. Now she should do the ironing, to free up the washing basket that she would need as soon as the washing machine was finished.

'Life's too short to iron,' she told herself, pulling a few things out of the pile that would cope with being put away without ironing.

She was half-way through sorting out the pile when her phone rang. Putting down the T-shirt she'd been folding, she picked up her phone, expecting it to be a cold call or perhaps her mum calling for an hour-long chat. Her mother often seemed to instinctively pick inconvenient moments.

But it was Ben. She felt her heart race as she answered it.

Stupid reaction, she told herself. He's just a friend – remember that. He will probably only ever be a friend.

'Hi, Lisa. Just calling to . . . well, to see how you are. I've . . . missed you, this weekend. Hope you got up to something fun?'

'Hi, Ben. Yes, I was at Gaby's, walking in the South Downs. You?'

'Working for Dad, mostly. And starting to sort through the old family letters and junk.'

'Oh, that's good.' It was about time he got on with that research, she thought. He'd been promising to for ages.

Ben was silent for a moment and Lisa held her breath, wondering what he was going to say next. 'Listen, Lisa. I need to apologise. I'm sorry. Sorry I can't be what you want me to be. Sorry I led you on, with that kiss after the concert and what I said on the plane before . . . you know. But I can't put you in danger. I've spent the week thinking about it and trying to tell myself it's all a load of superstitious nonsense, but I just can't make myself believe it.' He sighed. 'But can we still be friends? I mean, proper friends, meeting up often, going out . . . just without the romantic stuff? Because I genuinely love being with you.'

She smiled, though her heart sank at his words. Still friends. Only ever friends. 'Of course, Ben. Apology accepted, though I don't think you led me on. You're being honest about your feelings, and that's the best way to be.'

'Thank you. That bloody diamond . . . I wish . . .' He sighed, and she imagined him shaking his head sadly at the situation. 'Anyway. Listen, if you're free next weekend, shall we get together at the British Library to properly get going with that research? Are you up for that?'

'Definitely! I have a reader's pass for the British Library anyway. No idea how to start with the research but we can have a go.'

'I promise I'll have gone through all the family papers and letters by then, and hopefully that'll give us a starting place.'

Lisa hoped so, otherwise it felt like finding the original owners of the diamond would be an impossible task. She'd already tried googling *Chamakta Sitara* and had found nothing about a diamond. But even if they found nothing useful, she was still looking forward to a day in Ben's company. Friendship was better than nothing.

Chapter 22

Wilfred, July 1947

After Celia left for the station with Sita and Sanjit, Wilfred finished his breakfast in peace, lingering over a second cup of coffee and the paper. With his daughter now away in Simla for a month or more, that was one less thing to worry about. He would be able to focus fully on his work – there was a lot to accomplish before independence – and when not at work he could simply relax and unwind without worrying about what Celia was up to. It would be a productive and pleasant way to spend his last few weeks in India.

And yet, the house already seemed too quiet with Celia gone. It felt hollow and empty. She had a way of filling the space and banishing silence. Just like her mother before her.

Wilfred realised he had read the same paragraph in his paper several times now. His mind wasn't on it – it was on Alice, his dear, much-missed Alice. Would he miss her more or less when he returned to England, he wondered. He'd met Alice in England during his final year at university but had spent very little time with her there. She'd been dating Cyril, but dropped him when she met Wilfred. They'd decided to marry very quickly and he'd brought her out to India as soon as he could. Partly to get her away from Cyril, in case she changed her mind. But thankfully she never had, constantly reassuring him that she loved him and that she knew she'd picked the right brother in the end. So he hadn't many memories of Alice in England, unlike in India, where every corner of his houses, both in Agra and Simla, reminded him of her. Perhaps moving home would mean he wouldn't find himself thinking of her quite as often. Well, it was not long now before he found out if that was the case.

It would be so different, back in England. Celia – he wondered how Celia would cope? She'd surely make new friends. She'd need to learn how to be English again, how to be a lady. He'd been too lax with her; he'd allowed her far too much freedom. Her friendships with Sita and Vijay – he should have put a stop to those. He should have dismissed Sita when Celia no longer needed a nursemaid. He should have found English girls of around Celia's age or perhaps a little older for her to befriend and learn from. But over the years since Alice's death, he'd just immersed himself in his work and left Celia to fend for herself. And now this was the result – she was now a girl of almost sixteen whom he could scarcely control, who could barely look at him sometimes. Yet he loved her dearly.

Wilfred sighed and put down his paper. He wasn't taking anything in anymore. He was only brooding. He needed to snap out of it. There were only a few more weeks, but so much work to do before they moved back home. And there was no Celia to worry about during that time.

'*Sahib, sahib*! I am frightened, something is wrong!' Sanjit came charging into the breakfast room, without even knocking. That was unusual in itself; he was normally the most polite and unobtrusive servant in the household.

'What is it, man?' Wilfred stood up from the table, alarmed at Sanjit's agitation.

'*Sahib*, I went to fetch a trolley for the luggage, and when I returned to the motorcar with it the ladies were gone!'

'Gone? Had they found a trolley themselves?'

'No, *sahib*, the luggage was still there in the car but the ladies were gone. I checked in the station, I went to the platform and to the café and the ticket hall, and I found someone who checked in the facilities, but they were nowhere to be found!' Sanjit was running his hands through his hair, pacing back and forth as he spoke. 'They have vanished, pfft! Like that!'

'Calm down. I will go back there now and look again. The train they're booked on has not yet left, I am sure I will find them. You stay here in case they return.' Sanjit, Wilfred thought, was in no fit state to drive. He marched from the room and out to the front of the residence where Sanjit had left the car.

A few minutes later he was at the station, striding into the main building, scanning the crowds for Celia and Sita. He called a station porter to him. 'Have you seen an English girl of about fifteen, with dark hair, accompanied by a short middle-aged Indian woman?'

The porter stared at him wide-eyed and shook his head, then hurried away to return to his work. He possibly hadn't understood, Wilfred thought. He needed someone more senior. He found an official and demanded to be taken to the station manager.

'You need to stop all trains from leaving, and put someone at every exit to look for them. And call the local police. We need to search the surrounding area for them.'

'Sir, I cannot stop all trains from leaving. There is a timetable—' the station manager began, but Wilfred put a hand up to stop him.

'I don't care about your timetable. This is my daughter we are talking about. She has gone missing from *your* station, and I intend to hold you fully accountable until she is found.'

'Perhaps you ought to have taken better care of her,' the station manager said. Wilfred was astounded by the man's insolence. It was as well the British were leaving India, he thought, if the local population thought they could treat him like that.

'Perhaps you ought to take your station security more seriously,' he retorted, jabbing a finger at the man's chest.

'As I understand it, they had not yet come into the station. They were outside, in a car that was parked on the street. I do not think it is my problem,' the manager replied.

'Where else would they have gone?'

'To a shop, perhaps?'

It was a good idea, he had to admit. There were stalls and shops in the station's vicinity and perhaps they had wanted to buy something for the journey, some food or a book . . . Or one of them had forgotten to pack something and they'd decided to buy it in Agra before they left . . . Wilfred turned and half-ran out of the manager's office without saying another word. He had to check all the shops. Celia and Sita wouldn't get on a train without their luggage, which was still in the car. Maybe even now they were standing by the car, wondering why it had moved position, and were looking about for Sanjit.

He dashed outside but no, there was no sign of them near the car. People were milling about in the street, pushing carts, hawking wares, hurrying towards the station or over to the market area. He crossed the street and began checking in the nearby shops, asking the same question each time – had any of them seen a young English girl with a middle-aged Indian woman?

One shopkeeper nodded, but his face looked worried. 'They were standing by a car over there. They got into a van.'

'That car?' Wilfred pointed back to his own.

'Yes, *sahib*. Though it was parked in a different spot.'

'What van did they get into?'

'I don't know. There were some men.'

Wilfred stared at the shopkeeper, a knot of pure horror forming in his gut as the implications of this news sank in. Someone had taken Celia. For what purpose he had no idea. 'Men? What men? How many?'

The shopkeeper shrugged. 'Three men, I think.'

'Indian? English?'

'Indian.'

'Have you seen them before?'

'*Sahib* there are a lot of people living in this city. I do not know them all.'

'Were they roughly handled? Pushed into the van perhaps? Describe the van.'

'It was blue. I do not know what kind it was. They were pushed, I think. I do not know.' The shopkeeper was getting agitated now, and Wilfred realised he'd get little more from him. Better to go and alert the authorities so that a proper search could begin. And he could telephone the maharajah, who would be able to advise him, and who had men at his disposal who could help search.

He hurried back to the car and drove home, praying silently as he drove that somehow they'd have turned up back at the bungalow in his absence.

Sanjit met him at the door and one look at his face told Wilfred that no, they hadn't returned, but something else had happened.

'A note, *sahib*. Brought by a boy on a bicycle. It is addressed to you, *sahib*.'

'Put it on my desk, I've no time for that now.' Wilfred waved it away.

'Sir, I think it is to do with the ladies . . .'

Wilfred snatched it from Sanjit and tore open the envelope roughly, then scanned the single page of badly written English, the feeling of horror mounting with each word.

Your dorter will not be hurt if you do what we say. We want the dimond that is called the Chamakta Sitara. You bring it to this place by four o'clock today and you will get your dorter back. You come on your own. No police.

A ransom note! Wilfred read it twice more. There was an address given at the bottom – it was on the edge of the city, he thought. He mentally ran through his options. It was not possible to comply with the kidnappers' demands within the timescale.

The diamond was in a safe place much too far away. In any case, he had no intention of handing it over. Could he, somehow, give them an imitation jewel in its place? Would it be possible? His head was spinning with mad ideas, ways in which he could get Celia back safely.

Arriving at the location at four o'clock with a group of armed men could be achieved with the help of the maharajah, but might Celia be hurt if he did that? Or maybe he could go and offer money instead of the jewel. But how much would he offer? How much would the kidnappers want? The jewel was priceless. He didn't have the funds. Unless perhaps the kidnappers had no clue as to how much it was worth, and would accept . . . how much? Whatever he could give them? He could probably put together a few thousand rupees if he had a few days . . .

A plan was taking shape. He'd go at four o'clock on his own, and offer money, but he'd have to explain he needed time to get it together. He'd insist they release Celia to him today. They could keep Sita as assurance that he'd keep his word. Then when he had Celia, he'd go immediately to Delhi and book flights to England, and take her out of this damned country. He'd write to the governor to explain. He could leave Celia with Cyril and return on his own to complete his duties here.

Wilfred paced back and forth in his office, deciding how best to act. He needed to talk it through with someone. He needed advice. He picked up the telephone and dialled the number for the palace. The telephone was answered as usual by Arun Gupta, the maharajah's servant.

'Wilfred Fforbes-Whyte calling, to speak to the maharajah. Please tell him it is exceedingly urgent.'

'Of course, *sahib*, I shall fetch him at once.'

Wilfred waited a moment and then the maharajah, Devraj Kaur, was on the line. He quickly told him what had happened. Devraj made a few grunts of understanding as he spoke. 'This all sounds very frightening, Wilfred. What are you going to do?'

'I am calling for advice, Devraj. Of course I cannot give them the diamond. Should I get the police involved?'

'I think the police are too busy dealing with the riots, Wilfred. I do not think they will care about the fate of one girl and one woman. And the note says no police, didn't you say?'

'What if I offered money instead, do you think that would work?'

'Hmm. No, I do not think it would. They have specifically asked for the diamond, by its name. Perhaps because it is a sacred diamond for this state.'

This was not at all what Wilfred wanted to hear. 'But I cannot give it to them.'

'You must. Otherwise . . . I fear . . . who knows what these ruffians will do to your dear Celia? You cannot risk it, Wilfred.'

'I cannot risk Celia being hurt, you are right. But you don't understand. I *cannot* hand over the diamond at four o'clock today.'

'What? Do you mean you don't have it, Wilfred?' The maharajah sounded shocked.

'I took it . . . somewhere else . . . for safekeeping.'

'Where?'

'Somewhere safe. Out of Agra. I'm sorry, Devraj, but the fewer people who know its whereabouts the better, don't you think?'

'Then you must go to wherever you hid it, my friend, and fetch it back. It is the only way, Wilfred, to be sure they won't harm Celia or her *ayah*.' Devraj sounded exasperated.

'But I will not be able to retrieve it by four o'clock, Devraj.'

'Hmm.' There was the sound of scratching, as though Devraj was rubbing his chin. Wilfred imagined him deep in thought. He'd done the right thing, phoning Devraj. The maharajah had contacts, he had plenty of servants – he practically had an army he could call on. He'd have a solution.

'I suggest you set out immediately to fetch the diamond. This afternoon I will send Arun to meet the men and he will tell them that you agree to give them the diamond but that it will take longer. He can offer them money instead, in case they decide to take that option. And he will obtain assurances that they will look after Celia well in the meantime.'

'But won't they be expecting me? The note said I had to go on my own.'

'Arun is resourceful. He will be able to explain. Have faith, Wilfred. All will be well if you follow my suggestion.'

Wilfred considered. He realised he probably didn't have any other option but to do what Devraj suggested. 'All right. I will set off immediately. Promise me . . .'

'I promise I will do everything in my power to ensure dear Celia is kept safe, and her *ayah* also. Believe me, Wilfred. I would not like to see either of them harmed in any way. Arun is my trusted man, he will do a good job as liaison. Now, you should go, and I will speak to Arun. He will go to the place at four o'clock.'

'He'd better go alone or they'll think I've sent an army.'

'He will go alone. Goodbye, Wilfred. Travel safely.'

As Wilfred hung up, he felt cold with fear but at least he now had a plan formulating, though not quite the one the maharajah thought. There was not a moment to lose. To ensure the safety of both Celia and the diamond, he needed to go to Delhi and then London, and back as soon as possible. He grabbed his trusty metal briefcase and shoved a few items in it – a newspaper, his book, a few other things. He wasn't sure when the next flight to London was but the sooner he began the journey the sooner he'd have Celia back at his side, safe. At least, he hoped he'd get her back safely. The alternative didn't bear thinking about. He called to Sanjit to take him back to the station, this time so that he could catch the train to Delhi on the first leg of the long journey.

Chapter 23

Lisa, 2023

Lisa met Ryan the following Thursday night, in a trendy bar tucked into a Soho backstreet. Gaby had put them in touch, as she'd promised. 'You'll really like him, Lisa. I only met him once, but I think he's just your type.'

'What, like Rupert?' Lisa had been aghast.

Gaby had laughed. 'The exact opposite, mate.'

And so Lisa had contacted Ryan and they'd arranged to meet after work on Thursday. 'I might be a little frazzled when I arrive,' Ryan had said, 'but it'll be nothing that a couple of pints and some decent company can't sort out.' He'd seemed nice on WhatsApp and she was looking forward to meeting him. Even though he wasn't Ben, a little voice at the back of her head kept reminding her. Hopefully, spending an evening with Ryan would help her move on.

She arrived at the bar before him, and found a small table where she could watch the door and spot him as soon as she arrived. The bar was small and decorated with some huge floor-standing plants, which gave each table a bit of privacy from the others.

Lisa ordered herself a glass of wine to sip while she waited. She was a little early. Ryan had said he'd be there by seven, or sooner if he could manage it, so she'd arrived at six-thirty.

And now it was ten past seven and he still hadn't arrived. At what point should she send him a message, she wondered, but decided to give him another ten minutes. He worked, she knew, as an IT project management consultant, earning good money but being expected sometimes to stay late to deal with overrunning projects.

She'd almost finished her glass of wine and was beginning to wonder if she'd been stood up when he finally arrived, wearing a business suit with his tie slightly askew, and clutching a laptop bag. He entered the bar and stared about him, reminding her a little of a deer caught in headlights, before he spotted her. He gave an awkward wave and came over. 'Lisa? Sorry if I'm a bit late. Got hauled into a meeting at six that overran.'

'Not a problem. Can I get you a drink?' He looked like he needed a moment to compose himself.

'Ah, cheers. I'll get the next one then.'

'Sure. What'll you have?'

'Um . . .' Oh dear, Lisa thought. He had the expression of someone who looked as though choosing a drink was using up the last remaining bit of brain power he had. Conversation might be a little tough to get going, at least until he loosened up. He'd warned her of this; that he took a while to unwind after work. 'Drink. Yes, right, what are you having?'

'They do a nice Rioja here. I'm having that.'

'Yes, perfect.' He looked relieved he hadn't had to actually choose himself. Lisa went to the bar to get the drinks. First impressions, she thought, as she waited at the bar, is that he was probably a nice enough person who worked too hard.

She lingered over ordering the drinks, allowing another couple to be served before her, to give him time to relax. Out of the corner of her eye she could see he'd removed his tie, tucked his laptop under a seat, and was now jabbing at his phone and frowning. Still working, then. She sighed. This was quite possibly not going to be a good evening.

As she brought back a bottle of wine and two glasses, the bar's menu tucked under her arm, she noted with approval that Ryan had the grace to turn off his phone and slip it into his pocket. He smiled at her. 'Sorry again. That was the last email I'm responding to today. I know. It's rude.' He poured himself a large glass and took a long swallow of it before pouring hers.

'You look like you need that. Tough day?' she asked.

'They're all tough. So. Lisa. Tell me about yourself – job, favourite films, where you live, family. All the usual, eh?'

Well, that was one way to get the conversation started, she thought. She launched into a monologue about herself, aware that he still needed time to unwind. As she spoke, she got the impression he wasn't really listening. His mind was no doubt still on his work. And her mind was half on Ben, who had a way of listening to her speak as though she was the only person in the universe.

A few minutes later he poured himself a second glass. 'We're gonna need a bigger bottle,' he said, and she smiled at the reference to the film *Jaws*.

'Looks that way. So, your turn.'

'What?' He glanced at the half-empty bottle.

'Tell me about yourself.'

'Oh. You've finished? Sorry I was . . .'

'Not listening. I know.' She smiled. 'I could tell.'

'Yeah, just this project at work, it's kind of at a critical point. I'm not normally this distracted.'

'What's the project?' She offered him this as an opening, but he simply shrugged.

'Some financial system. Nothing of interest. You're in IT too, are you?'

'Sort of. Data analysis for the Civil Service.' She'd told him this not five minutes earlier.

'Ah, sorry, thought you worked for Capgemini. My bad. That was . . . someone else I had a date with. Didn't work out with her.'

And it's unlikely to work out with me. 'That's a shame.'

'Not really. It meant I was free to meet you. So, how do you know Gaby?' He topped up his glass again as he spoke.

'Known her since we were five years old. We started school together. You?'

'I only vaguely know her via a mutual friend. Look, I'll get us another bottle. I seem to be ploughing through this one. Rioja again, if that's all right with you?'

'Er, sure.'

He got up and went to the bar. She looked at the empty bottle in amazement. She'd only had one glass and that was still half full. He'd polished off the rest himself.

Ryan was back a moment later with another bottle, and a bag of crisps. 'Better soak up some of this alcohol,' he said, as he pulled the bag open. Lisa had been hoping to order a meal but he didn't look as though he was going to have anything more than crisps and wine.

After the first glass from the new bottle he did appear to relax and unwind, and began chatting about funny things his sister's dog had done. Lisa listened. She might have thought him amusing and good company if he'd started out like this, and if he wasn't well on the way to being drunk in less than an hour of them meeting.

She managed one small glass from the second bottle before that too was empty. By then, Ryan had gone beyond the funny, lively phase and was slurring his words, being belligerent towards someone who accidentally kicked his chair on the way past, making lewd suggestions to Lisa as to what they might do next. 'Yours or mine, eh? Ha ha. The ol' cliché. I'd say mine but s'not tidy. Not fit for a girl to see. S'go to yours, shall we?'

'Actually, I think we'll call it a night. It's been fun. I'm going to go now, Ryan. Work tomorrow.'

'Yeah, I've got work t'morrow too. But s'early yet.' He peered at his watch, clearly struggling to focus on it. 'Loads of time yet.'

She wanted to tell him he'd had too much to drink, but she'd seen enough to know that he was the type of drunk who wouldn't take kindly to that. Visions of the inebriated man on board the flight to Dublin ran through her mind, and now she just wanted to get away from him. 'I've got a really early start. Sorry, Ryan. Got to go.' She stood up and picked up her bag.

'Was just going to get another bottle,' he said, with a frown.

'Not for me. Bye, then.'

'I'll call you. I got your munber.'

She smiled at his mispronunciation and made a mental note to block his number. What had Gaby been thinking, saying that Ryan might be suitable for her? Gaby had said he was good-looking and good fun. Well, she couldn't deny he was easy on the eye, and she supposed that if you met him when he wasn't just out of work or three bottles in, you'd consider him good fun. But that had been a short window this evening. Quickly, before he could say anything more, she gave a cheery wave and left the pub, hurrying around the corner to lose herself in the Soho crowds. To be certain he hadn't managed to follow her she took a few quick turns, left and right, through the narrow streets of that part of the city, and then she ducked into a branch of Pret a Manger to get something to eat.

Seated at the back of the restaurant, in case Ryan went past, she pulled out her phone and messaged Gaby. *Date with Ryan over. Won't be repeating it.*

Oh? Darn it. Abi said he was a good bloke. The reply came quickly.

Thought you knew him?

No. Friend of a friend. I only met him once, at a wedding. Sorry it didn't work out.

He may be a nice bloke. Works too hard then drinks too much. And not Ben.

Lisa smiled wryly to herself. Gaby had hit the nail on the head, there. Ryan wasn't Ben. And, therefore, she didn't feel inclined to put in the effort to find out what sort of a person he was when he hadn't just come from a tough day in the office. Perhaps she wasn't being fair to him. Perhaps she ought to book a daytime date at the weekend with him to see what he was like then. But maybe it was better to step away and let him find someone else who wasn't obsessed with a man she couldn't have, someone who would give Ryan a chance, maybe even help him get that drinking under control.

You're right. He's not Ben, she replied to Gaby's message.

And then she smiled, remembering that in two days' time she was meeting Ben to get going with the research into the diamond's provenance. At least the date with Ryan had made it clear in her mind that there was no chance of moving on from Ben by finding someone else. She needed to put all her efforts into Ben, and that meant doing everything she could to help them succeed at finding the diamond's original owners.

As if by thinking of Ben she'd conjured him up, at that moment her phone rang, and it was him.

'Lisa, you free for a quick chat?'

'Yes, sure.' She pushed away her half-eaten food, which could wait until after the call.

'So I was going through boxes of papers in the family archive like I promised, and I found a bundle of letters from Wilfred to my great-grandfather, Cyril, and Cyril's diaries from when he was a child in India. I haven't read them all, but they're definitely of interest.'

'Do they mention the diamond?'

'Better than that.' She heard the sound of papers being shuffled around. 'I'll read you a bit of one of the letters. It's from October 1945. Wilfred goes on about having returned to Agra from Simla after an enjoyable summer season in the hills, then refers to the war being over, and Celia's growing up fast but they still both miss Alice, yada yada. And then it says, *The maharajah is throwing a party at the Shahi Palace next week. I am debating whether to allow Celia to attend. I don't think she is quite old enough to be trusted to behave, although Devraj has extended the invitation to her. She and Vijay continue to be friends, playing tennis daily since we returned from Simla. I think he lets her beat him on occasion.*'

'This maharajah he mentions . . . the palace . . . you don't think . . .'

'Yes. I think it might well be the same palace from where the diamond was looted during the Indian mutiny. Granddad said it was a palace in Agra, and that's where Wilfred lived and worked, and so it must be the same one.'

'Who are these people, Devraj and Vijay, that he mentions?'

'From what I've read in other letters, Devraj Kaur was the name of the maharajah. He was a friend of Wilfred, and had even been at university in England with him and Cyril. I think Vijay is his son, a friend of Celia's.'

'So . . .' Lisa was pondering the implications of this, 'on the assumption Devraj and Vijay are descendants of the person the diamond was stolen from in 1857 all we have to do is track them down, or rather, their descendants. I would guess Devraj is long gone but Vijay, if he was Celia's age, could possibly still be alive now.'

'He'd be pretty old. We're more likely looking for his son.'

Lisa coughed. 'Or his daughter.'

'Oops! Of course. But we have a surname, Lisa. It's a start. I'll bring the letters on Saturday. I've also ordered some books at the library to be put ready for us. Indian genealogy and history. Hopefully . . .'

'. . . we'll find the Kaur family from Agra,' she finished, grinning broadly. It was a good starting place.

'And with luck they're the right family,' Ben continued. 'If not, I don't know where we'll go from there.'

Chapter 24

Celia, July 1947

Celia could not tell for how long they'd been held. It must have been a few hours by now, definitely. She cursed the fact she had not put her watch on that day. It was too hot to wear it, and as so often at this time of year she'd decided not to. It was packed away in her luggage, that as far as she knew was still in the boot of Papa's car.

Papa. Would he know by now that she'd been taken? Had the kidnappers made their demands? Yet again she wondered what those demands might be, and whether Papa would agree to them.

'How are you, Sita?' she asked, for the hundredth time. Her *ayah* was sitting on the floor in a corner, her head bowed, shoulders slumped. She was handling the situation very poorly, Celia thought. So far, they had not been treated badly. She had bruises forming on her thigh and shoulder from being bundled into the back of the van, but on the plus side, they'd been brought fresh water and some bread and mangoes to eat. The room was basic but it was relatively cool, making Celia think that the building must have thick walls.

'I am so sorry,' Sita said, looking up at Celia with red-rimmed eyes.

'It's hardly your fault.'

'I should have protected you, stopped this happening.'

'Sita, you couldn't have. There were three big men and we had no chance against them.' Celia felt vaguely irritated by the way Sita was acting, as though it was all her fault. Even though Papa had said Sita was in charge, it wasn't as though Celia was still a small child who needed looking after. Sita hadn't failed to protect her – there'd been nothing she could have done.

Sita sniffed and dipped her head again. No matter what Celia said or did, there seemed to be no consoling her. It was odd. Celia had always thought of Sita as a strong, brave woman. She'd have imagined it would take more than this to frighten her. But Sita hadn't struggled against the men when they were grabbed at the station, or even shouted anything at them. Not like Celia had. And now, all the older woman could do was cry. To be sure, the situation was scary – they had no idea what was going to happen to them or what the kidnappers wanted – but for now they were safe enough. Surely it was better to stay calm, to keep a grip of one's emotions and spend their time working out a plan to escape, in case a chance to get away presented itself? But whenever she'd suggested this to Sita, the other woman had shaken her head and commenced sobbing once more. It was better to leave her be. If she wanted to wallow in self-pity, let her.

It was up to her, Celia realised, to work out a plan. The next time one of the men opened the door to bring them something, she was going to question him. So far the men hadn't responded to anything she'd said. But next time she'd ask in Hindi. Perhaps they didn't realise she spoke the language, but Sita had taught her the basics over the years. Perhaps the men didn't speak English. Maybe if she spoke in Hindi, they'd answer her. The more information – any information – she could get out of them the more likely she'd be able to formulate an escape plan.

She thought too of Vijay. He, or rather his father, had a lot of influence in this town. If she could somehow get a message to him, he would talk to his father and they'd manage to do something to release her and Sita. But how could she do this? How could she get in touch with Vijay? What might she say to one of the captors to manage it? Perhaps she could offer money if they'd bring her writing materials and then deliver a note? She had only a little money on her, but maybe it'd be enough . . .

She lay down on the hard little bed that was positioned against one side of the room to think. If they had to stay overnight, she and Sita would have to share the narrow bunk. It'd be uncomfortable, but that would be the least of their problems.

Judging by the angle of the sun that she could just about see through the bars of the single, small window in the room, Celia reckoned it must be midafternoon when she heard voices again. Male voices, right outside their room. And one voice was familiar. She listened hard. She'd expected – she'd hoped – to hear Papa or Sanjit but it was neither.

'Sita, listen.' She beckoned Sita to join her by the door. 'That voice. That one, there! Do you recognise it?' She spoke in an urgent whisper.

Sita stared at her wide-eyed but shook her head. 'No, *meri jaan*. I do not know who that is.'

'I do. It's Arun Gupta. The maharajah's man. He's answered the telephone to me often enough, so I recognise his voice. What's he saying?' He was speaking Hindi, and she could only catch some of the words. She listened hard again, but then there was the sound of the bolts being pulled back. Her stomach gave a lurch. Were they free? Had Papa asked the maharajah for help and he'd sent Arun to negotiate?

But it was one of their captors who came through the door. He was holding a heavy stick.

'Get back. Away from the door,' he barked, in English. Well, that was interesting, Celia thought. So they, or this one at least, did speak English. She caught hold of Sita's arm and pulled her back towards the bed.

Behind the man were the other two, and Arun was with them. He nodded when he saw her. Was he just checking they were alive and well? It seemed so, for the man with the stick immediately began closing the door.

This was it, possibly her only chance. 'Arun, tell Vijay where we are!' Celia screamed out as the door closed. Whether Arun had heard or not, whether he'd tell Vijay and whether it'd make any difference at all to their plight, remained to be seen. Why she thought it would help if Vijay knew, when she was already aware that the maharajah must know of what had happened or why else would Arun have been there, she couldn't say. But somehow the chance that Vijay, her lovely, dependable Vijay, would learn of their kidnapping made her feel a tiny bit better. He'd always looked after her, and he'd help her now if he could, she knew. She crossed her fingers as she thought of him.

'We'll be all right, Sita,' she said. 'Arun will report back, the maharajah will send men, and we will be freed. You'll see.' She hoped there'd be no violence involved in rescuing them.

But her words just prompted another wave of sobbing from Sita. Her *ayah's pallu* was sopping wet now, as she kept using it to wipe her face. There was nothing Celia could say to her to help. She sighed and went to sit down once more on the narrow bed. 'Sit beside me, Sita?'

Sita simply shook her head in response and resumed her previous position on the floor, leaning against a wall, her head in her hands. Celia shrugged. It was better to leave her be. Who'd have guessed Sita would be so useless in a crisis? Celia poured herself a drink of water and settled down to wait. There was nothing more she could do.

Later, as darkness fell, she heard sounds of distant rioting. So they were in a part of the city where the riots had been occurring, were they? There was no need for her to gather clues as to where they were, as the maharajah must know. But in case there was some way they could get out, it'd be useful to have an idea of where they were so she'd know which direction to run in.

The room they were in had no electric lights. A meal was delivered to them just before darkness fell – one of the captors opened the door and brought it in but as before, did not respond when Celia spoke to him in both English and Hindi. He simply placed a bowl of *dal* and some *rotis* on the floor. Not much but it was better than nothing.

Celia ate, but Sita took only one bite and declared herself not hungry. 'Come on, Sita. We need to keep our strength up.' But nothing she could say was helping to lift the other woman out of the pit of despair she seemed to have fallen into.

Celia lay down again on the little bunk. She might as well try to sleep, she thought. There really wasn't anything else to do. The distant sounds of rioting – the gunshots, shouts, screams and small explosions – abated after a while, and she dozed off.

She was woken by the sound of her name being called, urgently whispered. It wasn't Sita, who'd curled up on the floor and was snoring gently. The door to the room was still firmly closed. The voice came from the window. 'Who is it?' she whispered back.

'It's me. Vijay. I'm here, Cee.'

'Vijay!' She went to the window and yes, there he was, on the other side of the bars. She reached a hand through and he caught it and held it tightly.

'Are you all right, Cee?'

'Yes, we haven't been hurt. Sita just keeps crying. Vijay, I don't know what's going on! Why are we being held? Who are those men? Arun came . . .'

'Yes, I saw him, and I made him tell me where you were.'

'So your father knows too?' Celia frowned a little that Vijay had had to *make* Arun tell him where she was.

'Yes.'

Something about Vijay's answer seemed cagey. 'What do they want?'

'They want your father's diamond. The *Chamakta Sitara*.'

'The diamond!' Celia wanted to spit. 'How do they even know about it? I mean, it's not as if it's been recently taken. My family have had it for a hundred years.' She spoke carefully, waiting to see what Vijay's response would be. If only she could see his face, to gauge his reaction. But it was too dark to see his expression.

'It is my father who wants it,' Vijay said quietly. 'You know that it was originally in my family's possession, until it was stolen during the mutiny?'

'And these men will sell it to him, perhaps?' Was that the game? They thought that if they could get the diamond, they could then sell it to the maharajah?

'These men have been paid to do this, Cee. My father doesn't know I'm here. He doesn't know that I know what he's been up to. Arun wasn't going to tell me where you were, but I have a hold over him – I once saw him steal from my father and I've kept it quiet. I told him I'd tell Father of his crime and that was enough to make him come clean to me.'

'Your father . . . is he the one who paid the men to kidnap us? Are you saying *he's* behind this?' Celia could not believe what she was hearing.

There was silence for a moment, and Celia could hear Vijay sigh heavily. At last he spoke. 'Cee, this was nothing to do with me – you know that? And I am one hundred per cent positive my father would not allow you to be harmed in any way. He wanted only to put pressure on your father to return the diamond to its rightful owners.'

'That bloody diamond.' Celia never swore but if ever there was a moment to curse, this was it.

'Yes.'

Celia's mind was spinning with what she'd heard and what it meant for her and Sita. 'Papa has hidden it away somewhere. Out of the city, I think.' She realised with horror that meant she and Sita wouldn't be getting out of there any time soon, as it would take ages for Papa to retrieve the diamond, even if he did agree to exchange it for her. 'So, what happens now? Will you tell your father to let us go?'

'If I say a word to him he will want to know how I know, and he'll be angry, and Arun will lose his job for telling me where you are, and there's no saying what my father will do next.'

'Go to my father, then.'

'Your father is not at home. I went there first. Sanjit would not tell me where he was, only that he had received a ransom note. He was in a terrible state, blaming himself for not guarding you. Of course I could not say anything about my father's part in this. And then Sanjit told me he'd dropped your father at the station, and that he was talking about catching a train to Delhi.'

'Delhi! That's not where he's stored it, I'm sure.' Celia had envisaged it tucked away in a bank vault in Agra, or perhaps in Papa's safe in their Simla house. And then with horror she guessed what he was doing. 'He's running away! He's abandoning me! He's taking the diamond as far away as he can from the kidnappers. I always knew he loved that diamond more than me!' To her shame, tears began to fall.

'Oh, Cee. I can't believe it of him.'

'What, then?'

'I don't know. But Cee, I'll get you out. I'll think of something. You won't be hurt, I promise, and—' He broke off at the sound of shouts and crashes coming from somewhere nearby. 'I've got to go, Cee. I'll be back.'

'Vijay, don't take any risks—' But he was gone, and Celia suddenly felt completely alone, despite the presence of Sita who'd slept through it all. She must need the sleep, Celia thought, after all that crying. Hopefully, she'd be more positive and therefore more use in the morning.

She went back to the narrow bunk and sat down, considering

what she'd heard. The shouts outside subsided quickly. She hoped they were just from rioters nearby, and not from anyone connected with their kidnap who might harm Vijay if they found him at the window. So the maharajah had done this to get the diamond back? And Papa was going to Delhi to ensure the diamond was well out of reach. She couldn't believe it. Even though their relationship had been strained, surely she meant more to him than a piece of carbon? But it was clear she'd get no help from him to get her out.

Would Vijay be able to do anything? Without endangering himself? Or would it be just down to her and Sita to save themselves?

She lay down on the bunk, her mind whirling with all the questions, and waited in vain for sleep to wash over her.

Chapter 25

Lisa, 2023

As Lisa travelled across London on her way to the British Library on Saturday, taking the tube to Euston then walking the short distance from there, she couldn't help but think that even though the library was the obvious place to go to for research, she had absolutely no idea how they'd actually do it. Even with a name, how do you track down a family in India, starting from the mid-1800s, following generations forwards rather than backwards, to find living descendants? She just had to hope that Ben had more ideas than she had. It would be weird seeing him again, after what happened in Dublin, but he was still Ben; she knew she'd enjoy his company just as a friend. And if they did manage to get anywhere with the research it might just give them another chance. As she entered the library, she told herself to stop thinking along those lines. It could all come to nothing.

Ben arrived a minute after her, carrying a small, battered rucksack. He grinned as he approached her and gave her a quick peck on the cheek. 'Hi, Lisa. Thanks for agreeing to help me with this. Must admit, it feels like being a student again, turning up at a library ready for a day's research. And at the weekend and all!'

She chuckled. 'Yes. Back then if you'd told me I'd be doing this for fun on a Sunday I'd have laughed you out of town. But I genuinely want to get to the bottom of it all. What does your father think about us doing research to find the original owners?'

'Hmm. I haven't told him. I thought it best if we see how far we get with this first. Maybe if we're successful I'll be able to talk him into returning the diamond, but there's no point starting that conversation until I know it's possible.'

She gazed at him, into those gorgeous brown eyes. 'Ben, I really, really hope we are successful.'

'So do I, Lisa.'

They went through the library to the reading desks that had been assigned to them and took their seats. Ben pulled out a folder of documents and laid them on the desk. 'The letters I told you about. I haven't read them all.' He'd already ordered a few books on Indian history and those were stacked on the desk ready for them. Lisa looked through the pile. It was going to be a heavy morning.

'Ben, I have no idea where we start with this!'

He picked up one of the books and flicked it open. 'A genealogy of the maharajahs of northern India. Family trees and everything. So, here we go.'

Lisa grinned. 'Excellent. Want me to look at that book?'

'Maybe read these letters? Don't worry, there's nothing private in them. Wilfred and Cyril were somewhat estranged so these are just duty letters really. They seemed to write to each other just once or twice a year. But there might be more useful details in them.'

'OK. Pass them over.' She took her own notebook out of her bag and set to work, reading the letters. There were a few rather stilted letters from the early 1930s from which she gathered that the estrangement between the brothers began in their university days and involved a woman. Alice. It seemed that Cyril had been dating Alice before Wilfred muscled in. Cyril had never forgiven him, even though he'd later found someone else – Winnie – and married her. Lisa recalled the photo of the 1930s bride wearing the brooch. She felt annoyed at Ben's long-gone great-grandfather for holding a grudge against his brother for so long over this. Surely Alice had had a say in which brother she married? If she'd cared more for Cyril, she'd never have married Wilfred. She glanced over at Ben who was poring over genealogical charts in a book but decided not to say anything. For all she knew, there could have been more to it than that.

She read on. There were letters passing on news of the birth of Celia, one that included arrangements for Wilfred, Alice and young Celia to come to England for Cyril's wedding in 1938, and another congratulating Cyril and Winnie on the birth of Ben's grandfather, James. There was correspondence from the war years, in which it seemed both brothers were pleased to be just that bit too old to join up and fight for their country. There was a letter from Wilfred about the death of his beloved Alice, then one offering condolences to Cyril on the loss of his wife Winnie.

> *Tragically we are both now widowers. Both our wives wore the Chamakta Sitara on their wedding days. Coincidence? Or do you think there could be something in the legend of the curse? After all, our mother and grandmother also died prematurely. I find I am half-dreading the day when Celia is old enough to attend the sorts of events where she would be expected to wear it. Perhaps I am growing superstitious. You will tell me it is all rubbish, of course you will. And of course it is. I sometimes wish Grandfather had never acquired the diamond. Perhaps I should cross out this entire paragraph before sending this letter.*

But he hadn't crossed it out, Lisa noted. He'd written another couple of pages filled with news and thoughts about current affairs. And he'd sent it. She put that letter to one side to show to Ben, and read on.

There was a letter dated December 1946 mentioning a brief visit Wilfred and Celia had paid to England, lamenting the fact that he and Cyril had not managed to get on better.

> *Now we are older and dear Alice is no longer with us, I wish we could put it all behind us. In time I shall be moving back to England when India gains its independence, and I should like to think we can be friends and have a closer relationship than hitherto.*

A letter from 1947 interested her next. In it, Wilfred was making arrangements to come to England.

> *I shall bring Celia, put her in a suitable school to make an English lady of her. I shall put the diamond brooch into a safe deposit box at my bank and try to forget it even exists. Devraj says I should not bring it out of India, and reminds me of the shady means by which our grandfather acquired it . . .*

'Bingo!' She couldn't help herself squealing. A woman at a nearby desk glanced up and frowned. Lisa mouthed a 'sorry'.

'What?' Ben looked up from the book he was studying.

'Wilfred's writing about putting the diamond in a bank safe deposit box. He says, *Devraj . . . reminds me of the shady means by which our grandfather acquired it from his family*. So Devraj definitely knew of the diamond, refers to its provenance and therefore must be the descendant of the maharajah from whom it was stolen!'

'Yes, I was pretty certain, but great to get it confirmed from those letters.'

'And it sounds like he was planning to put the diamond in a bank in England, when he brought Celia.'

'But they were involved in the plane crash on the way.'

'Yes. I think that must be what happened. So very sad.' Lisa recalled the house and school details that were in the case. 'And the house details must have been from the earlier trip in 1946.'

Ben nodded. 'That must be it. So, in 1946 he and Celia were making arrangements for post-independence, looking at houses and schools and the like. Then they'd gone back to India. I would imagine Wilfred needed to do his job right up until independence day, though they actually left a little bit before.'

Lisa considered. 'What about the letter, though? The one Wilfred wrote to Celia on the day of the crash? Seems odd for him to have written to his daughter if she was there with him.'

Ben shrugged. 'Perhaps he was too reserved to tell her his feelings in person. We can't ever know what was in his mind. Next job is to determine what happened to Devraj Kaur and Vijay Kaur, and find any descendants they might have.'

'How?'

'Well, I'm hoping I'll get some clues in these books.' He tapped the pile of books about Indian princes.

'Let me help.' Lisa picked up one that covered Indian nobility post-independence and flicked to the index, looking for 'Kaur' or 'Agra'.

They worked in silence for some time. Ben pulled a laptop out of his rucksack and logged onto the library's Wi-Fi. 'I can use the library's subscription to various genealogy websites, that might help,' he told Lisa. 'Though it's hard tracking people forward.'

A little while later he nudged her and pointed to something on his screen. 'Birth of Vijay Kaur,' he said, grinning. 'And I've found a reference to Devraj's death, but not Vijay's. He might still be alive.'

'Yes, but living where?'

'Well . . . quite possibly in the same palace in Agra where his family always lived. So if we can find some contact details, a phone number, or an email address . . .'

It was Lisa's turn to grin. 'Or, perhaps we can simply find the postal address of the palace and then write him a letter, the old-fashioned way? That way, even if Vijay himself doesn't receive the letter someone, probably his descendant, will. If the palace still exists – but we can easily check that.'

'How?'

'What did it say in that letter Wilfred wrote about going to a party at the palace? The *Shahi* Palace, wasn't it?' She pulled out her phone and opened up Google Maps, searched for 'Agra' then searched for 'Shahi Palace'. To her delight a large building on the edge of the city was pinpointed. 'There. It still exists. So we can simply write to him.'

'We could do exactly that. You're a genius, Lisa!'

She grinned with pleasure at his praise, and they high-fived each other. A middle-aged woman at the next desk frowned at them and held a finger to her lips. Ben made a face like a child caught misbehaving by a teacher and Lisa had to stifle a giggle. She couldn't remember ever having such an enjoyable time in a library before. And best of all, their success meant they were a step closer to being able to be together. She hadn't dared mention that to Ben in case he'd changed his mind about her and was no longer interested in her romantically, but his excitement at each new piece of information they found suggested that he still was.

By the time Ben and Lisa left the library they had several pages of handwritten notes on the Kaur family and had determined the full address of the palace near Agra where they'd lived. 'So I'll write to Vijay Kaur at that address and I'll let you know what happens,' Ben said. He pulled a face. 'I'll also talk to Dad about taking the diamond back. I think we should. And it's time I stood up to him, as it's definitely the right thing to do.'

Lisa's stomach flipped over at his use of 'we'. 'Yes, though your father probably ought to agree to it.'

'Yep. That'll be the interesting part, getting his approval,' Ben said with a wry smile.

Outside the library Lisa turned to him. 'So, I'd better let you get home, then. You've lots to do still.'

'Yes.' But he didn't move. He continued standing there in front of her, his eyes fixed on hers. 'We're nearer, Lisa. Just need to persuade Dad, and hopefully hear back from Vijay or his descendant . . .'

'Long way to go, still.' She gazed at him, longing for him to take her in his arms and kiss her the way they had on that starlit night on the banks of the Thames. But he just gave her a half-smile then turned and walked away. All she could do was watch him go and hope that he'd be successful in his two missions.

Other than a text thanking her for her help, Lisa didn't hear from Ben again for almost a fortnight. And then she received a phone call on Thursday evening.

'Hi, Lisa. Just calling to . . . well, to update you. Thought you'd want to know the latest, regarding the diamond brooch? If you're still interested?'

Oh yes, I'm still interested, in you as well as the brooch, she thought. 'Yes, definitely. Go on, then. Don't keep me in suspense!'

'Ha. Well, the letter plan worked. I sent Vijay Kaur an airmail letter, and he's responded by email, which arrived this morning. He's an old man in his nineties now, as we'd worked out.'

'Wow! Well done!'

'He says he knows of the brooch; he remembers seeing Alice Fforbes-Whyte wearing it when he was a child. He also recalls his father often saying the diamond rightfully belonged to their family. And he hints that it was the cause of . . . hold on, let me open the email and get the wording right . . . ah, yes. The cause of "some upset between the two families".'

That was intriguing. 'Wonder what that was?' Lisa said.

'Probably what we read in the letters, about Devraj Kaur

reminding Wilfred about the "shady" way the diamond was acquired. I've emailed back to ask if he can elaborate on it. I'm waiting for a response, but I thought you'd want to know I've made contact.'

'Yes, thanks. Has he asked for the diamond back? Has your dad agreed?'

Ben spluttered. 'No, of course not. I told him I was sending a letter to Vijay, and he told me I was a damned fool, and that no matter what, he was not giving up the diamond to some unknown person.'

'Oh.'

'Anyway, I have a bit of a plan brewing. I'll call you again if there are any updates.'

It was only a day later that he called again, during her lunch hour. She took the call while sitting in her favourite café, a half-eaten salad in front of her.

'So, I told you I heard from Vijay?' Ben said. 'We've exchanged a couple of emails now.'

'Yes. Did he tell you anything more about whatever the "upset" between the two families was about?'

'No. He's being cagey on that. I don't blame him. He doesn't know me from Adam, and if it was Wilfred who did something to upset his father, perhaps he'd think that telling me about it might put me off. He's . . . kind of cautiously friendly in tone.'

'He sounds like a nice man.'

'Yes, I think he genuinely is.' Ben was silent for a moment. 'You know, I'd rather like to meet him.'

'You mean, go to India?' Lisa widened her eyes. Vijay Kaur was an old man. If Ben was going to visit, he'd be well advised to do it sooner rather than later.

'Yes. And . . . I want to take the diamond with me and give it back to him.'

'Has your father changed his mind about that then?' Lisa was puzzled. Ben hadn't mentioned any more discussions with David Fforbes-Whyte about returning the jewel.

'No, he hasn't. But one way or another I'm going to take the diamond with me.' He sighed. 'I think it's the only way.'

'The only way?' She frowned, confused.

'To break the curse.' He spoke quietly, almost in a whisper, as if not wanting anyone around him to overhear.

He still believed in it, then. Lisa was weighing up how to respond when Ben spoke again, earnestly.

'Lisa, that incident on the plane . . . you know how it unnerved me. I know it's all rubbish, I know I'm being ridiculous even entertaining this superstitious nonsense, but I can't help myself. I *cannot* allow anything bad to happen to you. And yet it did, or nearly did, that weekend. I can *feel* it's due to the influence of the diamond, and it's because it's still in my family's possession. The curse is still potent. So somehow, one way or another, I have to restore the diamond to its rightful owners. To Vijay.'

She stared down at her salad, wondering if he was saying what she thought he was saying. 'And if you do . . .?'

'If I give it back, it breaks the curse. I believe that. I *have* to believe it. And then I'm free . . .'

'Free?'

'To date you. If you still want to, that is.' There was a note of longing in his tone.

Lisa's heart leapt at his words and she felt a blush rising to her cheek. 'Ben, yes. I do still want to. Very much. The more I see you, the more I—' She broke off, not wanting to say too much, in case it put him off. 'You know that I don't believe the diamond can possibly have an influence. But I respect your belief that it does, and in your situation, losing your mum so young and everything, I might well have felt the same way. If you're sure you want to give it a go – give *us* a go – then you're right. We must take the diamond back to Vijay.'

'We?'

'Yes.' She hadn't realised herself, until the moment she said it, how much she wanted to be with him if or when he made this trip to India. 'Yes. I'll come with you, if that's all right. I'd like to meet Vijay. I'd like to talk to him, hear his stories, hear what he remembers of Wilfred and Celia.' She was thinking of that letter Wilfred had written to his daughter. The sealed letter that Celia had never read.

'Really? You really want to go too?' He sounded astonished. Delighted, also.

She grinned. 'Yes. If you can persuade your father to give up the brooch, I'll come with you to return it to its rightful owner. I've never been to India, and I'd like to. Agra, the Taj Mahal, I'd love to visit that!'

'Would you be able to get the time off work at short notice? Because if I can persuade Dad, I think we'd need to go as soon as possible, before he changes his mind. Next week, even.'

So soon! 'I can provisionally book the time off, yes. I'll do that this afternoon.'

'Right then, it's a date. At least, it'll be a date when we've handed back the diamond, if you see what I mean.'

'Can't wait!'

'There are lots of hoops to jump through first, I'm afraid.' Ben's tone was more reserved now. 'First I've got to persuade Dad to give up the diamond. That won't be easy – you heard yourself how reluctant he is. Then we've got to book flights and a hotel and arrange everything with Vijay. And then—' He broke off, and gasped.

'What?'

'You and me, on a plane together again . . . Oh, God.'

'Ben, it'll be all right. It won't happen again. Flying is statistically one of the safest forms of travel.'

'You're right, I suppose. I just won't . . . be able to relax, until that blasted brooch is in Vijay Kaur's possession.'

Chapter 26

Wilfred, July 1947

Never had the journey to Delhi taken so long. Wilfred hated that all the time he was travelling he was out of contact with the maharajah, and had no idea how the kidnappers had responded to Arun's message. He had no way of knowing whether they'd accepted that it would take time to retrieve the diamond. He didn't even know how Celia was, whether she was being looked after, or how she was bearing up under the strain of being held captive. She was strong, feisty and determined. All those qualities that had made it hard for him to be her father were almost certainly helping her through her ordeal. He hoped so. He longed to hear whether Arun had seen her, whether she'd sent back any message. But all he could do now, during the long hours sitting on a train to Delhi, then on the taxi journey to the airport, was brood.

Brood on how his relationship with Celia had deteriorated so badly. Consider how different things might have been if Alice had survived. Contemplate about what might happen if the kidnappers didn't believe he was fetching the diamond or weren't prepared to wait for him.

No. Not that last one. He didn't dare. Celia, dear Celia, was his only child. He loved her – of course he did, he was her father. They'd been through rough times, and they'd grown apart in recent years. He knew that and he hated it. She was growing up, becoming a woman, becoming her own woman. She was no longer the little girl who worshipped her daddy, who treated him as though he was some sort of wise deity who knew everything. She'd developed her own mind. And that was a good thing, wasn't it? You didn't want to raise children to never think for themselves. It was hard, though, when they first started doing it and you realised you were no longer the one in total control.

But he was still her father. And he'd do anything for her. Anything to keep her safe, to get her out of the clutches of these kidnappers. As Devraj had said, the best thing he could do was fetch the diamond. In the meantime, Devraj had promised to do whatever he could to negotiate, maybe even to get Celia released as soon as possible, providing that Wilfred would hand over the diamond as soon as he was able to. And Sita! He mustn't forget Sita, who'd been such a loyal servant for so long.

Had all this happened because of the curse? Devraj had warned him that he shouldn't take the diamond out of India. But he had. The diamond was in London. In a safe deposit box at a branch of the Midland Bank. It had seemed like a good idea to leave it there, back in March, when the riots were ramping up across India, but he regretted that decision now. If he'd left it somewhere in India he would now be in possession of it, in a much more powerful negotiating position.

Well, he was going to bring it back. Whether he'd hand it over to the kidnappers or not remained to be seen. There might, he still hoped, be another way. Though of course, Celia's safety was of paramount importance.

He arrived at the airport and hurried over to the ticket office to buy a ticket for the first possible flight out. Thankfully, there was a BOAC flight later that day for London via a couple of refuelling stops, and Wilfred was able to get a ticket. 'No. I have no luggage other than my briefcase,' he told the clerk at the ticket office. The clerk raised his eyebrows but Wilfred was in no mood to explain.

His next job was to find a telephone and place a long-distance call to Devraj. It was past four o'clock, and Arun would have arrived back at the palace by now. He'd be able to report on whether Celia was all right, whether she was coping, if she'd been hurt at all . . . His heart gave a lurch. If she was hurt, what would he do? Rush back to Agra and go to see the kidnappers himself? He should never have left. He should have stayed and negotiated with them himself. He could have persuaded them to take money in place of the diamond, perhaps with a promise (that he'd never fulfil) to give them the diamond later . . .

He found a travel agent who had a telephone he could use for a price, and made the call. It took several minutes to connect via the operator. At last, he heard the ring tone, but it was not Arun Gupta who picked up the phone, but the maharajah himself.

'Ah, Wilfred, I guessed it would be you. You are in the process of fetching the diamond?'

'Yes. But what news from Arun? Did he see Celia? Is she well? Is she hurt?'

'He did, and she is well. She has not been hurt. The *ayah* is also well.'

'And would the kidnappers listen to him? Would they accept money in place of the jewel? I could come back immediately and pay them, then fetch the diamond later . . .' And bring Celia to London with me, he thought.

Devraj let out a snort. 'No. They would not negotiate. They have promised not to hurt Celia or her *ayah* while you are away. But they want the *Chamakta Sitara*. They will accept nothing else.'

'And you trust them to keep their word?'

'They will keep it if you keep your word, my friend. You must not try to cheat them in any way. I fear that would change things for the worse. So now it is up to you. Retrieve the jewel with all haste and bring it straight to me.'

'To you? But—' Wilfred had imagined going straight to the kidnappers, handing over the brooch as Celia ran sobbing into his arms. Going to the palace first would surely just delay the transaction needlessly?

'While you are away, I will have Arun make arrangements for the handover. Your daughter in exchange for the diamond. So you must come to me with it first, to learn what the arrangements are.'

Wilfred sighed. That made sense. And maybe Devraj would come up with a plan, which meant the brooch wouldn't need to be handed over after all. 'Very well, I will do that. Thank you, Devraj. If there is any way you can think of, to get Celia released safely before I return . . .'

'I will take the necessary steps.'

'Thank you. I will be in touch again, when I return from London.'

As Wilfred hung up he pondered his good fortune that the maharajah was his friend. Devraj was certainly being a great help through this awful ordeal. An awful thought crossed his mind. When he returned to the palace with the diamond, might Devraj want to keep it for himself? He'd sometimes said the diamond properly belonged to his family. When it was in the hands of these unknown kidnappers he'd have no chance of getting it back. Was there a danger Devraj would double-cross him? Was *that* why he was insisting Wilfred brought the diamond to him first?

As soon as he had this thought Wilfred dismissed it. Devraj was a good and loyal, long-term friend. They'd known each other for so many decades. They'd overlapped during their time at Oxford as students, albeit Wilfred being a couple of years ahead of Devraj. Their children were the best of friends. No, there was no possibility that Devraj would do such a thing. He'd be saddened that the diamond would be out of his reach but happy that Celia was released unharmed. Devraj was fond of Celia, Wilfred had always thought. He was doing everything he could to secure her freedom. All Wilfred had to do was get on that aeroplane out of Delhi, and then on the planes that would take him on subsequent legs of the journey, retrieve that blasted diamond, then do the whole journey in reverse.

There was a bar at the airport, and he went in and ordered a double brandy. Early to be drinking but he needed fortifying, and there were a couple of hours to wait before his flight. As he slumped back in the deep-buttoned leather seats he pondered the situation. The diamond had brought his family nothing but bad luck. All the women, all the Englishwomen in his family who'd worn the brooch had died young.

Devraj had always said the diamond was cursed, and that if it was taken out of India, possessed by a non-Indian, its magic would cause anyone who wore it to suffer an untimely death. Wilfred had always dismissed this as superstitious mumbo-jumbo, something Devraj was saying as a feeble ploy to get Wilfred to give him the diamond back. Indeed, when they were students at Oxford, hadn't they joked about it? *The Curse of the Shining Star Diamond.* 'Sounds like a book Agatha Christie might write,' Devraj had said back then, with a laugh.

'More like a Sherlock Holmes mystery, I'd say,' Wilfred had responded and the two had spent an hour or so coming up with a crazy plot for a book with that title.

But perhaps there was something in it. Perhaps the diamond *was* cursed. In which case, Wilfred was glad that at least Celia would now never wear it. She would never risk the curse becoming true for her. Now, he couldn't wait to be rid of the thing and to have Celia safely back in his care.

One thing he promised himself – the moment he had her back, he'd take her to England. He'd allow her time to say her goodbyes to Sita and Vijay, and then he'd take her on the next possible flight home. He could leave her with Cyril while he returned to India to tie up loose ends in the run-up to independence. She'd be safer in England. If only he'd thought of this before – he could have taken her with him back in March when he'd taken the diamond away. Both she and it would be safe now.

As he finally boarded the aeroplane for the first leg of the journey, he cursed himself for having not taken better care of her. That would all change when he got her back. *If* he got her back.

Chapter 27

Lisa, 2023

After Ben's call, and her decision to go to India with him as soon as he had his father's permission to return the diamond, Lisa could think of little else. All weekend she imagined what it would be like – a week or so in Agra, perhaps visiting Delhi too, meeting Vijay Kaur, seeing the Taj Mahal . . . and being in Ben's company throughout, without the 'curse of the diamond' hanging over him. She dared not think too much about what might happen between them, in case . . . something went wrong, something changed.

To take her mind off Ben, she spent some time in her apartment going back through all her notes about the provenance of the diamond, the Kaur and Fforbes-Whyte families and the plane crash. She reread the Wikipedia article she'd found way back at the beginning of the research and something struck her.

'That . . . can't be right,' she muttered, but she read it back again and, assuming Wikipedia had the correct facts, it was right. It made no sense, and blew their assumptions about what had happened out of the water.

She messaged Ben. *Just rereading Wikipedia re the plane crash in which Wilfred and Celia died. We have it wrong – the plane was en route TO India, not from it. Wilfred was bringing the diamond from London back to India, not the other way round. Why? Why would they be going back to India when they were planning to leave it for good?*

He replied quickly. *Must have been making some arrangements for houses, schools etc. But my grandfather's story was that he was in the process of moving back to England when the crash happened. Perhaps he had it wrong? He was only a child when it happened.*

She pondered this – it would explain the house details that had been in the case, that she'd assumed were from the earlier 1946 visit. She sent another message. *But why would he bring the diamond with him?*

Perhaps he never liked to be parted from it. Perhaps he always travelled with it.

It must be that, she decided. She'd been so certain that Ben's family legend was correct, and that Wilfred was on his way to London when the plane crashed. It didn't really matter – the end result was the same. He and his daughter had died; the diamond had been lost for decades, but now it was found and soon, if David Fforbes-Whyte would listen to reason, it would be restored to its original owners.

'Good weekend?' Justin asked, when Lisa settled at her desk on Monday morning.

'Yes, thanks. Didn't do much, though.'

'Didn't you see that chap you keep talking about? Ben, isn't it?' Justin waggled his eyebrows suggestively at her. 'I had the impression you were rather keen on him, going off to Dublin to see a rugby match with him, him saving your life on the plane and everything.'

'Yes, I like him but... nothing happening there.' *Yet*, she wanted to add, but stopped herself. She couldn't stop the corners of her mouth twitching into a smile though.

Justin laughed. 'Soon though, I'm betting, eh? Good on you. He sounds a lot better than that tosser Rupert. Anyway, it's Monday and the monthly reports are due by lunchtime today and I have a sneaky feeling you haven't written yours yet.'

'Blast, no I haven't.' She quickly opened her laptop and navigated to the saved report template she always used. Normally she wrote the reports on a Friday afternoon but other things had taken priority last week. No matter, there were a few hours before the deadline and the reports never took her too long.

She worked at speed but even so it took up the whole morning. She managed to submit it just before the deadline then headed out for a well-earned sandwich and cup of tea from a nearby branch of Pret a Manger.

As was her habit, she pulled out her phone to scroll through news and social media while she ate. One minor news story caught her eye: 'Minister's home broken into, jewellery stolen'. She opened up the article to read it fully, her eyes widening as she took in the details.

It was David Fforbes-Whyte's home that had been broken into. Ben's father. The thief had made a mess of his study, it seemed, and had somehow broken into a safe. An item of 'immense value' had been taken, along with a few other items of less monetary value 'but just as important to me for sentimental reasons,' David was quoted as saying.

Lisa thumbed a quick message to Ben. *Sorry to hear of burglary at your dad's. Was the broo—*

Brooch stolen, she'd been about to type, but then she realised he might not have heard the news yet. This was not the way to break it to him. She deleted the message.

She sat, staring into space, considering the implications of this news. 'Item of immense value' certainly sounded like it referred to the diamond brooch. And if it had indeed been stolen, then there was no way it could be given back to Vijay. The chances of the police recovering the lost items were slim. The brooch would be broken up, the diamond perhaps split, and it'd quickly become untraceable.

And what would that mean for the curse? Would its powers transfer to the thief, or stay with the Fforbes-Whyte family? She mentally rolled her eyes at herself for even thinking about it in those terms. 'Powers' – poppycock! The 'curse' was fictional. It was just a myth, a legend. The diamond was an inanimate object that didn't care or know who it belonged to. It was a lump of rock. Albeit a lump of rock that was keeping her and Ben apart.

When Ben's ancestor had acquired the diamond from another thief, the misfortunes for the family had begun. Maybe this time the burglar would begin experiencing bad luck. Perhaps it would start with him or her being caught. And then – having to return the diamond?

'Everything all right, miss?' One of the café's employees was clearing tables around her and had obviously spotted her sitting motionless, her food uneaten.

'What? Oh, yes. Sorry. I was miles away.' Lisa flashed him a smile and finished eating her sandwich, reading the rest of the news article as she did. She decided that if she didn't hear from Ben by midway through the evening, she'd contact him. She had to know more details of what had happened, and whether the diamond brooch was among the stolen items. She vaguely recalled Ben saying his father had put it in his safe. And the news article said the safe had been opened. Which would mean the diamond was almost certainly gone.

'Not a very good safe then,' she muttered. Unless it had been left open, or one of David's staff was the thief . . . She knew he had a housekeeper and a secretary who would have access to the study if not the safe.

Ben would know. She couldn't wait to talk to him about it. It was going to be a long afternoon.

* * *

Lisa left work on time that evening and hurried home. There'd been no word from Ben, and twice she'd almost broken her resolve and messaged him. But he'd be at work, at one or other of his jobs, and it'd be unfair to text him about the break-in if he didn't already know. It was his home too. For all she knew, his room might have been rifled through and things taken.

The thought made her grow cold. Burglaries were so intrusive. The idea of a stranger going through your things and taking anything they fancied was awful. Poor Ben, and his father.

When she reached her flat she dropped her bag and coat onto the sofa and flicked on the TV, tuning in to a news channel to see if there were any more details. She let the news play out in the background while she made herself a salad for her evening meal. And then she tuned herself back in to the TV when she realised David Fforbes-Whyte was being interviewed about the break-in. He was standing in the driveway of his house.

'I've lost pieces that held enormous sentimental value,' he was saying, looking rather less self-assured than he usually did. The burglary had clearly shaken him badly. 'And one item in particular has been taken which was a family heirloom and is priceless. It's an item of jewellery that can't be sold on as it's too distinctive. A description has been passed to the police and advertised to all gemstone dealers in the capital.'

There was no doubt that the brooch had been taken, then, Lisa thought. She had mixed feelings about this. She'd hoped so much that somehow she and Ben would be able to return it to Vijay Kaur, but on the other hand, Ben might believe that the 'curse' had been broken now that the diamond was in the hands of the thieves, and that he was now free to date her. The more she considered this the more she thought that even if he didn't reach that conclusion himself, she would probably be able to persuade him. Yes, the theft of the brooch was almost certainly a good thing, for them.

'Mr Fforbes-Whyte, do you have any idea how the burglars

got in? The items of value were locked in your safe, were they not?'

'They were. Well, it's a bit of a mystery. It happened this morning, while I was on my way to London for the week in Parliament. My housekeeper arrived midmorning as she always does on a Monday, to clean the house. It was she who found the door to my safe open and items missing. And the burglar or burglars left an awful lot of mess in my study – there were papers strewn everywhere as though the burglar was looking for something specific.'

'Can you speculate as to what they were looking for?'

'Among the papers – I have no idea. I don't, of course, leave any sensitive parliamentary papers out on my desk. They're always locked in the safe, or kept with me in my briefcase. Among the jewellery – well as I said, it was the family heirloom that they were no doubt searching for. It's priceless.' He frowned. 'I don't even know how they knew I had it.' Because you'd only recently acquired it, Lisa thought.

'And how did they get into the house?'

'That's the real mystery. There's no damage to any door or window, though a window round the back was found to be open. I'm certain it had been locked when I left the house.'

'Could it have been someone who had a key?'

David Fforbes-Whyte shrugged. 'Who knows. I am not prepared to speculate any further at this point. I have the utmost faith in our police force and am supporting them fully as they investigate the crime. Thank you.' He moved away from the reporter then, back into his house.

'Well, there we are, a mystery indeed,' the reporter said, wrapping up. 'And now we go back to Krishnan in the studio.'

Coverage of the crime ended and the next report was on the latest inflation figures. Lisa switched off the TV and sat down, pondering once more. No sign of a break-in from the outside pointed to the theft being an inside job. A member of David's staff? Perhaps even the housekeeper, who'd then pretended to discover the burglary to cover up her crime?

Or, the most obvious person of all. The one who knew there was a diamond brooch, knew exactly where it was, probably knew the combination code for the safe, had a key to the property and of course, had a very good reason for wanting to take the diamond. Ben.

She gasped as she came to this conclusion. Was it possible that he was behind it? Would he do such a thing?

She'd barely had a chance to consider the possibility when her doorbell rang. Composing herself she got up to answer it, speaking into the intercom. 'Hello?'

'Lisa, it's me. Ben. Can I come up?'

'Ben! Sure.' She buzzed the door release and quickly straightened cushions and put dirty coffee mugs into the kitchen while she waited for him to take the lift up to the flat. Her salad, half made, still sat on the kitchen worktop but that would have to wait.

He arrived a minute later, looking flushed as though he'd run there from the tube station. His expression was a curious mix of excitement and fear. It was clear he had important news to share, and she had no doubt as to what that would be. He was carrying a large rucksack, which he dumped on the floor by the door.

'What is it, Ben?'

'Developments!' he said as he collapsed onto her sofa, still breathing heavily. 'Just give me a minute.'

I can guess, Lisa wanted to say, but decided against it. Let Ben tell her in his own words what had happened. 'Can I get you a drink?'

'Beer, if you have it. The type with alcohol in this time, please. I came by train and tube.'

'Sure.' She went to the kitchen and came back with two bottles of beer from her fridge. He'd gotten up and was standing by her window, looking down into the street. He closed her window blind then took the beer from her and sat back down on the sofa.

'Thanks.' He took a long swig and smacked his lips. 'That's better. Needed that. Do you want to sit down? While I tell you—'

'—that you broke into your father's study and took the diamond?' Lisa couldn't help blurting it out.

'Yes. Oh, my God. I can't believe I did it.' For a moment he hid his face in his hands, shaking his head. 'But it was the only way. I damaged nothing, and I'll return the other items and come clean about it, as soon as we've given Vijay the diamond. Look.' He put a hand into his pocket. Lisa assumed he was going to pull out the diamond in its little box, but it was his phone he pulled out. He tapped on it a few times and handed it to her.

'What am I looking at?'

'Air tickets. To Delhi, leaving tomorrow afternoon. You said you'd be able to go at short notice, I hope this isn't too short?'

'Well . . . no, it's fine,' she said, mentally composing an email to her boss that she would send that evening. 'So tell me, how . . . what . . .' She waved a hand vaguely to encompass the whole situation.

'So I asked Dad again about giving the diamond back. But he was adamant it wasn't going anywhere, that he'd never give it back, no matter what. I spoke about the curse, and he said it was all mumbo-jumbo. I told him about our research and that I'd found Vijay Kaur, and he became angry and told me to forget it because he'd never give it up.'

Ben shook his head again. 'I should have known. Push Dad and he digs in, doubles down on his stance and won't listen to any other point of view. So then I told him about you, and that I didn't feel I could have a relationship with you all the while the curse of the *Chamakta Sitara* hung over our family, but he just laughed and told me to "man up". That was when I had the idea. If he wouldn't give me the diamond, I'd simply take it. After all, it would be left to me eventually to do what I want with. Dad had said he wanted to pass it on to me, and my children if I have any. So, you know, I'm just speeding that process along a little.'

He gave her a wry little smile and took another slug of his beer. 'Anyway, I went out this morning as though I was heading off to work, but actually, I doubled back to the house once I knew he was out. Vanessa, the housekeeper, never gets there until after half past ten, so I had plenty of time. I was going to simply take the diamond but knew that he'd immediately guess it was me and we'd have an almighty row.'

'You still will,' she said, 'when you come clean about it.'

He grimaced. 'Yes, but that won't happen until after we've done the deed and returned the diamond. It won't matter then. I figured that if I took a few other bits and made a small mess, it'd look more like a burglary from outside, and give me more time to take the diamond out of the country. I opened a window in the dining room to make it look like the burglars got in that way. Vanessa and Dad certainly thought it was a genuine burglary.'

Lisa had her hand over her mouth. He was effectively a criminal on the run. But she wouldn't dare say that to him. 'Have you spoken to your dad since? Did you see his TV interview?'

'Yes, I spoke to him. He called me as soon as he got back home. He was quite agitated, telling me my laptop had been taken too – it had, it's in there.' He pointed to his rucksack. 'I rushed over and helped him work out what had been "stolen". He's actually most upset about a necklace that was Mum's. It's not worth much but means a lot to him.'

'Oh, Ben, are you sure you didn't go too far?'

'Lisa, it was the only way. Mum's necklace is safely hidden in my bedroom, along with the other bits and pieces. I'll call him from India as soon as possible, and tell him where they are, I promise.'

'Are you sure he genuinely believes it was a burglary? Because there was no sign of a break-in. He said so to a reporter, on the news.' David Fforbes-Whyte was an intelligent man. It wouldn't be long before he put two and two together and worked out that Ben must be the culprit.

Ben twisted his mouth. 'I considered breaking a window. But

I didn't want to damage anything. I'm hoping he'll think that window was mistakenly left open or at least unlocked . . .'

'Or he might blame Vanessa or someone else who has a key?'

'Forty-eight hours, Lisa. In forty-eight hours or less we'll be in Agra, handing Vijay the diamond. Then I promise I'll call Dad and come clean, and take any flak.'

'What if . . . what if he wants to press charges against you?'

'It's actually up to the police to charge a person or not. I might be in trouble for wasting police time, but if so, I'll just have to face the consequences.' Ben tipped his head to one side and regarded her. 'Lisa, please don't be cross with me. It's the only way we can take the diamond to where it belongs. And then, you and I . . . if you still want me?'

'Ben, yes, I do. I just think . . . it was a bit extreme. And I don't want you to be in trouble.'

'Dad will forgive me. He confided that he only really wants Mum's necklace back.'

'Despite how keen he was to hold on to the diamond?'

'He lived all his life without possessing that brooch. He can manage the rest of it. I'm sure he'll come round.' Ben held out a hand to her. 'Trust me, yeah?'

She squeezed his fingers. 'Yeah.'

For a moment they held each other's gaze, then Lisa broke away. 'Would you like some dinner, Ben? I was making a salad . . .'

'That'd be great, if you have enough. Um, any chance I can stay here tonight? If not, I'll get a hotel room, but it might be easier to be here.'

'No problem. I can make up the sofa-bed for you. And I suppose I ought to pack.'

'Yes. Ten days in India, as we discussed on the phone. I've already emailed Vijay to say we're coming over, so he's expecting us.'

'Right, I'll get on to it.' Lisa went out to the kitchen to prepare the salads. She had some feta cheese in the fridge so she turned what she'd begun preparing into a Greek salad, with some crusty bread on the side. She had some white wine chilling too, which would go well with it.

When she brought the plates back to the sitting room, Ben was sitting on the sofa, hunched over something. As she put the plates down on the coffee table, she realised he was holding the brooch, turning it over and over, letting the diamond catch the light. He looked almost obsessed by it. He was right. The sooner they got rid of the damned thing the better.

Chapter 28

Celia, July 1947

Celia managed to sleep for a few hours, and woke up to daylight streaming in through the tiny window. Sita was sitting at the end of the bed, watching her, waiting for her to awake. She'd stopped crying at last, Celia was pleased to see.

'*Meri jaan*, they have brought us some breakfast,' Sita said, as soon as Celia opened her eyes.

Celia sat up, confused, wondering why she hadn't woken up when the breakfast was delivered. 'Who brought it?'

Sita shrugged. 'One of the men who doesn't speak. He unlocked the door and I opened it and took the tray from him.'

'Was he alone?'

'I think so.'

Celia sighed. If she'd been awake and had seen only one man at the door, then perhaps the two of them could have rushed him and forced their way out. But that chance was gone now. 'What did he bring?'

'Mango, *lassi*, bread. Shall we eat?'

'Yes. You go first, you ate nothing yesterday. We have to keep our strength up.'

Celia was pleased to see that Sita nodded and picked up a slice of mango. She seemed in a better state than yesterday. Celia picked up a glass of the *lassi* and drank it quickly. You couldn't buy it in England, she recalled Papa saying. It was yet another thing she'd miss about India.

'What I don't understand,' she said to Sita when they'd finished eating, 'is how the men knew we'd be at the station yesterday morning. Who told them when we were leaving for Simla?'

In answer, Sita shrugged and picked up a glass of water, inspecting it as though the answer was beneath the surface.

'I mean, only you, me, Sanjit and Papa knew. Even the other servants didn't know we were leaving until yesterday morning. I remember cook was cross that no one had told him, because he'd ordered in too much food.'

'Someone must have heard us talking about it.'

'But when, Sita? We didn't talk about it. We only made the decision the day before, didn't we? When Papa came home with the railway tickets.' She remembered how Papa had called her and Sita into his study and told them to pack. She'd been annoyed because the short notice hadn't given her time to say goodbye properly to Vijay. She'd had to call him on the phone, while Sita had run out on some last-minute errand. 'When did someone overhear us, Sita?'

'Maybe it was Sanjit,' Sita said quietly, not looking at Celia as she spoke. Her attention now seemed to be on a smudge on her sari that she was trying to remove by rubbing it between her fingers.

'You think he betrayed us? He never left the house that day, after Papa told us we'd be leaving.'

'At the station, when he went to get the trolley, maybe.' There was no conviction in Sita's tone.

'But he was only gone for a minute or two. Not nearly long enough to tell the kidnappers we were there and for them to arrive in their van. I think they were already there, waiting for us. I'm sure I saw that van parked across the street as Sanjit drove us to the station. So they already knew our plans.' Celia shook her head. 'No, it can't have been Sanjit. And it wasn't me. And of course it wasn't Papa.'

'You called Vijay to tell him goodbye.'

'I did, yes. But I don't believe it was him either.' Even though his father had ordered the kidnap attempt, Vijay had come to her last night and promised he'd do what he could to get her out. It couldn't possibly have been him. Which only left one person.

'Sita?'

'Yes, *meri jaan*?'

'Sita, look at me?'

Still the *ayah* kept fiddling with the stain on her sari. She couldn't look Celia in the eye, Celia realised. 'Sita?'

'Oh, *meri jaan*, he said he'd hurt my family!' Sita burst out. 'My little nieces and nephews, my parents . . . he threatened them all if I did not tell them a time when you and I would be out of the house together . . . and when the *sahib* said we were to go to the hills I knew it would be the last chance and I had to tell them the time of the train . . .'

'So, it was you?' Celia couldn't believe what she was hearing. She had known Sita all her life, trusted her with every secret she'd ever held, and now Sita had betrayed her like this. She felt cold at the thought. 'I can't believe it . . . *you*, Sita?'

'It was me, *meri jaan*, and I am sorry, very sorry, but I had to do it! You must understand . . . he made me! I cannot risk my brother's children and my parents . . .' Sita buried her face in her hands, sobbing, her shoulders heaving.

'*Who* made you?' Celia spat the words out.

'The man, the one with the beard who came here yesterday . . . I thought I recognised him but at the time I did not know where from. But now we know – *meri jaan*, he is the maharajah's man, which means the maharajah ordered this! Your Vijay must be a part of it too!'

'No, not Vijay . . . We – I – can trust him. Sita, why didn't you tell my father that you were threatened?'

'He said to tell no one or he'd hurt them. That man . . .'

'Arun Gupta.'

'Yes, I remember him now. When they dragged me into that back room near the market, I did not remember him. He had those other men with him. Two of them held me while he spoke. I was frightened, *meri jaan*, but they promised me you would not be hurt. I would *never* allow you to be hurt! I would rather die, rather they kill me than let you be hurt!'

It was on the tip of Celia's tongue to retort that Sita would rather risk Celia than her brother's children but she thought better of it. Sita's nieces were only very small. And her parents were old and frail. No wonder she'd thought she had no option but to do what the kidnappers demanded, rather than risk her family being harmed. Celia couldn't believe it. She'd always thought of the maharajah as a decent man. He'd been aloof and distant towards herself and Vijay when they were children, but hadn't he always been a friend of Papa's, since *they* were boys? How could he do this? Not only kidnap her and Sita, but threaten Sita's family if she did not help them? And all for the sake of a stupid diamond!

And Sita! Sita who'd been like a mother to her all her life. Sita, the one constant after the death of Mama, after Papa turned bad-tempered and became so easily annoyed with her. Sita had betrayed her. Celia would never forgive her; she knew that. But there was no point being angry with her now. They needed to work together to find a way out of this.

'They will not hurt me, and they will not hurt you or your family either,' Celia said firmly. It all made sense now – why Sita had done nothing but sob yesterday, why she'd taken it all so badly. It was because she felt guilty about her part in this. Guilty that she'd put her charge in danger, even if she had felt forced into it by the threats against her family.

Celia sat in silence for a while, letting it all sink in, thinking through the implications of everything she'd heard. All those years, her whole life, when Sita had been the one person she could trust above everyone else, above even her father – that period was suddenly over. It was now up to Celia to get them out of this situation. Vijay might help if he could, her father might be taking steps, but the only person she could rely on one hundred per cent was herself. *So this is what it feels like to be grown-up*, she thought wryly, as she felt a pang of longing for those wonderful, carefree innocent days of childhood that had so abruptly disappeared over the horizon.

A little later came the sound of the bolts being shot open, and two of their captors appeared at the door – these two, Celia had worked out, were simply lackeys, and were not in charge. One was tall, the other short and rather fat. One of them came into the room to pick up the tray of breakfast things and the bucket they'd been using as a toilet. Celia glared at him as he crossed the room. The other man stood guard at the door.

'I know who you're working for,' she said, first in English and then in Hindi. Sita stared at her in alarm but Celia ignored her. 'My father will get me out of here. You'll see. And then you'll be reported to the authorities and you'll be punished. Or, alternatively, you could help me get out and my father will reward you. I promise he will make it worthwhile.'

The two men said nothing but Celia noticed a glance pass between them. One shook his head, and then they left the room, re-bolting the door behind them. Celia ran over to it to listen. As she'd guessed, the two men were discussing what she'd said, debating in Hindi whether her father would pay them more than what Arun Gupta was paying them.

'But her papa has gone away,' one of them said. 'I heard his house is empty. He has gone to find men to break her out.'

'He has gone to raise the ransom, Gupta said.'

'Do we trust Gupta?'

'He told us we'd only have to hold her for a few hours. Then he said a day. Now he says it could be longer, maybe up to a week. I have other things I could be doing. He is not paying us enough to do this for a week.'

'If we don't do what he says it will be trouble for us.'

'Well, I think that . . .' The voices trailed off as the two men moved away from the door. But Celia had heard enough. One of them was wavering, and could perhaps be bought. When or if Vijay returned, she could tell him this. Or the next time the door was opened. Trouble was, she didn't know which of them to appeal to – the tall one or the fat one – as neither had spoken in her presence.

She sat down to think of a plan. One of the men at least would be back soon to bring them fresh water, and maybe then she would be able to get them to speak and work out which one was her best bet.

Celia had to wait until the evening before anything of note happened. When their bucket was replaced and food and water brought, it was always all three men. The leader, the man with a moustache, was the only one who'd speak to them and it was clear he could not be turned.

Darkness fell and Celia tried to prepare herself for a second night in the room. She'd persuaded Sita to sleep on the bed as her body was stiff and sore from sleeping on the floor the first night.

Celia had no intention of sleeping yet. By her reckoning, Vijay had visited around midnight the night before, and she hoped that perhaps he'd do the same today. And so she was awake, pacing up and down in the little room, sometimes sitting for a while at the end of the bed where Sita lay, once again snoring softly. She'd had plenty of time to think. And she had the beginnings of a plan.

At last, when she was beginning to give up hope that he'd

come and resigning herself to settling down alongside Sita, she heard an urgent whisper at the window.

'Cee! Are you there?'

She quickly hurried over to the window. 'Yes, I'm here. I'm so glad you've come!'

'Cee, I have news for you. But I fear you won't like it.'

'What? Tell me.' She took his hand that he'd passed through the bars and held it. Its warmth and familiarity was somehow reassuring.

'Your father, he's gone to London.'

'London!' Celia gasped.

'He purchased a one-way plane ticket. He's not planning to come back, my father says.'

'Of course he'll come back. For me.' But Vijay's words confirmed her worst fears. They'd had their differences, and they'd parted on a bad note on the day of the kidnap, but she was sure he loved her, at least enough to do whatever was needed to obtain her freedom. Wouldn't he?

'*Pitaji* says he won't. He tried to tell me that your father had taken you to England too. He insisted that you'd gone to Delhi with your father. He doesn't know I know you are here. I had to pretend to be upset that you had left without saying goodbye.'

'I would never do that, Vijay.' Celia thought hard. 'The diamond . . . perhaps it is in London?' Hadn't Papa gone there in March? Maybe he'd taken it then? She could only hope that was the truth, and that even now he was in the process of fetching it back. But if not, then it was up to her to do something.

'If it is, it'll take him days to get back with it,' Vijay said.

'Yes. That's why we must find a way to get me out. Listen. I think one of the men holding us here could be bribed. If we pay him more than Gupta is paying him, I think he'd accept it.'

'Which one? I spied on them earlier. The tall one or the short one? Or the one with the moustache?'

'Not the moustache – he's the boss. One of the other two, I

don't know which. I only know the voice. It is the one whose voice is a little higher-pitched than the other. They never talk in front of us. But Vijay, I think there are times when only one man is left here to guard us.'

'All right. So we need a moment when only the one that might be bribed, whichever he is, is guarding you. And then I approach with a fistful of money and he opens the door. And then the two of you run out.'

'And run where?'

Vijay shrugged, and they were both silent, trying to work it out. It was Celia who spoke next.

'Sanjit. Tell him to bring Papa's car somewhere close by, but out of sight of the entrance to this place. When we get out, we run to him.'

Vijay nodded. 'I can arrange that.'

A thought occurred to Celia. 'How will you know only that one fellow is guarding us? And how will you know which he is?'

'I'll watch and wait, Cee. I'll spy on them. Trust me. We're like this, remember?' Through the bars of the window he crossed his fingers, one over the other. She did the same.

She did trust him. She had to, didn't she? She could no longer trust Sita, even though she fully understood why Sita had betrayed her. She glanced over at the sleeping form of her *ayah*, who thankfully had not heard any of this conversation. She'd decided not to tell Vijay of Sita's betrayal yet.

Papa had left the country. Which meant Vijay was the only person besides herself she could rely on. 'All right. Thank you.'

'Get some sleep, Cee. I'll see you tomorrow. Be ready.'

Somehow she did sleep, at least a little, squashed beside Sita head to toe on the narrow bunk. When morning came and the guards brought them breakfast, she tried once more to get them to talk, to work out which was the one who might be bribed.

'Thank you. We appreciate it,' she said, as the taller of the men placed a tray on the floor. He nodded at her words but said nothing. Had there been something behind his eyes that said he was wavering, open to a higher offer to let them out? She wasn't sure. And she couldn't risk suggesting anything more to the wrong man.

When the door was bolted again, she sat on the bed and called Sita to her side. 'Listen. There might be a chance we'll get out today. When I say, you come with me, all right? We'll have to move quickly.' She spoke in an urgent whisper, scared that the men might be listening by the door.

'But . . . my family . . .'

'They'll be safe. I promise.' She'd send Sanjit or some other servants of Papa's to watch over them if necessary. Or she'd bring them all into Papa's bungalow where they could lock the gates; they'd be safe there. 'You have to do what I say.' She spoke firmly. Sita had done enough damage.

It was several hours later when she heard voices behind the door. The higher-pitched guard's voice, and Vijay's. It was happening! 'Sita! Come on!' She pulled her *ayah* to her feet and waited. Any moment now the door would open and Vijay would be there.

And then – yes! The bolts were shot back and Vijay pushed open the door. 'Come on, run! The car's round the corner.'

Celia grabbed Sita's hand and they hurried out of their cell, through the other room, which was empty save for a table and chair, out into a courtyard and onto the street. She spotted the tall guard running off in the opposite direction, stuffing a bundle of rupees into his clothes as he ran. He glanced back over his shoulder at them and she felt her heart pound. What if the other kidnappers were nearby, and this man raised the alarm? 'Come on, Sita, we need to run faster,' she urged, hoping that Sanjit had been able to park the car nearby.

Vijay led them into a side street and around a corner and there was the familiar sight of Papa's car. For one wonderful moment

Celia thought it was Papa himself behind the wheel; Papa who'd come to rescue her, who loved her after all. But it was Sanjit, of course, starting the engine as soon as he saw them.

They all bundled into the waiting car and slammed the doors closed. 'It worked!' Celia gasped.

'Good to see you again, Miss Celia,' Sanjit said as he rammed the car into gear and took off, wheels spinning.

She was about to reply when she saw to her horror a familiar van approaching from the opposite direction. In its cab were the moustachioed man and the stouter of the guards. 'That's them! Find another way!' she screamed, and Sanjit took a sudden right turn, sending a couple of chickens that were in the road squawking and fluttering through an open door. They just missed hitting a man on a bicycle who wobbled against a wall and shouted something. Celia was thrown sideways across Sita's lap, and Vijay, in the front seat, was clinging on to the dashboard. She twisted round to see if the van was following them but it had overshot the turning. Had the men spotted them? Had they recognised the car?

'It's all right, Miss Celia. They will not catch us. This car is quick,' Sanjit said, as he steered the car out of the side street and onto another broader road.

But a moment later she saw that the van was still following them.

'Drive faster!' Celia shouted. Sanjit glanced in the rear-view mirror and said a word in Hindi that she didn't recognise, but guessed was a swear word. He hit the accelerator. He was right: the car was fast and he was a good driver, weaving in and out of traffic of all kinds – carts, bicycles, trucks and rickshaws. The van was still chasing but dropping back. Sanjit swerved around a bullock cart that was emerging from a side street and to her relief, Celia saw that the van didn't make it past before the cart blocked the road. The cart's driver seemed to be arguing with the men in the van, and Celia prayed that he would refuse to move his cart long enough for Sanjit to drive them out of sight.

It worked. Sanjit took a few more turns, left, right, left again, mingling with other traffic.

'Well done. I think we've lost them,' Vijay said at last.

Sanjit nodded. 'Where shall I take them, Mr Vijay? The kidnappers will surely come to the bungalow looking for them first.'

'Well, er . . .' Vijay began, but Celia leaned forward from the back seat to speak to them both. Sanjit was right – they couldn't go home. Instead, she'd had an idea that just might work.

'Take us to the palace.'

'What?!' Vijay twisted round. 'But my father will be there . . .'

'Exactly. I shall appeal to him for help.' She looked pointedly at Sanjit, who didn't know who was behind the kidnapping, and back at Vijay.

'I don't understand,' Vijay said quietly.

'Trust me,' she replied, with a small smile.

Vijay held her gaze for a moment and then nodded. 'Very well. To the palace, then.'

Sita let out a small gasp. Celia's instinct was to take her hand, reassure her that it would be all right, that she wouldn't let anything bad happen to Sita, but she stopped herself. The woman had betrayed her. If she was frightened now then so be it. Celia had been terrified enough locked in that room, not knowing why or by whom, hadn't she?

The journey passed in silence, with Vijay keeping a look out in case the men in the van came in sight again, and Celia mentally rehearsing exactly what she was going to say to the maharajah. It was a gamble, she knew, but if it worked it was definitely the best plan.

At last they turned into the road that led to the palace, and Sanjit brought the car to a halt inside the gates. 'Sita, stay here with Sanjit for a minute. Vijay, let's go,' Celia said. Her heart was pounding. If she got this wrong, she'd be locked up again . . . or worse.

'Let me go first,' Vijay said, as they walked through the entrance hall towards the maharajah's study. A servant showed them in. The maharajah was at his desk, poring over some paperwork.

'*Pitaji*,' Vijay said, and the maharajah looked up, surprised. When he saw Celia behind Vijay his mouth fell open and he looked from her to his son and back. 'What the— Vijay, what is this? Why . . . how . . . is she here?'

'Sir,' Celia began, stepping forward. She forced herself to smile as though this was a social occasion just like all those other times she'd been in the palace. 'I understand you would like the *Chamakta Sitara* returned to you. I understand also that my father is en route to London to retrieve it. Assuming he doesn't know that you are behind my . . . abduction, I imagine he might contact you for advice when he returns, or if he doesn't, you could offer him your help. I'm proposing that I stay here, quietly, and when he returns you pretend to set up a handover – the diamond for me. I promise I will say *nothing* to him of what has really happened, ever. As long as you let me live here freely in the meantime.'

'But I—' the maharajah began, then he broke off and rubbed his chin. 'He has already contacted me, and I told him to come here once he has the diamond, and that Arun Gupta would make the exchange. So I suppose . . .'

'I might as well be kept here, in comfort, rather than in that horrible hovel with a bucket for a toilet.' Celia smiled brightly, though inside her stomach was churning with nerves.

'I suppose you might.' The maharajah nodded.

'And . . .' Celia began.

'More demands, child?' The maharajah spoke gruffly and Celia once more steeled herself.

'Sita, my *ayah*. You must also promise that you will call your thugs off, and that no harm will befall her or her family.'

He nodded. 'Arun will pay the men what they are owed. Her family will not be harmed. She is to stay here also until I have the diamond in my possession. Go. You and your *ayah* can use the Mumtaz suite. Vijay will show you.'

'Thank you, sir.' Celia followed Vijay out of the office and let out a huge sigh of relief. That had gone very well, she thought.

Vijay turned and hugged her. 'You're a genius, Celia. This way everyone gets what they want. My father gets the diamond, which then remains in India where it belongs. You stay here in comfort until your father returns. He gets you back safe and well.' His eyes softened. 'And I . . . I get to spend a little more time with you before you go to England.'

Celia looked up at him and smiled. 'Yes, it'll all work out well. Let's go and tell Sita she's safe, then you can show us the rooms.' As long as her father *did* return with the diamond, he was right – everyone got what they wanted. And if Papa didn't come back . . . well, she'd worry about that later.

Vijay showed them into a suite of rooms, which were sumptuously furnished in Indian style. 'There are two bedrooms leading off this sitting room. You can access the grounds from here but it's probably best you don't go anywhere else. No one else must know you are here.'

The grounds were enormous, Celia knew, so keeping to them would not be a hardship. Sita immediately lay down on the bed in her room to sleep, and Celia closed the door.

'When we hear that my father is on his way here, we'll stay out of sight in these rooms. And once the diamond is handed over, I can go home with Papa.' Assuming her father returned with the diamond, she thought. But he would. Of course he would.

Vijay nodded. 'It's a good plan.'

'Where's your room?' Celia asked. Suddenly she felt as though she wanted to know Vijay was nearby.

'It is just along the passage.' He smiled. 'I think now you ought to rest, and I'll bring some food for you both. And then, I'd rather like a game of tennis.'

'You're on,' Celia replied, with a grin. She might enjoy living here at the palace for a few days, after all.

Chapter 29

Lisa, 2023

It was a rush, getting ready for the trip to India; that was for certain. Thirty hours after Ben turned up at her door with the brooch, Lisa was on a flight to Delhi, sitting beside him. She was thankful she'd provisionally booked the time off work as that had made it easy to arrange the trip that morning when she'd made a brief visit to the office. 'No problem,' her boss had said. 'Have a good time.'

And Justin had winked at her, knowing she was going away with Ben and guessing that this trip would be make or break for their relationship.

She'd been back home by midday, in good time to pack. Ben had spent the morning cleaning her flat, to her great surprise. Rupert had never lifted a finger to help her with housework, even when he'd stayed there for several days at a time. 'Ben, you didn't need to do that!' she said, as she gazed at the immaculate kitchen, the shining bathroom and vacuumed floor.

'Ah, but it's nice to come home to a tidy place,' he replied, then he clapped a hand over his mouth. 'Oops. Not suggesting it wasn't clean and tidy before . . .'

'But you're right. It wasn't. I often get massively behind with household chores. That's something you ought to know . . .' She looked at him sideways.

Ben laughed. 'Just as well I'm tidy, then. I actually rather like housework. Cooking and preparing food, however, is not my thing. I eat a lot of takeaways. That salad you knocked up last night – I wouldn't have a clue where to start.'

'Right then, I'll cook, you'll clean. Seems like a deal.' And then she realised what she'd said – what their conversation had implied. They were making plans on how they'd organise their lives when they lived together, as though it was a foregone conclusion. It just all seemed so right, so natural with Ben.

'Anyway, I couldn't go out,' Ben said, pulling a face. 'Police might be looking for me, if Dad's guessed.'

She made him a lunch of stir-fried vegetables with strips of chicken, using up whatever was left in the fridge. Once again, he seemed impressed that she'd been able to make something so tasty with little effort.

And then in the late afternoon, checking a thousand times that the diamond brooch was safely stowed in Ben's hand luggage, they left the flat and took the tube out to Heathrow airport. Lisa offered to look after the brooch. 'I could put it in my handbag, or wear it,' she said, but Ben stared at her with horror.

'There is no way on earth I am letting you touch that thing. We don't know the extent of its power.'

She was going to reply, but decided against it. She knew there was no point appealing to his sense of reason where that diamond was concerned. And there was a tiny piece of her that knew she wouldn't be able to relax until the diamond had been handed to Vijay Kaur. Not only because that meant that at last Ben would feel free to let their relationship progress naturally, but because he believed in the curse so strongly it was beginning to rub off on her. Maybe there *was* something in it. Maybe that incident on the way to Dublin had unnerved her more than she'd realised at the time.

'In any case,' Ben went on, 'if we're challenged going through airport security with it, it has to be me who's detained. Not you.'

There was also the outstanding question of just how much trouble Ben would be in, when he told his father what he'd done. Plenty to worry about. She bit her lip nervously, staring out of the window of the tube at the darkness of the tunnel they were passing through.

'What's wrong, Lisa?' Ben asked, sounding concerned. 'You're not worried about the flight are you? After . . . what happened.'

She turned back to him. 'I sort of am. But no, not really. I'm just . . .'

'. . . looking forward to it all being over, and us being free?'

'Yes. That.' She gave him a tentative smile. He looked at her with longing in his eyes. In any other situation she would lean over and kiss him, but . . . not now. Soon, but not yet.

They arrived in good time at Heathrow, went through check-in and the security control – thankfully with no trouble despite the diamond brooch nestled in Ben's hand luggage – and settled themselves in a bar to pass the time. 'Do you think we should have brought Vijay a present?' Lisa said. 'I mean, I know we're giving him the diamond, but if he's putting us up . . .?'

'He is. And yes, we should. We don't want to arrive with one arm as long as the other, as my Irish mother would have said. Let's get him a bottle of good whisky in the duty-free shop.'

'Does he drink?'

'Hope so.' Ben grimaced. 'It's the gesture that counts. Right, we'll go there after we've had this drink. We've got loads of time.'

'That's good. I hate having to rush when I'm travelling.'

'Me too.'

Later, with a bottle of ten-year-old Bushmills in a carrier bag, they boarded the aeroplane for the long flight to Delhi. Most of it was overnight, so after eating a meal and watching a film they slept. Lisa woke once in the night to find she'd been sleeping with her head on Ben's shoulder. He was still sound asleep. She gently tucked his blanket around him and settled back down in what felt like the most natural position leaning against him.

She awoke the next time to find dawn was breaking, people were pulling up the window shutters and watching the pink and orange glow spread across from the east. They'd be landing in a couple of hours, in the early morning. From Delhi they'd take a train to Agra. Ben, bless him, had managed to book the rail tickets in advance. Lisa had seen TV programmes about the vagaries of the Indian railway system so she was glad they already had their booking. It was one less thing to worry about.

Beside her, Ben stirred, and rubbed the sleep from his eyes. He yawned and glanced at his watch. 'They'll be coming round with breakfast soon, then before we know it, we'll be landing. India, here we come!'

'Yes!' She gripped his hand and he grinned at her.

The plane landed and they made their way through the airport and into a taxi to take them to the train station. They were heading straight to Agra. 'We could have spent a day or two in Delhi first, but I'd rather get the important part of this trip done first,' Ben said, and Lisa nodded.

'Absolutely. Anyway, we've got time in Delhi at the end, haven't we?'

'Yes. A few days to explore.'

The taxi drove past airport hotels then into the city along a wide, busy highway teeming with all manner of vehicles, from scooters to articulated trucks. Lisa saw whole families balanced on mopeds – mum, dad and three or four small children. Green and yellow motorised rickshaws with their noisy two-stroke engines sped past on both sides of them. Beyond the highway were dusty fields and rundown shacks with corrugated iron roofs, until they reached the edges of the city and the highway turned into a tree-lined boulevard and larger buildings began to appear.

The taxi wove its way through increasingly busy streets, navigating around Connaught Place that marked the centre of the modern city, past a mix of colonial-era and modern buildings. Now there were fewer trucks but more bicycles on the roads, as well as brightly painted cycle rickshaws and the occasional cart pulled by oxen. Lisa stared out of the window the whole way, and Ben did the same. Shops and stalls lined the streets, selling everything from leather sandals to spices, mobile phones to cooking utensils and clothing. Everywhere was teeming with people going about their business.

At last, the taxi pulled up outside the railway station, a modern building that looked more like an airport terminal than a station. Ben paid the driver and they headed inside. There was time for a cup of tea before their train was due to leave, so they headed over to a café and ordered.

When the tea came it was milky and already sweetened. 'I generally drink it black,' Ben said, 'but hey, when in India we should drink it the Indian way.'

'Yep. Not sure I'll get used to it like this though,' Lisa said, after tasting it.

The train was old but clean and serviceable. They had first-class tickets and soon were settled on worn but comfortable seats in an air-conditioned compartment.

'How long to Agra?' Lisa asked. 'I don't think I want to read, I want to just look out of the window and take it all in.'

Ben checked the booking confirmation on his phone. 'It's about two hours. We can get a meal on the train if you're hungry. I've messaged Vijay to say we're on our way and he says a car will be at the station in Agra to meet us.'

'He's being very kind.'

'I think he's just happy that after a century and a half the diamond's being returned to his family.'

'I can't wait to meet him.' Lisa pictured a frail old man, living in a large house – no, a palace, she reminded herself – full of faded grandeur. Would he live alone? She imagined he'd have servants. At the age of ninety-three he'd need help with the house at least. A question occurred to her. 'Did Vijay ever marry? Does he have kids?'

'I don't know. He's never mentioned any family in his emails. I imagine he would have, though. We'll soon find out.'

As the train left the station Lisa kept her eyes focused on the view through the window. The jumble of city buildings gave way to open countryside, dusty fields with villages in the distance. Women in saris worked in the fields, men led ploughs pulled by oxen, children ran alongside and waved excitedly as the train passed by.

A few hours later they arrived at Agra. Lisa had kept her eyes focused on the view from the train windows, looking out one side and then the other, desperate to get a glimpse of the Taj Mahal but she hadn't spotted it. 'We'll visit it before we leave here, don't worry,' Ben said, guessing her thoughts.

As they emerged from the colonial-era station building, they spotted a young man holding a placard which read: 'Mr Fforbes-Whyte and Friend'.

'That's us,' Lisa said, nodding in the man's direction.

'Come on then, Friend,' Ben replied, and they headed over.

'Welcome, welcome Mr Fforbes-Whyte,' the man said, as they introduced themselves. 'I am Abhijeet. I will take you now to Mr Kaur's house. He is looking forward to meeting you.'

Abhijeet hauled their rucksacks into the boot of the car as they got in the back.

'Excited?' Lisa said, noticing Ben's apprehensive expression.

'Yes, but also . . . not sure what to expect.' He spoke quietly, obviously not wanting Abhijeet to hear from the front seat.

'You are ready? We are going.' Abhijeet gave them a huge grin and started the car. They drove through busy streets that looked similar to some they'd seen in Delhi – bustling markets, white-washed houses with peeling paint and crumbling woodwork, roads filled with all manner of vehicle. Here, she thought, there were more mopeds and scooters and carts pulled by mules or oxen than there'd been in Delhi. Some side roads were simply dirt tracks and there was certainly more litter than Lisa had noticed in the capital city.

'Will we pass the Taj Mahal?' Lisa asked Abhijeet.

'Nearby, but you will not see it well,' he replied. 'You can go there tomorrow maybe. I will take you.'

'Thank you.'

'*Dhanyavad*,' Ben said, and Lisa looked at him in surprise.

'Hindi for thank you, though I am not sure I pronounced it correctly,' Ben explained.

'You did well,' Abhijeet said, with a smile.

It was just like Ben, Lisa thought, to make an effort to learn a few words in the language of the country they were travelling in. An image flashed through her mind of Rupert yelling in English at a Frenchman on their last holiday together. She quickly dismissed it. There really was no comparison between the two men. She shifted a little in the back of the car, so that her thigh pressed against Ben's, and he turned to give her a secret little smile.

Look at me, she thought. Here in exotic India. About to do something culturally significant, which was partly brought about by my own doing. Look at me with my new-found self-confidence. *This* is the real me, and being with Ben's helped me find myself. She felt quietly pleased with the way things were turning out.

Then they were driving through a smarter neighbourhood, with large houses. Some modern, others that appeared to date back to the days of the British Raj. At last Abhijeet turned into a driveway and stopped before a set of gates. He leaned out of his window to wave a keycard at a reader, and the gates opened automatically. Beyond the gates was a large garden, filled with enormous bushes bearing colourful flowers. Lisa had no idea what any of them were but resolved to find out. Abhijeet drove the car up a long gravel driveway and parked in front of a large whitewashed single-storey house.

'We are here. Mr Kaur will come out in a moment.' He opened the car door for Lisa and she climbed out, looking about her. There was a set of steps leading up to the house's entrance, and a veranda on either side, that she imagined stretched right around the house. At the far end of the garden beyond some trees Lisa glimpsed a tennis court. It looked like a lovely place to live.

'Mr Fforbes-Whyte? Miss Statton? Come in, come in. Abhijeet will take your bags to your rooms. I am delighted to meet you.' A tall, thin and very old man had appeared on the veranda, coming through patio doors that opened onto it. He was smiling broadly, and was dressed in loose cream linen trousers and a baggy shirt.

Ben stepped forward and shook his hand. 'I'm glad to meet you, Mr Kaur.'

'Please, call me Vijay.'

'And you must call us Ben and Lisa.'

'Of course. Please, come and sit down. I'll ask Abhijeet to bring us refreshments on the veranda. You must be tired after your long journey?'

'A bit. But we both slept on the plane,' Lisa replied, as she sat on a wicker sofa filled with cushions. Ben sat beside her. Around them was the scent of geraniums which were in full flower, planted in pots and flower beds all around. 'You have a beautiful home, Vijay.'

'It's my wife's, really. My house is the old palace. But we haven't lived there for many years. We moved here soon after we married.' Vijay put a hand to his cheek as though suddenly recalling his manners. 'My wife, I am sorry, she is resting at present. She will join us a little later.'

'No problem. I'm looking forward to meeting her too,' Lisa said. She imagined a tiny, grey-haired woman in a sari.

'Have you other family?' Ben asked.

Vijay smiled. 'We were blessed with two sons and a daughter.

And seven grandchildren. Abhijeet is one of our grandsons – he lives here with us and helps us take care of the house and garden. He has offered to cook for us too, but I'm afraid we don't like his cooking. So instead, there is a local woman who comes in every day to make our food.'

'Sounds like a perfect set-up.' Lisa smiled at Vijay's frankness about his grandson's culinary abilities.

At that moment Abhijeet arrived bearing a tray with tea, iced lemonade, and a plate of scones. He put it down on a side table then left, saying something about needing to trim some bushes. 'He will join us for dinner,' Vijay said. 'He wants to give us time to get any business out of the way first.'

'Talking of which,' Ben said, 'I have the diamond here.' He patted his small hand-luggage bag, which he had not let out of his sight during the entire journey.

Lisa watched as Vijay glanced at the bag. An odd look crossed the old man's face. Was it fear? Or worry? She couldn't quite tell. There was something strange about his expression. In her understanding, the trouble the diamond had caused was all to the Fforbes-Whyte family, not Vijay's. But something about his expression told her there was more to the story than she and Ben were aware of.

'Should I bring it out now?' Ben asked, looking puzzled as Vijay had not replied.

'Let's wait for my wife to join us. Tell me, Lisa, the story of how you found it, please?'

Lisa nodded and began relating the story of her walk in the mountains above Chamonix with Gaby. How long ago that seemed now! She told how they spotted the briefcase at the edge of the glacier, and pulled it out. How they'd found the diamond tucked in its little box and had initially wondered whether it was real or not. How she'd gone through all the paperwork, researched on Wikipedia, and pieced together the story. 'I recognised the surname Fforbes-Whyte, because Ben's father is a politician, so that's how I got in contact with him. And he confirmed that his great-grandfather's brother Wilfred, and Wilfred's daughter Celia had died in a plane crash in 1947. Then we—' She was going to mention how they'd used Ben's family archives and gone to the British Library to find out more but stopped speaking when she saw Vijay's eyes widen with surprise.

'Celia?' he said. 'Celia didn't die in that plane crash. Only her father.'

'But . . . what happened to her, then?' Lisa asked. She was confused. Beside her Ben gasped and clapped a hand to his mouth. Once more the assumptions, his family's legend, was proving incorrect.

'I married her. Not immediately – she was only fifteen and I wasn't much older. But she came to live with my father and me, and we'd always been friends since we were small children. That friendship grew into love, and we married when she was twenty-one and I was twenty-two.'

'And we've been happily married ever since,' said a woman's voice from behind Lisa, 'although there've been times when we've driven each other bananas. But I suppose that's true of all couples.'

Lisa twisted round to see an elegantly dressed white woman standing just inside the house. She was wearing a long, floaty dress and her grey hair was wound into a loose bun on the top of her head.

'Hello, you must be Ben and Lisa,' she said. 'I'm Celia. I'm sorry if I've shocked you, by . . . um, by being alive!' She laughed, and Vijay chuckled too.

'Celia!' Lisa cried, and they both jumped to their feet to shake the old woman's hand, but Celia pulled first Lisa and then Ben in close for a brief hug. 'I'm sorry, we always thought . . . Ben's family believed . . .'

'Yes, that I was dead. I knew this, back then. I knew that's what they all thought, as I'd apparently disappeared around the time Papa died. I wondered many times if I should write to my

Uncle Cyril and tell him that I was actually alive, but I decided against it. You see, I'd have had to leave India. Uncle Cyril would have insisted I went to live with him and his son in England. I barely knew them. I was born in India, and apart from a few trips to England I had always lived in India. I also didn't want to leave Vijay.' She shot him a tender look that he returned. 'So I let them carry on believing I was gone. I thought if Cyril or someone came over to pack up my father's house – this house – I'd have to come clean but no one ever came. I think with all the kerfuffle there was surrounding Indian independence, they must have decided just to abandon everything. My father and Uncle Cyril hadn't been close for years. There'd been a falling-out. Over my mother, I believe.'

Celia smiled. She seemed warm and friendly, and Lisa instinctively knew she'd like her a lot.

'Vijay's father took you into his home after your father died? That was kind of him.'

'Hmm. Yes, he did give me a home. He felt responsible, in a way, for my father's death. He and my father had been friends for many years, but there were some . . . shall we say difficulties between them in 1947.'

'Because of the diamond,' Vijay added.

'Yes. Because of the diamond,' Celia agreed, and shot Vijay a look that Lisa couldn't read.

'I see . . .' Ben began, but Celia held up a hand to stop him.

'No, I don't think you'd ever guess the whole truth. But we owe it to you, and we'll tell you the whole story. There are things we've always kept quiet about but we agreed, Vijay and I, that it was time, after all these years, to have it all out in the open. First, let's put the *Chamakta Sitara* on the table between us. It's the start and end of the whole thing, so it deserves to be centre stage while we talk.'

Ben reached for his bag, opened it, and pulled out the little velvet box. Vijay and Celia appeared to be holding their breath as he opened it and placed the open box down on the table where it caught the light, sending sparkling shards of light across them all.

'It's just as I remember it,' Celia whispered, but made no move to pick it up. 'I can picture it now pinned to Mama's evening gown. I never wore it myself. My father deemed me not old enough.'

Vijay picked up the brooch, his hands shaking a little as he turned it to catch the light. 'So much trouble, and all caused by this piece of rock.'

'Do you mean the curse?' Ben whispered.

'Curse? Oh, you mean the stories my father used to tell about it. That all the while it was out of the hands of the Kaur family it would bring bad luck, and women in particular would die?' Vijay gave a little laugh. 'That was all made up, by my father and grandfather, as one of the ploys to try to get your ancestors to return it.'

'Made-up? But . . . so many women in my family did die young. Even when we didn't have the diamond in our possession, when it was buried in a French glacier. My grandmother, my mother . . . all died prematurely.'

'I am very sorry for your losses. But no, there's no "curse" – it was all invented. Even so, the diamond caused a lot of trouble. I can't hate it, however. Because if it wasn't for the diamond, or rather, my father's lust for the diamond, Celia would have been taken to England by her father in 1947 and I might never have seen her again.' He smiled at his wife, who waved a dismissive hand.

'Poppycock, Vijay. You'd have taken up your place at Oxford University and you'd have visited me from there. We were always destined for each other.' She rolled her eyes. 'I'm sounding like a character in some corny Bollywood movie now, aren't I? Anyway, we said we'd tell you the story, and so now we must do exactly that.'

Lisa listened in astonishment as between them Celia and Vijay told the story of how Vijay's father had kidnapped Celia, with the help of her loved and trusted *ayah*. And how Vijay had broken her out, and then Celia had persuaded the maharajah to house her until Wilfred returned with the diamond.

'But of course my father never returned,' Celia said. 'We heard the news of the plane crash some days later.'

'My father had to accept then that he was never going to get the *Chamakta Sitara* back. And he was sad to lose a friend, but I told him it was all his own fault. After all, he was the one who'd sent Wilfred half-way round the world to fetch the diamond.' Vijay's expression was one of deep sadness.

'His only way to make amends for all he'd done was to offer to continue to give me a home for as long as I wanted to stay. Sita, too – she was my *ayah*. He'd put pressure on her to help with the kidnap. I didn't blame her, though of course I never fully trusted her again. We all lived together at the palace for years. We moved here after we married, though Sita stayed at the palace taking on a new role as housekeeper. I think every time she looked at me, she felt too guilty. We'd always loved this house and grounds and in those days we used to play a lot of tennis.' Celia waved a hand in the direction of the tennis court Lisa had glimpsed through the trees. 'Sadly, not now, though. These old bones won't take it.'

'I still own the palace,' Vijay said. 'That's how I received your letter. But it's in a poor state of repair. One of our grandsons wants to open it as a museum, so I'm in the process of handing it over to him to do just that.' Vijay nodded at the diamond. 'And I am thinking that will become the first exhibit.'

'I certainly never want to wear it,' Celia added, with a shudder that made Lisa think perhaps she did believe in its curse, a little bit. Or was it just the memories of all the horrors it had caused. Being kidnapped must have been terrifying, and then to lose her father as a result . . .

'It must have been awful for you, when you heard your father had died in the plane crash,' Lisa said gently.

'Yes . . . it was.' Celia sighed. 'But he and I had not been close.

We hadn't got on well since Mother died. I always thought he didn't love me, that he saw me as a burden, a nuisance.'

'I'm sure he didn't,' Lisa said.

'We used to fight all the time. At least, all the time if he even bothered to notice me. I used to try to keep out of his way because everything I did seemed to disappoint him. We'd even argued on the morning when I was kidnapped – the last time I saw him. I hadn't known the brooch was in London and when I first heard he'd left town after I was abducted, I thought he was running away with the diamond, choosing it over me. I always thought he loved it more than he loved me. Oh, I know, you're going to say no, he didn't, but that's the way I remember it.' She stared at some distant part of the grounds for a moment before continuing.

'And when days had passed and he hadn't returned, I believed it even more. It was a fortnight before we heard of the plane crash, and Vijay's father made enquiries and discovered Wilfred had been on the plane and on his way back. So I suppose he must have loved me more than the diamond after all. We'll never know.'

Lisa looked at Ben, who gave her a small nod. This was the moment. 'Celia, there was something else in that briefcase I found. Something that you should have.'

'If it was in Papa's papers, I don't really care,' she said. 'There can't be anything of any importance now, after all these years.'

'I think,' Lisa continued gently, 'that this is important.' She dug into her bag and pulled out the letter Wilfred had written on the day of the plane crash, and handed it wordlessly to Celia.

Chapter 30

Wilfred, July 1947

Wilfred settled back in his seat for the first leg of the long journey from London back to Delhi. He tapped his metal briefcase for the hundredth time, making sure it was safely there by his feet. He had refused to put it into the aeroplane's hold, or into any other storage space on the plane. It was staying right there with him where he could reach out and touch it as often as he wanted. It wasn't the case or even its contents that was so precious. It was the fact that it represented his darling Celia's wellbeing. He had to get the case and the jewel inside it safely to India, and then hand it over to the kidnappers in exchange for his daughter.

Quite how that would all play out he had no idea. Devraj would advise and help him, no doubt.

In London he'd gone straight to his bank at the earliest opportunity and collected the brooch. He'd spent one night in a hotel and booked a flight back for the following day. He'd not bothered to contact Cyril at all – it was too difficult to explain why he was back for so short a visit. As soon as he'd collected the brooch, he'd sent a telegram to Devraj and had a reply, saying that Arun Gupta had contacted the kidnappers and explained there would be a delay fetching the diamond. *CELIA AND SITA BOTH WELL*, the telegram also said. *ADVISE WHEN BACK IN DELHI STOP.*

The moment he landed in Delhi he would send another telegram to Devraj. Presumably the maharajah would then send Gupta to make arrangements for the exchange. Wilfred gave a shuddering sigh. He wouldn't relax for a single moment until Celia was safely back with him. His vague plan to get a paste copy of the brooch made had come to nothing. He'd been mad to consider it even for a moment. Why did he even need the jewel that only brought back painful memories of Alice? All he needed was Celia, safe by his side.

The plane taxied out to the runway and took off. At last he was on his way. The first stop and change of plane would be at Milan, followed by Beirut and finally Delhi. And then he'd take the train back to Agra, where Sanjit would pick him up. He'd go straight to the palace where Devraj would be able to advise him on arrangements for the exchange.

He reached down again to check the briefcase was there. That blasted diamond. Now, he couldn't wait to be rid of it. And to think that only a few months earlier he'd been taking it across the world in the other direction, to keep it safe and to ensure it stayed in his family's possession!

An air stewardess was making her way along the aisle of the plane serving drinks. Wilfred ordered a gin and tonic. Anything to calm his nerves. There was a young girl across the aisle from him, with long dark hair like Celia's. She smiled at him as if she thought he was unaccustomed to flying and needed reassurance. He forced himself to return the smile. He envied her innocence. If only she knew of the events that had brought him here!

And it was all far from over. If it had taught him anything it was that Celia meant more to him than anything in the world. He'd always known that deep down, but somehow that fact had been buried by his job, by what was going on in India. He'd allowed himself to forget that she was the most important thing in his life. He'd let their relationship deteriorate as she grew older. He hadn't made allowances for the fact she was almost a woman, growing up without a mother. She was a wonderful, spirited, beautiful girl and he was proud of her. Yet when had he last told her so? Had he ever told her how much he loved her? One might always assume one's children simply knew that as a fact, which didn't need to be stated, he supposed, but on the other hand, what was the harm in saying it aloud? It wasn't the British way to show affection openly, but by God he was going to do just that when he was reunited with Celia! He'd hold her tight and stroke her hair and tell her how scared he'd been for her, how much he loved her, how sorry he was that their relationship had been so strained lately. And how different it was all going to be from now on. Returning to England would be a new start for them both.

Yes, he'd tell her all this. He sipped his drink and considered the exact words he would use. He should write it down, he supposed. He should write her a letter. He'd tell her everything in person of course, but in case he clammed up or the words came out wrong, he'd also hand her a letter. She'd have it all in writing. That would prove to her how much he meant every word of it.

He pulled his briefcase onto his lap and opened it up, taking out a pad of writing paper and his fountain pen. He touched the box to check the brooch was still in there before closing the briefcase back up again.

Taking the lid off his fountain pen he paused, as he decided how best to begin the letter. He should simply let it all pour out onto the page, he decided. It wouldn't matter if his sentences were badly formed; she'd recognise his emotion and sincerity all the more if the letter was clearly from the heart. As it was. It really was.

To his utter surprise he found tears forming at the corners

of his eyes. He hadn't cried since the day dear Alice died. And yet now, at the thought of pouring his heart and soul into this letter – this letter that his wonderful daughter Celia would read in just a couple of days, he found himself choked with emotion.

Seize the hour, he told himself. Write it while you are feeling it so acutely. Write it now, and don't hold back.

My dear, darling Celia,

I have not been the best father to you of late. I have been distant and aloof. I have been more concerned with India's future and my job than with you, and I am sorry. I am sorrier than I can say that I have allowed all these external events to come between us. I have not paid you enough attention, I have not noticed what a charming and wonderful young woman you are fast becoming. I have treated you as though you were still a child, an annoyance, a drain on my time.

It has taken these awful events for me to realise, to truly understand, how much you mean to me. How empty my life would be without you. Your darling mother, God rest her soul, would have reminded me daily how lucky I am to have you. She would never have allowed us to drift apart the way we have. Day by day you remind me of Alice as you grow more and more like her. But you are also your own person, and I have been slow to accept that, slow to grant you the independence you need as you reach adulthood. I am sorry, my darling, for all of it. For being a controlling, cantankerous old man. For snapping at you, for picking fights where none were justified, for not respecting that you were growing up and not accepting that you have your own rights and needs and personality.

I love you, Celia. I know I may not have said it enough times in your life, maybe I haven't said it at all. I hope you have never doubted it, however badly I behaved towards you at times. I love you with all my heart. I would give up everything

I own to keep you safe, if that was what was needed. You are my life. You are my reason for being. You are everything to me, my incredible, darling daughter.
Papa

He read through it once again. Yes, that said everything he wanted to say. He resolved not to tweak it or amend it at all. She should read it in all its raw honesty. He folded it once, slipped it into an envelope and sealed it, to remove the temptation to reread it and fret about whether it was right. He wrote her name on the envelope and slipped it into his case, checking once more as he did so, that the brooch was still there in its little box. There. That was done, and it felt good. Now he just needed to get back to India. He sat back to try to relax for the rest of the journey.

It was growing dark outside, and they were passing through thick cloud. The flight grew bumpier as they hit an area of turbulence – more than once the plane lurched downwards uncomfortably. An air stewardess was making her way along the aisle, collecting empty drinks glasses. She needed to hold on tightly to the back of each seat as she moved along.

'Just passing through a storm, sir. We'll soon be out the other side and into some smoother flying time before we descend to Milan. Fasten your seat belts, if you would. Thank you.' She smiled and reassured people as she made her way along. Wilfred smiled back as he clipped his seat belt across his lap. It didn't look like an easy job, and he didn't envy her it. He hoped the storm would pass over soon. Presumably the pilot couldn't gain altitude to fly above it as by now they must be not far from the first stop, in Milan. That meant they must be somewhere over the Alps.

Was turbulence worse when you flew over mountains? Wilfred couldn't remember it being so on previous trips. But they were going through a storm too. He could see flashes of lightning around them in the clouds outside his window. He felt a momentary longing for the old days, when one had no choice but to travel by ship to India. They'd leave Southampton docks, sail along the Channel and across the Bay of Biscay, through the Mediterranean to the Suez Canal, through the Red Sea and across the Arabian sea, to dock once more in Bombay. Back then as a young man, he'd hated the long journey. It had made him feel too far removed from his homeland, and he'd hated the dead time while they were at sea. Flying was so much better, allowing one to complete the journey in a matter of days.

There was a sudden jolt as the plane once more hit an air pocket and plummeted. Loose items flew around the cabin. The poor air stewardess's feet left the floor and a passenger grabbed her arm to try to keep her upright. Wilfred frowned. This was definitely much worse than usual. He put a hand on his metal briefcase and grasped the handle tightly, to reassure himself it was safe, the diamond within it was safe, and it would get back to India and release his darling Celia. Nothing else mattered.

And then there was another immense lurch, another gut-wrenching plummet and finally, as the plane plunged to the ground near the summit of western Europe's highest mountain, a sickening crash. For Wilfred, and for everyone on board, it was over immediately. All were thrust into oblivion as the plane broke up amid the rock and ice at the top of a glacier. The storm raged for another two days, meaning there was no chance of mounting any kind of rescue attempt. By the time the storm abated, the wreckage was completely hidden by several feet of snow.

It would be many decades before any parts of it were seen again, inexorably carried down the mountain by the movement of ice, and ultimately revealed as global warming caused the glacier to shrink and contract. Wilfred's case, the letter within it and the diamond, were swallowed by the glacier and did not see the light of day for three-quarters of a century.

Chapter 31

Lisa, 2023

There was complete silence from the group as Celia read the letter. Lisa watched as her eyes scanned down the page then back up to the top again to reread it. And then she folded the letter carefully, almost reverently, and tucked it back into its envelope, not meeting anyone's eyes, not saying anything. She lightly stroked her fingers across the envelope, across where Wilfred had written her name, and from this small gesture Lisa knew the letter had hit home.

At last Celia lifted her head and gazed around at each of them in turn. To Vijay she whispered: 'He did love me. He really did, and he was sorry.'

'Oh, Cee,' Vijay said, reaching out his hand to her. Celia grasped it as though she was drowning and he was saving her.

'He really loved me,' Celia said again, in a whisper. Her eyes were wide, and Lisa could see tears forming, about to spill. 'He'd have given everything he had for me.'

'I hope this hasn't upset you,' Lisa said.

'No . . . it hasn't. Not at all. I mean, it's been such a long time . . . but I'm glad you brought me this letter. I'm glad that before I . . . leave this earth I have heard his voice one last time, and know that he realised . . . that he knew, he understood, and that he was sorry.' She took a long, shuddering breath. 'I probably didn't make it easy for him. I was headstrong—'

'You certainly were,' Vijay added affectionately.

'—and for a man bringing up a daughter on his own, in those days . . . it can't have been easy. I wished he'd remarried but he always said my mother was the love of his life and that no one could ever replace her.' Celia looked down again at the letter in her hands. 'He wrote this on the day of the plane crash, didn't he?'

'I believe so. It's certainly dated that day,' Lisa confirmed.

'He died thinking of me.' Celia nodded. She tipped her head back, speaking to the sky. 'Papa, thank you for your letter. I forgive you. I'm sorry we quarrelled that last day.' She took a long, shuddering breath. 'And, Papa, I love you too.'

Celia looked overcome by emotion. It was the right time, Lisa thought, for them to retire to their rooms, to give her some time and space to process everything. She yawned ostentatiously and Vijay, ever the gentleman, got the message. 'You must be very tired. I expect you'd like a nap before dinner. Come, follow me, I'll show you to your rooms.'

He led them through a sitting room into a hallway and then along a corridor alongside a central courtyard to what seemed to be a bedroom wing. There he showed them into two rooms, side by side with a connecting door, in which Abhijeet had already put their rucksacks. 'There is a bathroom opposite that is just for your use. Please, make yourself comfortable. Our house is yours to enjoy for as long as you wish to stay.'

'Thank you. You've been very kind offering to put us up.'

'It's the very least I could do.' Vijay nodded and left them alone.

Ben looked at Lisa and exhaled. 'Now that we've handed over the diamond, I need to make a phone call.'

'To your father.'

'Yes. To my father.' He sat on an armchair beside the window that overlooked the garden. They were in the room allocated to Lisa.

'Want me to . . .?' She waved a hand towards the connecting door and the other room.

'No, no. It's all right. I don't mind if you listen in.' He pulled out his phone, took a deep breath, and tapped on his father's number. It was answered quickly. Midafternoon in India would be breakfast time back home, Lisa calculated.

And then she listened while Ben explained that he'd been responsible for the 'break-in', that he'd hidden his mother's necklace and the other items, and taken the *Chamakta Sitara* to India, which he had now handed over in person to Vijay. 'The other things, Dad, you'll find in my room. Look in the bedside cabinet, bottom drawer, under the jumble of phone chargers and other stuff that's there. There's a brown envelope containing it all. But the diamond is back where it belongs.'

Ben fell silent but Lisa could hear his father speaking angrily into the phone. She couldn't make out the words but the tone was clear enough. David Fforbes-Whyte was furious. Ben grimaced as he listened, but made no attempt to explain himself further. 'Do what you have to do, Dad. I'll face up to it,' he said, sounding resigned to his fate, whatever it would be.

It was uncomfortable to witness. She decided to leave the room, and went out to the hallway to check out the bathroom, which she needed to use anyway. She spent a while in there, freshening up, then pulled out her phone and sent a WhatsApp message to Gaby. *Don't think I'll be climbing Mont Blanc with you after all!*

A reply came within seconds: *Ben? Squeeee! You go, girl!*

Lisa laughed, then went back out to the hallway. There were no sounds coming from either room. Ben must have finished his phone call. She tapped on the door and cautiously entered. Ben was where she'd left him, sitting on the chair by the window in her room, his phone lying on a side table. He looked drawn, as though it had been a difficult conversation.

'What happened?' she asked.

'He shouted, then shouted some more. I suspect we'll have another enormous row about it when I get home. But he's relieved not to have lost Mum's necklace, and he said he'll explain it to the police and persuade them not to charge me.'

'OK. I think that's the best you could hope for.'

'Yes, it is.' Ben took a deep breath then looked straight at her. 'I feel good about it, Lisa. For the first time ever, I've faced up to him and done what I thought was right. I feel free of him. And in a strange kind of way, I think he's secretly proud.'

She smiled at this. She understood all too well the joy of feeling no longer under another person's control. 'That's good, Ben.'

'It'll be all right, I think. He said that, in the end, what's really important to him is my well-being. And given that I've "swallowed all Granddad's stories"—' Ben made quote marks with his fingers as he said this '—then giving the diamond back is clearly the only way for me to be happy, though I should have OK'd it with him first rather than pull this stunt. He said, in time, he thinks he'll accept the diamond's loss even though right now he's angry about it. So, yeah, it'll be all right in the end, I guess.'

'Thank goodness for that.'

Ben gave her a small smile and stretched out a hand to her. 'We're free, Lisa. Free of the curse of that diamond, at last. Even though Vijay insists it was all made-up, we're free of it.'

Free to be together? If that was still what he wanted? Suddenly Lisa felt awkward, standing there holding his hand, with her bed just behind them. After weeks of friendship, keeping each other at arm's length, how did you then make the first move towards a closer relationship?

'Let's rest for a bit,' Ben said, as though he'd read her thoughts. 'We're both exhausted. Then let's see if we can get a lift to the Taj Mahal this evening. I know you've been longing to see it, and sunset is supposed to be one of the best times to go.'

'Good idea,' she replied. Ben stood up and went through to

his own room, leaving Lisa alone to unpack and then lie sleeplessly on her bed for an hour, her mind too active to relax as she thought through all that had happened and all that she hoped was soon to happen.

She must have dozed off eventually, for the next thing she was aware of was Ben tapping on the connecting door. 'Abhijeet's free to take us to the Taj Mahal before dinner, if you're ready?'

'Oh! Yes, give me five minutes.' She rubbed the sleep from her eyes, got up and brushed her hair, then went to the bathroom to splash water on her face. Looking at her reflection in the mirror she decided to put a bit of make-up on. It wouldn't hurt to look her best, would it?

A few minutes later they were back in the car with Abhijeet, driving through the city to the Taj Mahal. Abhijeet dropped them off at one of the gates.

And then, after purchasing their tickets, they were in the grounds, walking past a rectangular pond lined with carefully pruned shrubs. Spotlessly clean, paved paths with benches at intervals led them alongside the pond, beside neatly tended lawns towards that iconic white marble building. The Taj Mahal rose pure and gleaming above its red sandstone base and even though Lisa had seen a hundred photos of it in the past and watched documentaries about it, the sight of it there, right in front of her, still managed to take her breath away.

Inside, they marvelled at the intricate decoration on every surface, the semi-precious stones inlaid into detailed designs, the ornate stucco work and detailed mosaics spelling out verses from the Koran. Under the central dome sound reverberated for twenty or thirty seconds.

'It's quite eerie,' Lisa whispered.

Ben nodded. 'Let's go outside to get some photos.'

They walked away from the building, back along the side of the pool, only turning back to look at the Taj Mahal again when they reached the end of the pond where there was a raised viewing platform. There they could stand exactly in line with the building and see *that* view for themselves.

'It looks most impressive when you position yourself so that it's perfectly symmetrical,' Ben said, and Lisa had to agree. The main dome, the minarets and arches, the perfect reflection in the still waters of the pool were all exquisite in the evening sunshine, the marble mosaics glowing pink and orange. They sat on a stone bench admiring it, and reading the leaflet that explained its history.

'It's a monument to love,' Ben said. 'Shah Jahan built it to commemorate his deceased wife.'

'It's beautiful. Look how the tiles are beginning to change colour as the sun goes down.'

'It really is gorgeous,' Ben said. He took her hand, and she realised he was not looking at the building but at her. There was a longing in his eyes. A need, a hunger. 'Lisa, we're free . . . the diamond's gone . . . if you're still interested?'

She smiled and put a hand up to his cheek. 'Yes, Ben. I think after all this, we should at least give it a go, eh?'

'I am so, so very glad you said that,' he whispered, as he leaned in close, his eyes dropped to her lips, and then, at long, long last, there was the kiss she'd dreamed of, the kiss she'd waited for and longed for, and it was every bit as good, as warm and loving, as she'd hoped it would be.

In front of them, the Taj Mahal, the most famous building in the world, stood impassive as they deepened the kiss and forged the bond between them. A bond that, Lisa thought, no diamond or curse could ever break. He was hers, she was his, and that was all exactly as it should be.

Author's Note

The idea for this novel has been kicking around for a few years, with notes and research relating to it saved in a folder on my laptop entitled 'Novel – Mont Blanc'. It was inspired by a newspaper article I'd cut out and kept, about wreckage from a plane crash that had resurfaced at the nose of a glacier in the Chamonix area. An engraved watch had been found and there were enough clues for it to be reunited with descendants of its original owner. Readers might well imagine my excitement on reading that article – it has 'dual timeline novel' written all over it!

I'd pitched the initial idea to my editor years ago and it was approved, but I kept putting off writing it and instead wrote several others. It was only when I decided to research the true-life plane crash, and discovered it was an Air India plane, that the story began to take shape. Why not set the historical parts in India? And what better time period to use than the last days of the Raj? (The real-life plane crash actually happened a few years later, post-independence, in the early 1950s.)

Colonial-era India makes me think of diamonds such as the Koh-i-Noor, which was passed into Queen Victoria's hands as part of a treaty signed in 1849 and is currently set into one of the crowns in the collection held in the Tower of London. That large, imperfect stone is said to be cursed, and I liked the idea of inventing my own cursed diamond for my story to revolve around. Koh-i-Noor means Mountain of Light. I love the idea of naming large gemstones – it almost gives them a personality of their own.

I visited India back in 1988, which is almost exactly the midpoint of the two eras written about in this novel. As well as researching it online and reading several books on Indian history and the journey to independence, I mined my own memories and photos for some of the descriptive passages. So if my descriptions seem too modern for 1947 or too dated for 2023, now you know why!

The walk described in Chapter 1, to La Jonction on the flanks of Mont Blanc, is one I did myself with family and friends on one of my most memorable days ever in the mountains. If you're ever staying in Chamonix and enjoy mountain walking, I can thoroughly recommend it.

Acknowledgements

Firstly, enormous thanks to my editor Priyal Agrawal who was the perfect person to help me make this novel as good as possible. Thank you so much, and I hope you're as proud of the finished product as I am!

Thank you also to Teresa Palmiero, the eagle-eyed copy-editor who has worked on several of my books, and whose attention to detail is phenomenal. Thanks too to everyone else at HQ who was involved with this book. It's hard to believe but this is my 15th novel with you.

I owe a debt to my friends Gabrielle and Trevor who took me and my family on the walk to *La Jonction* that I describe in Chapter 1. It was a long time ago now, but as you can see it made a huge impact and has finally made it into one of my books.

My son Connor helped me out once again discussing ideas for this novel while we went out for 'plot walks'. He's moved away now and I miss those walks, but my lovely husband Ignatius is shaping up to be good at helping me with plots too. A writer always needs to bounce ideas off someone, and talk things through when they get stuck, and I am lucky to have supportive family around me. Thank you, Ignatius, Fionn and Connor.

And finally, thank you to all my readers, bloggers and reviewers everywhere. I'm fortunate to have such loyal fans and I love hearing from you. I hope you enjoy this book as much as the previous ones! To be the first to hear news of forthcoming books please sign up to my mailing list at https://kathleenmcgurl.net/home

A Letter from Kathleen McGurl

Thank you so much for choosing to read *The Lost Diamond*. I hope you enjoyed it! If you did and would like to be the first to know about my new releases, sign up to my mailing list.

I hope you loved *The Lost Diamond* and if you did, I would be so grateful if you would leave a review. I always love to hear what readers thought, and it helps new readers discover my books too.

Thanks,
Kathleen McGurl

https://kathleenmcgurl.com
https://twitter.com/KathMcGurl
https://www.facebook.com/KathleenMcGurl

Dear Reader,

We hope you enjoyed reading this book. If you did, we'd be so appreciative if you left a review. It really helps us and the author to bring more books like this to you.

Here at HQ Digital we are dedicated to publishing fiction that will keep you turning the pages into the early hours. Don't want to miss a thing? To find out more about our books, promotions, discover exclusive content and enter competitions you can keep in touch in the following ways:

JOIN OUR COMMUNITY:

Sign up to our new email newsletter:
http://smarturl.it/SignUpHQ

Read our new blog www.hqstories.co.uk

X https://twitter.com/HQStories

f www.facebook.com/HQStories

BUDDING WRITER?

We're also looking for authors to join the HQ Digital family!
Find out more here:

https://www.hqstories.co.uk/want-to-write-for-us/

Thanks for reading, from the HQ Digital team